Court

of

Lies

&

Cinder

Courting Books Publishing

Court

of

Lies

&

Cinder

A
Dark
Cinderella
Retelling

Autumn Kaufer

Contents:

L'Evrope

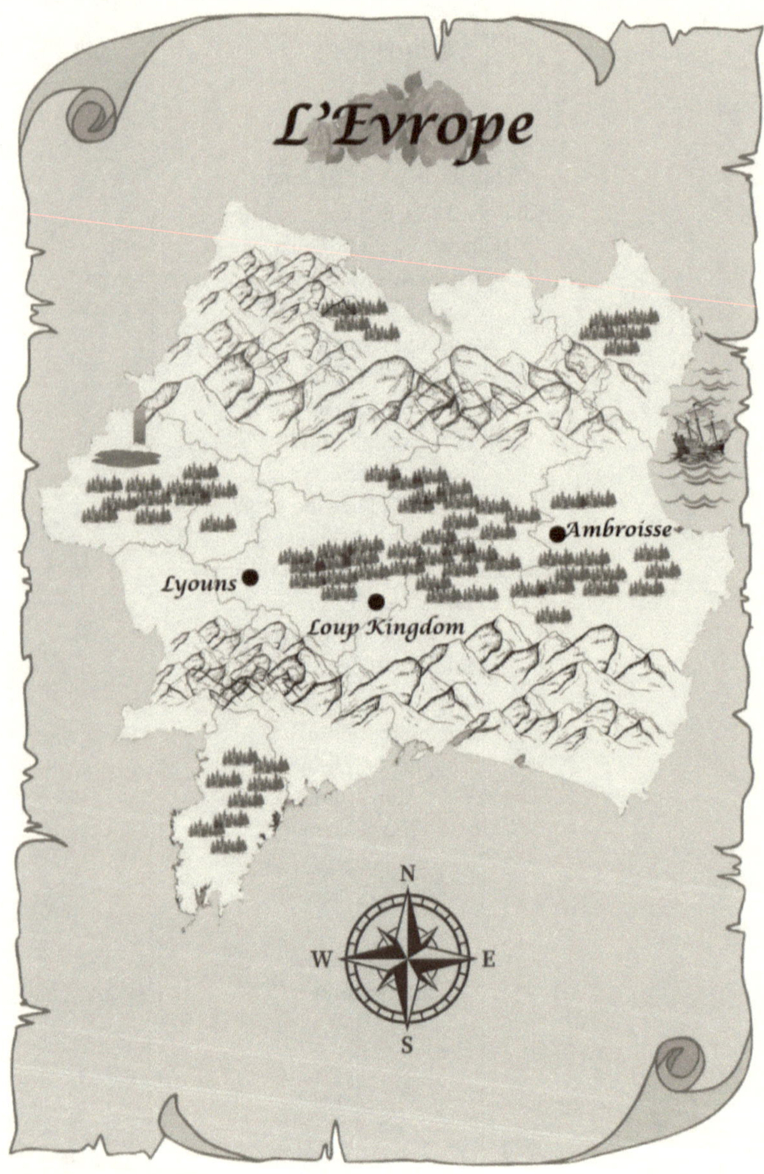

For Kevin, my knight in shining

armor. You have become my home, and

I am forever grateful for you.

Once
upon
a
time....

"With love's light wings did I o'erperch these walls, for stony limits cannot hold love out, And what love can do, that dares love attempt." -*Romeo & Juliet*

Prologue

i'lady, this came for you," the messenger said as he handed her the envelope. The woman could only see his silhouette, dimly lit by the hallway torches. Anxiety and eagerness both filled her. Would this be the news she'd longed for?

"Thank you," she said as she closed the door.

The flickering candlelight cast eerie shadows on the walls, heightening the woman's anxiety. With a trembling hand, she ripped open the envelope.

It's done. You and your family will be safe now.
-L

A sigh of relief escaped her. Her daughters watched as she raced across the room. She pried up the loose floorboard and removed a knapsack before turning to the young girls. Her daughters sensed the gravity of the situation, their wide-eyed stares and silent compliance conveying their understanding of the imminent danger.

"This is the day I warned you about. Gather your things quickly. We must leave at once."

"Yes, Mother," the oldest responded, grabbing her sister's hand as they went to their room.

The young girl stood still, unsure of what to do, as the older one collected their bags. She then picked up a few books and toys to add in before they left.

"Where are we going?"

"Mother said she is taking us somewhere we'll be safe. She told us that when she made us pack. Remember?" the older sibling responded.

"But why—"

"No time for questions. She is waiting for us."

They returned to their mother, who held a small, swaddled toddler in her arms. She slept soundly.

"We have to be quiet and move swiftly," their mother instructed. "Do you understand?"

The girls nodded.

"Momma, can I help?" the older one asked.

"Yes, take this," she answered, handing her one of her bags. "Carry this, and not another word until we leave the kingdom. No matter what."

Opening the door, she peered into the empty hallway before gesturing them to follow. The chiming clock signaled the imminent dawn. There was no time to waste.

Their footfalls were silent. Every shadow jumped out, every door shutting could be guards alerted to their presence. Her heart thudded so loudly in her ears, the sound consumed her until they reached the exit.

Despite the short time, fears raced through her mind, stretching the seconds. They left the palace and went straight to the dirt path. She glanced down at her girls as they made their way.

The scent of damp earth filled their nostrils as they ran through the dense woods, adding an earthy intensity to their desperate escape. The iron gate came into view, and her pace quickened, eager to reach the freedom awaiting them on the other side. Her children struggled to keep up with her long strides.

A faint rustling sound reached her ears, causing her to glance nervously over her shoulder, fearing they had been discovered.

"Halt!" a guard yelled at the sight of them.

"Don't stop," she said to her daughters. "We must keep going, no matter what."

They clung to her gown, and she encouraged them to move faster. The wall came into view. A few more steps, and they would be closer to leaving everything they knew behind.

"Close the gate!" The words shot past her as swift as an arrow.

The family made it through as the wrought metal iron slammed shut behind them, effectively cutting off their pursuers. The woman laughed.

Running through the woods, the river came into view. The mother stopped and paced for a moment before finding the shallow section she had previously discovered. They safely crossed and rested on the other side. She assured her daughters that everything would be fine.

"Momma, won't the king come looking for her?" the oldest asked, staring at the bundle held tightly in her mother's arms.

"He can search all he wants, but he won't find us."

"I want dada," the youngest pouted. "Where is—"

"Why can't we stay?" the oldest interrupted.

"It isn't safe here, not anymore," their mother explained as her patience wore thin.

"But why?"

"Hush, child. We need to rest a moment before we continue our journey to the colony."

The long road ahead held potential peril, but the risk was worthwhile. For the sake of her daughters and herself, sacrifices had to be made.

With a bag of valuables taken from the palace, she ensured they would still have nice things. It wouldn't hold a candle to the life they lived there. The thought of no longer living in luxury hurt her heart, but it was necessary.

"Come, let's continue."

Hope waited for them, hope of living a life of quiet peace, free from violence, and away from the royal intrigues. Her daughters were her number one priority, and she would do whatever necessary to protect them, to see to it every need was met.

She knew they would have to stop from time to time, but as long as they remained in the woods, off the path, they should be safe. The toddler in her arms squirmed, and the woman wondered if taking her had been the right decision. It didn't matter now. It was too late to turn back. Death only awaited her, should she return to the kingdom.

So far, everything had gone to plan. Next, she had to meet her contact in the colony who would help them hide. After enough time had passed, they would move into the Ambroisse colony and live a quiet life.

Imagining her daughters learning to dance, drinking high tea with nobles, and living their well-deserved life brought a smile to her face. As they headed towards their new future, she reassured her girls in a calm manner.

She had no bed to go to,
but had to sleep by the
fireside in the ashes. And
on the account she always
looked dusty and dirty,
they called her Cinderella.

-The Brothers Grimm
Cinderella

Chapter 1

Little Cinderella

t twenty years old, Luella had grown into her beauty. Her platinum blonde hair, nearly white in the sun, with her porcelain skin and piercing blue eyes made her the envy of many colonists of Ambroisse. Her melodic laughter and kind heart endeared her to the locals.

Seen as compassionate, she took care of those around her. Though it was often her stepmother, the Countess Clara, who took the credit. She would claim she sent Luella to help, or she made the stew Luella delivered to a sick neighbor.

This hid her cold-heart and conniving ways. For as warm and compassionate as Luella was, her stepmother was stoic and calculating. The countess and her daughters were lovely in appearance, with their strawberry blonde hair and green eyes. Attractive to look at, but their hearts were dark as night and hard as stone.

Madison was most like her mother, being the oldest and easily shaped by her. Aubrey attempted to be like her sister, but she wasn't quite as cruel.

They wore fine gowns, attended high tea, and did nothing to help Luella around the manor. Luella wore a simple, dark blue work dress with a cream-colored apron.

The sisters spent their time attending lessons with their mother, learning to behave like nobility so they may ensnare a wealthy suitor.

One evening, Luella swept around the chimney while the stew cooked over the fire. The aroma of beef and rosemary filled the kitchen.

"There you are," Madison said as she walked in. "Why is my dress not mended yet?"

"I will finish it after dinner."

"Of course. It is important you clean your bed first," Madison said with a cruel laugh.

Luella faced her, keeping her expression neutral, while she continued. "Whatever do you mean?"

"You sleep down here more than in the attic." Madison glanced over her shoulder when Aubrey walked in. "Isn't that right?" she asked with a smile.

"What is?" Aubrey asked with a furrowed brow.

"Little Luella sleeps in the fireplace." She giggled while Luella's face turned scarlet. "Oh, take a joke, cinder girl!"

Aubrey barked at her sister's insult. "Luella, queen of ash and soot." She gave a playful bow.

"I got it! I got it! Our little Cinderella," Madison cried out. The girls fell against each other as tears rolled down their cheeks.

Luella put the broom away and tightened her apron. "Dinner will be ready shortly."

Her stepsisters left without another word, though she heard their laughter fade down the hallway. Luella walked to the fireplace to check on their meal. Seeing it was nearly ready, she loaded the tray with drinks, bread, and cheese. After ladling three bowls, she added them alongside the rest of the food.

Carefully, she carried the tray to the dining room. She spread everything out, rang the bell, and waited. The countess entered first, followed by Madison and Aubrey.

"Luella," she said with a sigh, "I do wish you would at least clean yourself up *before* serving us. You are causing me to lose my appetite."

Aubrey's expression was sympathetic, but it only lasted a moment until her sister giggled at the comment. She laughed as well. Luella turned on her heel and promptly left.

In the kitchen, she dampened a linen and cleaned her face. The bell rang as she finished her meal. It pulled her from her thoughts, of her upcoming birthday, of leaving home. Slowly, she rose from the table and returned to the dining room.

"Yes, madam?"

Clara gestured her forward. "Well, at least you appear a little cleaner this time. I am ready for my nightcap."

Luella went to the small corner cabinet, removed a decanter of brandy with a matching glass, and filled it before taking it to Clara.

"Anything else?"

"No."

Luella hurried from the room. She went to the small washroom to get ready for bed. After making her way upstairs, she stopped at the foot of the steps leading to the attic. The thought of climbing so many overwhelmed her, tired as she was.

Cinderella.

With determination, she made her way up and to her small, drafty room. There was no bed or mattress, only half a tattered blanket.

When she asked Clara why she wasn't allowed a bed, she refused to answer. Instead, she grew angry at Luella's incessant questions. Finally, she snapped, throwing the blanket at her and telling her it was all she would have.

Luella's exhaustion rolled over her in waves. She curled up on the floor and fell asleep.

The pleasant weather made Luella smile. Finding the market mostly empty, she made her purchases and headed home in a short amount of time.

"Why do you continue to reject my advances?"

Luella spun around to find Anthony following her on the path. The governor's oldest son, he was taller than Luella, with light brown hair and hazel eyes. Seeing no one else around them, Luella forced a pleasant expression while trying to figure out a way to escape.

Though somewhat handsome, he was known as a brute and a bully. Nearly everyone in the colony avoided his path when possible, for fear of what he may do to them. Luella had become his latest obsession.

"What advances? You and your brother tease me, call me names, taunt me. I hardly call that showing interest in someone," she replied as her heart thudded in her ribcage.

"What, calling you skunk?" He glanced at her hair. "It's a joke. You should think it's funny."

"And why is that?"

His smile twisted into a frown. "Because of your white hair. I figured it was rather obvious."

"I was unsure if you were making fun of me for that or saying I smell bad. Or worse, comparing me to the animals who rule over us from their kingdom."

He remained serious a moment longer before erupting into laughter. "I would never compare you to a dirty shifter. No, I meant it as a term of endearment."

"You can understand my confusion. If you'll excuse me, I need to return home. They are waiting on me."

"Are they? Or is it the other way around?"

"What do you mean?"

Anthony stepped in front of her to block her path. He caressed her cheek down to her chin and neck. Her breath caught in her throat as her skin flushed.

"I am aware it is your duty to serve them. What if I want to serve you? To have you for myself. Would you let me?"

She forced herself to step back, immediately aching at the loss of such an intimate touch. "You and Stefan are mean to the colonists. I've never seen either of you lift a finger to help. Most of all, you are cruel to me when other people are around. Since it is only the two of us here, I am expected to believe this is really how you feel about me?"

"My own feelings scared me," he admitted. "I find you to be ravishing, and I want nothing more than to have you for myself. I was afraid to admit it, because my father looks down on you as well. Given your status at the manor."

She studied his eyes, trying to determine if his intentions were sincere or if this was yet another joke. "Last time I saw you with Stefan, you both called me horrible names."

"I was trying to be the fun older brother, but I didn't mean any of it."

"I don't believe you." Her eyes trailed over his muscled arms and the tight fit of his shirt. She cleared her throat. "And what about you? You seem to look down on anyone who isn't of some higher status."

"I want you." He stepped up to her and brushed her hair behind her ear. "Please, Luella, I want you badly." He cupped her face.

"Really?" she asked, leaning into him. She ached for his touch, desperate for any contact.

"Tell me what you want."

"I want to be loved," she admitted, her breath catching in her throat at her own outburst. She studied him, waiting to see what he would say.

His smile grew wider, until he laughed so hard, tears streamed down. "As if anyone would ever love a skunk like you?"

She backed away, swallowed hard, and took advantage of the situation. While he could hardly breathe, she took off running as fast as possible.

Her eyes watered as she replayed his words. Even knowing what sort of man he was, she fell for his charm, and humiliation was her reward.

Arriving at the courtyard of the manor, she paused for a moment to catch her breath and clean her face.

Why did I almost fall for that? I know what a jerk he is. Her shoulders sagged. *I guess it's because I long for love, since I've never known it, and will take whatever attention I can get. I learned my lesson, and I will keep my heart closed off. At this rate, I will never find someone who will love me for me, regardless of my appearance or my status. It is not something meant for me.*

Chapter 2

A Chance Encounter

uella stoked the fire while she prepared lunch. She set everything up, then rang the bell. While waiting for the countess, she rearranged the utensils on the small buffet table against the side wall. When finished, she straightened the painting above the fireplace.

"You're still here?" Clara asked as she entered, sitting down and placing her napkin over her lap.

"I will be leaving to attend to laundry and the market for the afternoon. Do you need anything before I go?"

"No."

Luella went through the kitchen, going to the small back room where the laundry was piled up. She gathered the basket with blankets and carried it outside. The donkey saw her approaching and waited for her at the gate. She loaded the cart, then smiled as she let the donkey out. After harnessing him up, she attached him to the cart.

They took their usual path to the pond. After releasing him to pasture, she hummed and began to wash. Carefully hanging each blanket, she finished the last one when loud voices rang out.

"Stop!" a man yelled.

The sounds came from the woods, and she ran as fast as she could. Branches scratched her arms and face, but she paid no attention. Someone was in trouble, and she focused on getting to them.

When the trees opened to a clearing, she saw two men kicking something balled up on the ground. As she approached, she realized it was Anthony and Stefan, and the ball was a man trying to protect himself from their blows.

"What are you doing?" she screamed as her stomach churned.

Either they did not hear or chose to ignore her. "We don't want filthy shifters in our colony. Not even to visit. You don't belong here," Anthony yelled.

The man groaned at the contact and kept his arms wrapped around himself, attempting to stave off each hit.

Luella rushed to them. "Stop this at once!" she yelled.

They paused and looked at her. Using the momentary distraction, she ran between them and the man they were hurting just as they resumed. Knocked to the ground, she cried out when one of their boots made contact with her spine. Fire flashed before her eyes as pain exploded through her.

The man jumped to his feet, pulling her with him. He shoved her behind him, blocking her from their attackers. Her eyes remained unfocused for a moment until the pain began to ease. He maintained his grip on her wrist while watching them.

He glanced back to check on her, and she recognized him. His dark brown hair stopped below his ears, and he swept it back while staring intently at her with his deep, molten brown eyes. As though in a trance, he stepped towards her. His concentration shattered when she spoke.

"You are the herald from the palace!" She tried to see if he was injured or how severely.

Before he responded, Stefan stepped forward. "Why are you ruining our fun?" he asked Luella. Not a spitting image of his older brother, they shared the same hair color and masculine facial features. Stefan was a foot shorter than Anthony and not quite as built.

"He represents the king himself. They might sanction us, or worse, station soldiers here. What were you thinking?"

"Please, he's nothing more than a lowly herald."

"And a disgusting shifter," Anthony mumbled.

Luella scowled. "Are you even listening to me? He represents the monarchy. How could you do this?"

"He started it."

"I highly doubt that. What exactly did he do to offend you so?" She looked from Anthony to Stefan, watching as neither would meet her gaze. "Well?"

The man remained silent, watching the exchange. She clearly held her own against them, and it amused him to see.

"He came into the town hall and spoke with our father, asking him to please take down the black wolfskin hanging on the wall."

"And?"

"Our father refused. As he left, the herald called him a few choice names under his breath. Father didn't hear, but I did."

"He is a shifter. Of course the sight of a dead wolf would offend him."

"Still, he had no right to say such things."

Stefan and Luella stared at each other for a moment. "It is up to him whether or not he will seek charges for what you have done." Her eyes met that of the herald's, and her breath sucked in. She swallowed hard. "I am well aware I have no right to ask this, but please, be lenient."

"May I inquire as to why you're protecting them?" Remi asked, his voice betraying a mix of curiosity and suspicion.

"Because their father is our governor."

"Yes, I am aware," he said with a scoff. "So they shouldn't be punished because they are of some rank?"

"Absolutely not what I meant!" she shot back. "However, the way things work here, if you press charges their father will punish all of us."

"Why should I care?" he asked with a shrug.

"I make no assumptions about your life at the palace, but we are struggling to get by here. Please, don't make things worse for us."

He studied her for a moment before giving his attention to the two men who attacked him. They avoided his gaze while attempting to look remorseful.

"Very well. You're free to go."

Without a word, Stefan and Anthony took off. Luella stepped away from the herald. "Thank you." Leaning against the trunk of the nearest tree elicited a wince of pain.

"How badly are you hurt?" he asked, his voice soft with concern etched across his face.

"I'll be all right," she assured him.

"Soak in a hot bath. It will help."

Luella laughed. "Oh, of course. I shall have my servants prepare one for me as soon as I return."

He tilted his head and chuckled. "It was merely a suggestion. I am… Remi, by the way. Nice to meet you."

His smile sent her stomach into a flutter. She cleared her throat and collected herself. "I am sorry for what they did."

"It's not your fault, and I am fine."

"How are you not hurt?" she asked as she studied him from head to foot.

"They had only begun when you found me." His answer did not assure her, made apparent when her jaw clenched and her eyes narrowed.

"I need to return home."

"Wait, where do you live? I would like to see you again. To thank you," he added.

"That's not necessary."

"Don't leave yet. Please."

His words and demeanor calmed her. Though she didn't understand why, she stepped towards him as if pulled by some invisible force.

"Really, I must go."

"You are familiar to me. Have we met before?"

"No."

"At least tell me your name."

She stepped back and turned to leave. "Goodbye."

"Please, I am begging you. At least give me your name."

"Why?"

"You saved me. I would like to see you again."

She shook her head to clear it. "Enjoy the rest of your day."

Watching her leave, determination filled him. He would learn her name and where she lived. He smiled and whistled as he headed towards the market.

Thursday dragged on as Luella ignored the pain in her back and legs while attending to her chores. When bedtime came, she didn't even attempt to climb the stairs to the attic. She curled up beside the fireplace and fell asleep.

After preparing lunch, she started laundry, then traveled to the market while it dried. This was her routine on Wednesdays and Fridays.

She made her final purchase, then she walked along the path leading to the pond. Everything was neatly packed in her bag, and she enjoyed the late afternoon sun.

Footsteps approached from behind. She clutched her goods tighter, ready to turn around, when an arm wrapped around her waist. A hand clamped over her mouth as her bag fell to the ground. Strong hands carried her into the woods.

With brutal force, her back slammed into a tree, knocking the breath from her lungs. She attempted to remain standing, only to see Anthony and Stefan looming over her, each with a smug grin on their faces.

"Look here, little skunk. You had no right to intervene. For that, you will pay," Anthony said as he approached her.

Her head swam as she attempted to collect her thoughts. She could hardly hear herself over her heartbeat pulsing in her ears.

"You were hurting someone. I had to do something."

He slapped her hard enough to nearly drive her to her knees. "He is a filthy, no-good shifter!" His eyes burned with anger. "We have every right to protect our colony from them."

"No, but—"

The punch to her chest knocked the words from her. She fell backwards, landing against the tree. The rough bark bit into her skin. Anthony gripped her by the neck and pulled her to his face.

"You do not tell us what to do. We would've happily killed him, had you not interrupted us."

"The palace—"

"I'm not afraid of those freaks," he said with a hollow laugh. The air whooshed from her lungs when he shoved her backward. His lips grazed her neck and chin. "Hmm, I can't wait to taste you."

"Please, don't," she begged, glancing around and praying someone would find her.

Anthony dragged her to the ground, leaning over her, as he unsheathed his dagger. Her eyes went wide with fear, watching as he sliced open the front of her gown.

"Don't do this."

Stefan knelt beside Anthony. "You said I get to have her first!"

"I'm the oldest, so she is mine. Besides, I don't do leftovers."

"But you said I could!"

"This was my idea, I get her first. Wait your turn."

Stefan pulled Anthony off Luella and punched him in the jaw. Luella made it to her feet and about to run when Anthony grabbed her wrist.

"You aren't going anywhere."

His knuckles made contact with her ribs, and she went flying before hitting the ground with a thud. Stefan tackled Anthony, and punches flew left and right.

While they continued, Luella scrambled to her feet, struggling to catch her breath. She fled as quickly as she was able. Her steps were unsteady and her vision blurred, but she found her pack. Without another thought, she scooped it up and rushed to the manor.

Gratitude filled her when she entered the empty kitchen, as she did not want to have to explain her disheveled appearance. She assessed the goods before putting everything away. The bag of flour had burst open, but most of its contents remained in the pack. Since the storage container was nearly empty, she slowly poured it in.

Her adrenaline wore off as the memory overwhelmed her. She noticed her hand shook as she closed the pantry door. She went to the washroom, splashed cool water over her face, and assured herself she was safe. They could not hurt her here.

Chapter 3

The Bargain

uella set up breakfast, rang the bell, then left before anyone would see her. Normally on Saturdays, she swept and mopped, but she chose to work outside instead. She hoped in doing so, she would avoid any questions about the bruises on her face and arms.

After preparing lunch, Luella strolled through the woods. Work needed to be done, but fresh air was needed more. She arrived at the pond, gathered cool water into her hands, and washed her face. Once her hands were dry, she sat against a tree trunk and removed a small book from her apron pocket.

Always remember, my dearest Luella, kindness and hope will keep you going. Have courage, even in the darkest night, and especially in the face of despair. Do not let despair seep into your heart, since that is the home for love instead.

Your father and I agree on a lot of things, except he refuses to believe in the magic that is out in the world. Him, of all people! He knows the stories of fae and other creatures, but he says the story of a faery godmother is unbelievable. Why would a faery take an interest in people like us? But I believe in her. When the time is right, she will appear, and all will be good in the world.

I am due to give birth any time. I call you Luella, though we are uncertain yet if you are a boy or a girl. I know in my heart who and what you are. Your father hovers over me, but I am not worried. More than anything, I am excited to meet you. I cannot wait to hold you in my arms, kiss your forehead, and tell you how much I love you.

These words brought her a small measure of comfort when all else failed. They calmed her heart, and she knew her mother was right. At least, the part about having courage. She was unsure how she should feel about magic and faery godmothers.

This was her life for now, yes, but she did not despair over her situation. Better days were coming. Soon, she would turn twenty-one. As an adult, she would no longer be tethered to her stepmother or stepsisters.

"I hoped I would find you here."

The book nearly fell from her hand as Luella scrambled to her feet. She slipped it into her apron before glancing up to see the herald standing before her. In an attempt to hide her bruises, she lowered her head, but not fast enough.

He stepped up to her and gently gripped her chin to tilt her face towards him, to get a better look. His jaw clenched as he examined the blue and purple splotches on her cheek and eye socket.

"This was because of me, wasn't it?"

The bark pressed into her back, forcing her to stay where she stood. "I'm okay," she said softly.

"Do not lie to me. What did they do to you? I said they, because I assume it was the two men who attacked me. Tell me I'm wrong."

"Please, do not pursue this."

"I let them go after they attacked me. However, they hurt you, and I will not let this stand. They will be punished."

"No, you don't understand. I implore you. You'll only make things worse for me. Please—"

Remi lifted his hand, and one of the guards approached him. Tall and well-built, his uniform consisted of dark breeches and his shirt properly tucked in, with his weapons sheathed at his hip. Midnight hair swept past his chiseled jawline and continued down his back.

"Yes, sire?"

"Simon, this is Luella. I need you to do us both a favor. Go fetch the governor and his two sons."

"Right away," he answered as he turned on his heel and left.

"How do you know my name?" she asked without meeting his gaze.

Remi started to answer until he realized she trembled against him. "Why are you so afraid?"

"I am already an outcast here. The people are kind and polite but keep their distance. If you do this, you will be putting a target on me."

"They keep their distance? Is it because of your appearance?"

Anthony's cruel words ran through her mind. Her eyes watered. "It doesn't matter why. The merchants are civil because I am a customer. Otherwise, most people avoid me."

"Why would they treat you this way? After all, aren't you the daughter of the Countess Clara?"

"You… you asked about me?"

"After you refused to give me your name, I did." He sighed. "Look, I wasn't going to pursue this. What they did, I mean. I hoped by showing them compassion it would influence them to do the same. Clearly not the case."

"Remi, please, do not do this."

"I assure you everything will be fine."

"You say that because you are unfamiliar with how things are here!" she reiterated with a high pitch to her voice.

"Then tell me."

"It's not so simple. There are rules we must follow."

"Every colony has its own rules."

"No, but…" Her voice trailed off. "Our governor is cruel. If you do this, surely he will take his anger out at me and everyone else. I am begging you to let this go."

"You would let them get away with hurting you? And if I leave, what guarantee is there they would not do worse?" He stared at the marks on her neck and wrist. "I can only assume what they wanted to do to you."

Her mouth opened to respond, but the governor and his sons appeared in the tree line. Remi gripped her arm and led her to them.

"Governor Langdon," he said, his tone steady.

"Remi, why are you here? You've already made your announcements this week. Is something the matter?" He eyed Luella, wondering if she had done something wrong. "Has she been causing trouble for you?"

"Quite the opposite. I came to check on her, after she saved my life on Wednesday."

"We are in your debt," Langdon said to Luella with a smile that did not quite reach his eyes.

"Thank you," she responded, her voice low.

"So, why am I and my sons summoned here?"

"Because they are the ones who attacked me."

"What? Then why am I only now hearing about this?" Langdon demanded.

"Because I let them go at the time. Then I saw what they did to her."

Langdon examined her bruises. "What proof is there my sons are the ones who hurt her? Perhaps she did this to herself?"

"I have her word."

Langdon scoffed. "Her word means nothing to me."

"After what she did, it carries everything with me. Fine. If you will not take her word, then I suggest you take mine. It was your sons who attacked me. And she witnessed it. Will you believe us?"

His shoulders sagged slightly with resignation. "It doesn't look like I have any choice." Langdon looked at his sons. "What will happen to them now?"

"They will be arrested, tried, and if found guilty, they will be sentenced to five years hard labor."

"I beg you, grant them mercy."

Remi thought about it for a moment. "I granted them mercy when I let them go. Instead of taking it, they brought this upon themselves."

"I am the governor of this colony, and I need my sons to help maintain order. You cannot take them away." He glared at Luella. "Say something, girl!" he snapped.

Luella swallowed hard. "I fell and hit my head. My memory is fuzzy, so I can't be sure of what I saw. Perhaps we can—"

"Silence!" Remi commanded. Luella flinched at his raised voice. "If you do not wish to pursue charges, that is your right. However, they will see justice for what they did to me."

Luella lowered her gaze. "My apologies."

Regret filled him when her voice cracked, but he remained stoic. "They will be taken to the palace now," he said to Langdon.

The guards placed the two men in irons. Langdon hugged each son, assuring them he would do whatever was necessary to secure their freedom.

Langdon sneered at Luella. "This isn't over. Not by a long shot."

Remi stepped in between them. "I am warning you now, touch a hair on her head, I will personally see to it you are executed, and your sons will serve for the rest of their lives. Am I clear?"

Langdon laughed in his face. "You are a lowly herald and don't have the authority."

Remi did not look amused. "I may be a 'lowly' herald, but I carry the king's favor. He will listen to me before he would a human governor."

"We shall see." Langdon turned on his heel to follow the guards and his sons.

Once they were out of sight, Remi enveloped Luella in his arms. "I'm sorry I snapped at you. I had to maintain a cold persona. Any weakness I may have shown you may have made things worse."

His warmth and strong grip sent a shiver down her spine. Reluctantly, she pulled away. "As if you haven't already."

"I threatened him."

"Yes, and what good will that be when he kills me and buries me in the woods? Are you assigning one of these guards to protect me?" The look on his face told her what she already knew. "That's what I figured. Please, go now. I do not wish to see you again."

"Don't send me away," he implored. His softened tone caught her attention, as did his next words. "I can protect you."

Her brow furrowed. "How?"

"First, I will tell you the truth. Yes, I am a shifter." He reached for her when her eyes went wide, but she stepped back. "I mean you no harm, I promise."

"Then what do you want?" she asked as he took her hand firmly into his own.

"What I said, that I will protect you. As a shifter, I carry a small amount of fae magic. I can make a bargain with you. If you agree, the bargain will open a channel, allowing you to call out to me if you are hurt or in danger. In return, I will come to you as quickly as possible."

Consumed with worry about her own safety, she tried to convince herself he truly had her protection at heart. "If you care for my safety so much, why did you press charges against them?"

"Is it not obvious? I told you, I know what they wanted to do to you." His finger gingerly traced the bruise on her wrist. Her breath sucked in at the light touch. "If I had simply let them go, they would have accomplished that, then possibly killed you after. Getting them away from here was the best option I had."

"Do you really believe that?"

"I do."

"Now I am a target for their father, instead."

"Hence why I am offering this for you. What is your answer?"

Tears pricked her eyes as she shook her head. "You leave me no choice, because of the predicament you put me in."

"Luella—"

"I do not trust you, but what else can I do? Very well, I will partake of this bargain." Her gaze met his. "As long as you promise me, it will only do as you say. You will not be able to read my mind or feel my emotions?"

"I swear it." His hand gripped her wrist, and she did the same. "Luella, if you say you accept my bargain, your mind will open to mine, and we will be able to communicate through this channel. Do you accept?"

She hesitated for a moment. "Yes." A burning snaked around her navel, and she fell to her knees. "What is that?" she demanded while cradling her abdomen.

He knelt beside her, gripping her shoulder. "The bargain leaves a mark."

"Why didn't you warn me?" she asked as he helped her stand.

"Honestly, I forgot. This is not something I do lightly."

Luella turned away and unfastened the front of her gown. When she gasped at the sight of her mark, Remi pulled her to him so he could examine her.

His fingers trailed over the ring of vines and thorns that encircled her belly button. "Hmm, interesting."

"What does that mean?" she asked, hastily fastening up her gown.

"It's a unique pattern."

"Do you have a mark, too?" She looked him over but was unable to see anything different. He smiled in response. "This is permanent, isn't it?"

"It lasts until I free you from the bargain."

"I can't end it myself?"

"No, only I have the power to do so."

"So in other words, yes. It's permanent. If the countess sees this…" Her voice hitched. "I need to return home."

"Allow me to escort you there."

"You've done enough. Before I go, how exactly does this work?"

"If you are in danger, scared, hurt, concentrate on me. Focus as if I am the only person in the world. Our minds will connect, I will hear you, and if necessary, I will rush to your aid."

"You promise?"

"I do."

"You seem sincere in what you say."

"When can I see you again?"

Without answering, she turned and walked away. Her heart sank to leave him, but she convinced herself, it was for the best. This was the last thing she needed, for someone else to hold power over her. She reminded herself it was for her protection, but the thought failed to bring much comfort.

"You've been absent today," Clara commented when Luella entered the kitchen. "Where have you been and what have you been doing?"

"I took care of a few things outside," Luella answered while keeping her gaze low.

"Such as?"

"I fed the animals, fixed the chicken coop, then—"

"Look at me." When Luella didn't move, Clara grasped her chin and jerked her head up. "So the rumors are true, you are responsible for what happened to Anthony and Stefan?"

"No, I'm not."

"Do not lie to me. Madison heard all about it in the market. She informed me as soon as she arrived home. Do you have any idea what this will do to my daughters' reputations? I am already having a hard enough time finding suitors for them. They are past the point where they should already be married! Now, this?"

"But I didn't press charges," Luella insisted.

"I highly doubt that."

"I swear, Remi was the one who—"

"Remi, the herald you saved?"

"Yes."

"And you are on a first name basis with him?" Clara scoffed. "What else?"

"He had the governor's sons arrested. I had nothing to do with it. You must believe me."

"All he has done from the moment you met him, is cause trouble for this household. I forbid you from seeing him again. If I find out you did so behind my back, I will punish you until you learn your place. Do you understand?"

"Yes, madam."

"As punishment for keeping this from me, you will go to bed without dinner."

"Madam, please—"

"Prepare our meals, then retire for the evening."

"Of course."

Clara left the kitchen, and Luella brushed her tears away before dicing the tomatoes. The meat seared over the open flame as she continued with the other vegetables. She wiped the sweat from her brow with the back of her hand, removed the beef to the serving dish, then added the sides.

Luella set everything up in the dining room, rang the bell, then returned to the kitchen. Hidden under a table linen, she removed the plate and dined before washing dishes.

After climbing the stairs to the attic, she undressed and stood before her mirror. She examined the strange mark. Thinking of Remi caused her skin to go flush. He was attractive, but she knew she could never be with him. Even if Clara didn't forbid it, she was too low in status to be with a herald from the palace.

She slipped into her nightgown and curled up on the floor. Thoughts raced through her mind, being engulfed in his arms, resting against his firm torso. The fact he was a shifter escaped her attention as she focused on his comfort instead.

Remi paced in his chambers, debating how he felt about Luella. Part of him cared for her, he knew that much. There was more to her, more that he had yet to discover.

Something about her drew him in, and he couldn't stop thinking of her. Every waking moment away from her caused him pain, and he longed to see her more than anything. There were several beautiful women who came to the palace, but none of them ever caught his eye.

"The king is looking for you."

Remi startled at his voice. "Thank you, Simon. I didn't hear you come in."

He leaned against the doorframe. "You're thinking about her, aren't you? The woman who saved you, I mean."

Remi shot him a smile. "How did you know?"

"She is quite lovely and brave. The fact she stood up to two men who were hurting you is amazing. I wonder if she is available for courting."

"Why would you say that?"

"Because if you don't make a move, I will."

Remi bared his teeth, then barked with laughter. "Simon, don't be dense. I will talk to her when I get the chance."

Chapter 4

The Hunter

ave you finished mending my gown yet?" Madison asked as she entered the drawing room. "I need it for our afternoon tea." She approached Luella and tapped her well-manicured nails on the table while watching her work.

"Nearly there," Luella responded with needle and thread in hand.

"Well, hurry up!" Madison demanded.

At her childish tone, Luella smiled while continuing at her present pace. She completed the final stitch, tied it off, then held up the gown.

"All done."

Madison scoffed before snatching it away. "What, do you expect a thank you?"

"Of course not," Luella said as she slid from the chair and stood. "After all, only ladies with proper manners say that."

"You brat!" Madison yelled while storming up to her.

She nearly tackled Luella, but her mother grabbed her by the collar and yanked her backwards.

"This is not how you should behave," Clara scolded her. "What were you thinking?"

"She started it! How dare she talk back to me? She is a lowly servant, of no importance. I am the daughter of—"

"Silence!" Clara glared at Luella before returning her attention to Madison. "Even so, you do not attack her. Either use your words, or you come to me to deal with her."

"Yes, Mother."

"Get ready for tea. The Baroness of Lyndon will be joining us."

"And what of her son?"

"From what I understand, Henri is accompanying her. It is urgent you get dressed."

Without another word, Madison promptly left. Luella started for the door.

"And you, girl. What right do you have to treat my daughter in such a manner?"

Luella spun on her heel. "You don't even know what happened."

"Nor do I care. If all goes well, by the end of today she will be courting Lord Henri, a man of class and nobility. With any luck, it will be a brief courtship followed by marriage. As such, you will treat her with the same respect you would show him."

"Yes, madam."

"Tomorrow, we are attending the festival in Colmarre."

"I would love to attend," Luella blurted out.

Clara shook her head. "I dare not be seen with the likes of you. Anyway, we will be late returning, so I expect all of your chores to be done, the manor to be spotless, and not a single complaint from the colonists. Do you understand?"

"I do," Luella answered, keeping her gaze up while her spirits fell.

"Good."

Luella went into the kitchen to prepare for company. She stayed up late the previous night to clean and prepare the pastries. She set up the 3-tier stands with sandwiches, scones, jams, and cream before starting to heat up the kettle.

Clara answered the door, welcoming the baroness and her son, before leading them into the parlor. Luella entered a few moments later, offering tea. Henri stood by the table. She approached and filled each cup. Piercing grey eyes stared at her, before he offered her a smile.

"Child, your hair is the stuff of legend. I have only heard the story of one other with hair as white as yours. Why, it's almost silver, isn't it?" the baroness commented while dipping her scone in her tea.

"Thank you," Luella said with a curtsy. Clara's gaze remained fixed on Luella. "Did you need anything else?"

The baroness wore a large purple hat and matching dress. "No, dear. That is all. Thank you."

Clara laughed. "Oh, you need not thank the help. After all, that is what they are here for."

"Maybe you don't," the baroness said, "but we do."

Clara straightened up as she cleared her throat. "My apologies."

Luella left the room and went to wash the dishes soaking in the sink. Strong arms enveloped her waist as she dried the last one. Unable to turn, she glanced over her shoulder to see Henri, who stood at least a foot taller than her.

Forcing her way out of his grasp, she kept her head low. "Can I help you, sir?"

"I bet you have the spirit to match that hair, don't you? Wild and unruly, like me."

"I do not know what you mean, but if you'll excuse me." Her eyes darted to his when he refused to move. "I have things to do."

"Would you add me to your list?" he asked with a wink.

"If you are suggesting we court—"

He howled with laughter. "Of course not. I'm talking about a quick, fun romp in the sack."

"No."

"Why not?"

"For starters, this is wildly inappropriate. Also, you are supposed to be here for Madison, not me. If I may be so bold, perhaps it would be best if you returned to the parlor and left me to my own devices."

"Perhaps I could convince the countess to let me have some fun. She attempts to hide it, but I see the desperation in her eyes. Desperation for her daughter to be married off. I am sure if I insisted, she would include you in a package deal. Two for one," he said with a chuckle.

Luella's stomach flipped. "Sir, please return to the parlor. I am sure they are waiting for you."

"We aren't finished," he snapped as he sulked from the room.

Luella didn't understand why she attracted such vile men's attention, from Anthony and Stefan, and now Henri. She had to remain close by in case they rang for her, so she began meal preparation for dinner. Slicing up vegetables and focusing on spices helped distract her.

Luella rinsed the blanket once more before hanging it up. The weather remained fair, with the sun shining on her as she continued to wash.

"Would you like some help?"

She froze at his voice, contemplated her response, then picked up the next blanket. "I am fine, but thank you for the kind offer." Her gaze remained fixed on the laundry instead of the herald who stood behind her.

"I don't mind, really."

"Good day, sir."

"What have I done to earn such ire from you?"

"I… I simply wish to be alone, that is all."

"Aren't you alone enough?"

A shiver traveled down her spine, and the blanket nearly fell from her hand. She clutched it tighter for a moment before hanging it up.

"I beg your pardon?" she asked as she faced him.

He smiled at her, one eyebrow arched as he silently studied her, then gestured around them. "Every time I see you, you are by yourself. I only wish to learn more about you. Is that so hard to believe?"

"Why would you want that?"

"Why not?" he quipped with a grin.

"Because I am sure you have better ways to spend your time." Her breath whooshed out when he stepped up beside her, taking a corner of the blanket and attaching it to the line.

"Why do you fight me at every turn? Is it so difficult for you to have a pleasant conversation?"

"How can we have a conversation when every question you ask needs no answer?"

"Hmm, I could say the same for you." When he smiled at her again, her pulse quickened. "So tell me, what else do you do? Besides laundry and saving heralds, I mean. Do you bake, read, play piano?"

"What interests do you have?"

"Very well. If it will spark the conversation, I will answer first. If you promise to, as well."

"I will."

"I enjoy a great many things. Dancing, for one. I also enjoy hunting, and I am particularly fond of falconry."

"Hunting," she murmured as she stepped back. "Is that what you shifters call it, when you attack innocent people in the woods?"

"I was the one attacked."

"This time, yes. I know all too well how dangerous shifters are."

His eyes narrowed. "Watch how you speak of my kind."

"Given what they have done to me, I have every right to say whatever I want. Regardless of my feelings, I saved your sorry hide."

A low growl escaped him as his hands clenched. "If you hate my kind so much, why did you save me?"

"To protect the colony," she responded matter-of-factly.

"Bullshit. You don't care about it. You said yourself you are an outcast. So why would you care what happens?"

"Because, this is still my home. I will do what I must to protect it, even if that means saving an animal like you."

"Animal?" His spine stiffened as his eyes darkened. "I'll show you an animal."

He took three steps back. Before Luella could ask what he was doing, he began to shift. His face stretched out, then his arms and legs elongated as he fell to all fours. The final touch, deep brown and black fur covered him in his entirety.

Luella stood frozen in place, her mouth open in a silent scream as fear rushed through her very veins. Seeing her in such a state, Remi instantly shifted back. In her shock, she failed to notice his clothing reappeared, unharmed, as he took on his human form.

Remi rushed to her once he realized what he'd done. She flinched and covered her face in a futile attempt to defend herself. "Don't touch me!" she screamed. "Leave me alone."

"Luella—"

"Please, don't kill me," she begged with a sob.

Her final plea nearly broke him where he stood. He only intended to show her what he was, not scare or traumatize her.

"It's all right," he said in a gentle tone. "You're safe now. I am terribly sorry."

Her arms wrapped around her waist as tears streamed down her cheeks. "I am right about you. You are an animal! I never should've saved you."

She turned and ran, ignoring his pleas for her to stop. The thought raced through his mind, to give chase, to catch her and reassure her, but he chose to let her go. He would give her the time she needed to cope. They would talk, then everything would be all right. He assured himself as he started to walk home.

Thinking of the look on her face when he shifted made his heart fall into his stomach. The terror and unbridled fear nearly caused him to retch.

How could I do that to her? I never meant to scare her. I gave in to my anger, and in doing so, I may have lost her forever. Can you lose someone who isn't even yours? I will make this up to her and earn her forgiveness. If it's the last thing I ever do.

Comforted, he smiled on his walk. The guards joined him and led the way, except Simon. He remained by his side.

"So, your plan was to scare her?"

"Obviously not. Believe me, there is nothing you can say that will make me feel worse than I already do."

"What are you thinking?"

"You'll see," Remi answered with a grin. "For now, let's return to the palace. I'm ready to hear whatever lecture His Majesty has prepared for us."

"You don't agree with him, do you?"

"About the omegas? Absolutely not. It isn't their fault they are infertile. We still have yet to discover the cause."

"Assuming there is one. How long has it been now?"

"Nearly three hundred years. It's why each prince is expected to take a human bride when they come of age. The king made it law to ensure he would have an heir, and every king since has honored it."

"I see the logic behind it, to ensure the royal bloodline doesn't go extinct."

"Except I hate how the omegas are treated. The king uses them as his personal harem behind closed doors while spouting of chosen mates and faithfulness to your partner."

"I didn't realize you felt so strongly about this."

"We are all affected. Every one of us is expected to take a human bride, regardless of status. It is to continue building up our numbers. But whatever happened to love? Or even finding our destined mate?"

"There hasn't been a destined mate in a long time. Honestly, I don't think they exist anymore."

"But even my chosen mate should be *chosen*, not forced on me simply for being a human."

"Have you met a shifter you wish to court?" Simon asked, his voice low so as not to be overheard by the other guards.

"Of course not. Even if that was not illegal, I have had little interest in any of the females I've met. Well, until Luella."

Simon smiled at his response. "I think the two of you would make a lovely couple."

"I highly doubt she feels the same about me, especially after today."

Luella spent the next few days walking in a fog, completing her chores, and saying very little. At night, lying beside the fireplace, her dreams were plagued by the big bad wolf.

Wednesday rolled around, and she reluctantly returned to the pond. She gathered her courage and left the safety of the manor. The first blanket still clutched in her hand, her heart fell at the familiar voice wishing her good day. Ignoring him, she rinsed and hung it up.

"Good day, Luella," Remi said again as he approached her. She did not respond. "Please, speak to me. That is all I am asking for."

"You have done enough," she said as she hung the next blanket. "I have no desire to see you or to speak with you."

"Not even if I brought you a gift?"

"Sir, if you brought me the royal crown on a velvet pillow, my response would remain the same. No, thank you. Please, be on your way."

"It's a bookmark I made for you."

Her hand gripped the line as her gaze met his. "You… you made me something?"

He held it up to show her. It was a small, rectangular piece of wood containing dried flowers that were pressed on before being covered with a lacquer finish. The finishing touch consisted of a satin ribbon tied around the tiny hole at the top.

"I saw you reading here the other day and thought you might like this."

"You made me something?" she asked again, still in disbelief he took the time to do so.

"I did. Will you accept it?"

"No one's ever… I haven't…" Her eyes squeezed shut as she attempted to gather her thoughts. "Why would you do this?"

He stared at her for a moment. "Because I wanted to say I'm sorry for my behavior. I never meant to scare you. Plus, I wanted to thank you for saving me."

"Why was I the one to save you? Why didn't you shift when they attacked you?"

He sighed. "I was following something. My attention was wholly focused on it, and I didn't hear them come up behind me. I was about to shift when you appeared, so I decided to wait. I was curious to see if you were there to help them or help me."

"What were you following?"

He gave a shrug of his shoulders. "A scent." Once more, he lifted the bookmark. "Do you want this?"

Her hand visibly shook as she reached for it. "Thank you," she said softly. Their fingers brushed, and she sucked in her breath before admiring the bookmark. "This is beautiful."

"I'm glad you like it."

She startled when he stepped towards her. "That's close enough."

"You're still afraid of me?"

"I am. You can't possibly understand."

"Then help me to. Were you attacked by a wolf?"

"As a small child," Luella admitted.

"I didn't know. I sincerely apologize."

"You didn't care," she retorted. "Admit it, you only shifted because you were angry."

"I'll admit I was angry, yes. You called me an animal, so I showed you what I look like as one. Can you really blame me for that?" He studied her face. "You haven't slept well since then, have you?"

"How did you figure that out?"

"Your eyes are sunken in. This is because of me, isn't it?"

"I don't wish to discuss it. Actually, I need to get back to work."

"Do your sisters help as well?"

"What do you know about them?"

Remi sighed and shifted on his feet, getting agitated at her need to answer his questions with a question of her own. "Not much, I'll admit. I overheard the governor talking about them while we walked to the palace."

"What did he say?"

Remi hesitated to say anything, since this was the most she had shown any interest in conversing with him. He rubbed the back of his neck for a moment.

"Only that your mother wishes to marry them off to men of means or nobility, preferably both. It upset him she didn't consider his own sons to be good enough, and what happened would tarnish any chance they may have had."

"What else?"

"Nothing was said about you. Why is that?" His stomach knotted when her eyes narrowed, and he realized whatever progress he'd made with her was gone in the blink of an eye.

"It doesn't matter," she said, her voice terse.

"I didn't mean to offend you."

"Thank you for the lovely gift, but I wish you would go now. I have things to do."

"Luella, please—"

"Goodbye, Remi."

Watching her resume with the blankets, he doubted she would speak another word to him. He stepped up behind her, gently gripped her shoulder, and she froze when his lips graced her ear.

"Until I see you again," he whispered.

When she finally turned around, he was nowhere to be seen. A ghost of feeling haunted her skin, everywhere he touched her warm and igniting feelings in her she didn't quite understand.

"Well, that could've went better." Remi shook his head as the anger blazed in his eyes. "I believe she will not forgive me any time soon, nor would I blame her if she doesn't."

"If it's any consolation, her face lit up when you presented her with the bookmark. You made some progress today."

"Surely, you jest."

"No, I mean it. Though I am quite certain she would rather be with a handsome guard such as myself."

Remi pawed his shoulder. "Shall I challenge you to a duel for her hand?"

Simon chuckled. "Of course not. Give her some time, show her what a real charmer you are, then she'll choose me."

They erupted into laughter as they left the colony. Remi turned serious.

"Do you really think I have a chance with her?"

"Yes, I do."

"She is the most captivating woman I've ever seen. I get lost in her eyes, her smile, and her heart. She must surely be a siren, luring me in with her beauty and kindness."

"Whoa, sounds to me like someone is already in love." Simon's expression became more solemn. "You do realize—"

"Yes, I will have to gain my father's approval." His jaw clenched. "But why not her? She is the daughter of a countess, who is brave and compassionate. We would be quite good together."

"Then do not lose hope. Give her some time. See her again when you think she is ready for you."

"I appreciate that."

"Hey, we've known each other since we were pups. I know you better than you know yourself."

"You believe you do," Remi said with a grin.

Luella put away the mop before stepping outside for fresh air. Strolling through the woods invigorated her. It would rain soon, made apparent by the dark clouds looming overhead. Not wishing to be caught in the rain, she hurried towards the manor.

Her thoughts drifted to Remi, and she wondered if she would see him again. Such thoughts confused her, knowing he frightened her so. Yet she found herself inexplicably drawn to him. Something about the way he looked at her and spoke to her made her feel as though someone could actually care for her.

When he discovers who she really is, the servant of the countess and not her daughter, will he still look at her the same? It didn't matter, she told herself as she suppressed her feelings. She closed her heart and locked it up tight, knowing she had to protect it, no matter what.

She stepped inside the kitchen, shut the door, and watched as the heavens opened. Grateful she made it in time, she let out a small laugh. Then she noticed the fire needed tending, so she took care of it before she began to prep for dinner.

"Why do you always hum?" Aubrey asked while Luella chopped vegetables.

"It makes me happy, I suppose," Luella answered as she resumed.

"You serve us, having no life of your own, but you claim to be happy. How?"

"Because I do have a life of my own. It might be in books and dreams, but I can find joy there. I can read about a vampyr and his fated mate, or a merman king looking for a bride. I love reading those legends and stories, especially ones with romance."

"Mother says romance is for people who don't believe in themselves and need someone to make them feel whole."

"That is sad. While I don't believe you need a partner to complete you, I do think life would be better spent with someone who loves you, cares for you, and wants to be there for you."

"Mother…" Aubrey's voice cracked. "Mother used to be like that. I miss reading with her while she braided my hair. Then the incident happened, and—"

"What are you girls talking about?" Clara asked as she entered the kitchen.

"Romance books," Aubrey replied while keeping her eyes on Luella. "How silly they are."

"People who read cannot think for themselves, and they must rely on books to fill their heads with utter nonsense."

"I do enjoy a good story, though," Aubrey said.

Clara scoffed. "Dinner will be ready shortly," Luella said, smiling at Aubrey.

She and her mother left without another word. Luella continued to hum as she removed the meat from the open flame, before layering it on the tray with bread and cheese.

Once everything was set up in the dining room, she rang the bell, then promptly returned to the kitchen. After eating and washing dishes, she settled in front of the fireplace to read one of her favorite books.

When she turned the page, the bookmark slipped out and landed in her lap. She set the book down before taking a closer look. The pressed flowers were unfamiliar to her.

Her chest tightened as she thought of Remi. She looked out the window, relieved to see the rain had stopped. After returning the bookmark, she went outside, and stood on the hill overlooking the river. The wind whipped around her as the sky again grew dark. She raced for the manor as the rain began to pour, soaking her before she made it inside.

"Did little Cinderella get caught in the rain?" Madison teased as Luella stoked the fire.

Her teeth chattered, and her focus remained on the warmth of the hearth while she ignored her stepsister. After she dried off, she made it upstairs to her room, where her body flushed with fever. Curling up with her torn blanket, she fell unconscious.

"Luella, where is our breakfast?" Clara yelled from the bottom of the stairs. "If I have to come up there, you're going to regret it!"

When she received no response, she cleared her throat, and marched up the steps. As she reached the top, her gaze fell on Luella huddled in the corner and shivering. Clara approached her, then she knelt beside her to feel her forehead.

"You are burning up! Figures you would get sick today of all days. I have the baroness and her son coming. What am I going to do now?" She stood and placed her hands on her hips. "Aubrey, Madison, get up here now!"

"Yes, Mother?" Aubrey said as they approached.

"Luella is ill. What are we to do without her? Our company will be here at two o'clock."

"We will take care of her," Aubrey assured her.

Clara left them to it, going to the kitchen to be sure everything was ready for high tea. Relief flooded her at the sight of the pastries Luella made the night before.

She finished her final check when all three girls walked in. Aubrey dressed Luella in one of her fine pink gowns and covered with her cream-colored apron.

"You cannot be serious?" Clara asked, clearly mortified by the sight.

"She isn't coughing, and she can whisk in and out. They'll pay her no attention."

"Luella, how do you feel?"

"I'll be all right, madam. I need a little more rest, but I'll be up to serving your company."

"Take her to the fainting couch in the drawing room, close the curtains, and let her sleep."

Aubrey's jaw dropped. "Since when do you care about her well-being?"

"I don't," Clara snapped. "But I don't need her to pass out in front of company, either. There was that awful blood plague years ago, and we don't need them thinking she has something contagious! Fix her a cup of peppermint tea, then let her rest until a half hour before company arrives."

"I don't remember her ever being sick before," Aubrey observed.

"Neither do I," said Clara. "Now, see to her."

"Mother, but she—"

"Madison, I swear to the gods above, you better do as I say!"

"But who will help us dress?" Madison asked with a pout.

"Take care of each other," Clara snarled, having had enough of them both. "I need a drink." She left the room in a huff.

Aubrey took Luella into the drawing room while Madison attempted to brew a cup of tea. Aubrey helped her onto the sofa and covered her with a blanket.

Madison came in and handed Luella a teacup. Luella smiled as she took it, then tried to hide her grimace after her first sip.

"Thank you."

While she rested, they dressed in their fine gowns and helped each other with hair and make-up. Madison woke her up at 1:30, surprised to find her fever had spiked. Luella's skin was covered in a thin sheen of sweat.

"Mother, what are we to do?" Madison asked.

"I will take care of this. You two, set everything up. It's all arranged in the kitchen, move it to the dining room and lay it out. Make haste!"

Clara pulled Luella from the sofa, keeping her arm wrapped around her waist as she took her outside. Luella realized she was up and moving.

"Where are we going?" she asked in a daze.

"You will stay out here, away from my guests. I won't have you embarrassing me."

"Why not put me in the attic?" Luella murmured.

"Because, given the state you are in, I don't need you wandering in and scaring my company."

Clara led her into the woods, far away from the manor, and set her against a tree trunk. Luella slept soundly, and Clara shook her head as she headed home.

Chapter 5

The Wolf

hat's going on?" Luella asked with slurred speech when she was lifted from the ground. "What are you doing? Put me down at once!" she demanded while squirming in his arms, trying to break free.

"Luella, you have a fever. What are you doing outside?"

"Remi, is that you?"

"I'm here. I came to the pond, hoping we would have the chance to talk about the other day. You must've taken ill and passed out here."

"Yes, that's what happened," Luella mumbled, hating the lie pouring from her mouth. Shame tore through her as she considered telling him the real reason she was outside.

"I assume you have a doctor in the colony. Where does he live?"

"I... I haven't any money... on me, I mean."

"It's all right. We'll figure something out."

"His office is towards the center of town, by the bakery."

Remi rushed through the woods at inhuman speed, clutching her tightly to his chest. A memory stirred in Luella, but her foggy brain couldn't sort it out. Before she knew it, they arrived at the village.

People stared but said nothing as he ran past them. Luella guided him to the office, and Remi rang the bell as soon as he landed on the top step.

The door opened to a young woman dressed in a sterile nurse's uniform. "How can we help?"

"She is very ill and needs the doctor."

"Please, come inside."

He carried Luella across the threshold and into the small waiting area. A woman paced anxiously.

"The doctor is currently tending to her son. He will be with you shortly."

Remi held Luella tighter, sitting on a small open bench under the window. He ignored the confused look from the mother who continued to walk about the room.

"You'll be all right," he said softly to Luella, placing his palm over her forehead. "You're so warm."

The doctor walked out a few minutes later and spoke quietly with the woman to reassure her that her son was fine. He had broken his arm, but it was a clean break. Then he took her back to see him. He returned a moment later.

"I am Tiernan. How can I help?"

"Luella has a fever, and I'm not sure what else. I found her passed out in the woods."

Tiernan took her from Remi's arms, and the nurse followed him. "Please, wait here," she said to Remi as they left.

"Of course."

Remi glanced at the clock from time to time, anxiously awaiting any news. Her fever was high. She had no color, her skin was hot to the touch, and she barely looked human when he'd found her.

After thirty minutes, he was ready to march into the exam room to get answers. Before he had the chance, the nurse walked up to him.

"How is she?" he asked, jumping to his feet.

"She'll be all right. He is giving her medicine, but she needs to rest before traveling. We will keep her here until her fever goes down."

"I'm glad to hear it."

She shifted from one foot to the other. "I apologize, but there is the matter of payment."

"Does her mother not have an account here?"

"The countess? No, she isn't—"

He lifted his hand. "Say no more. I will pay for her. How much?"

After she gave him the total, he handed her the coin. "Thank you," she said as she placed it safely in the box. "The doctor will speak with you momentarily."

"Can you tell me where Luella lives?"

"No, I'm not allowed—"

The door opened, and Tiernan stepped out. "I'm afraid I am correct, that she is in no shape to travel at the moment. She'll stay tonight. We'll get her home tomorrow."

"Please, do. I'm sure her family is worried about her." Remi noticed the glance between Tiernan and the nurse. He started to ask.

"Thank you for bringing her here," Tiernan said, offering his hand.

Remi shook it. "Can I see her?"

"Sure, come on back. She's sleeping soundly, so she probably won't even realize you're here, I'm afraid."

He led Remi into the exam room where Luella slept. Remi approached her, saying nothing as he took her hand. Her face was relaxed and her color somewhat returned. Remi looked at the doctor.

"Can I stay with her tonight?"

"Sorry, son. Family only policy. I need to check on a few things, so you may visit for a while longer."

"Thank you."

The doctor left, and Remi watched Luella. Even asleep, she was the most stunning woman he'd ever seen. Her hair shone under the light. He felt her forehead before running his fingers through her silver strands.

He shook his head, wondering how someone so small, still practically a stranger to him, could have such possession over his entire being. There wasn't anything he would not do for her, would not give her, should she ask.

Tiernan appeared a few minutes later. Remi debated arguing, but he knew the doctor was right. Luella wouldn't know he was there. He thanked him, and with reluctance, he left the office.

"And how much do we owe?" Clara asked snidely when Tiernan returned Luella to the manor the next evening.

"The bill has been taken care of."

"How exactly did she end up at your office?"

"A young man carried her in. I believe he is the herald from the palace."

Clara cleared her throat. "Thank you," she said with a smile. Angry as she was at Luella, she needed to keep her emotions in check. Especially in front of the handsome doctor. "Say, are you still looking for courtship?"

"Ma'am, I am not interested. Not in either of your daughters. To be honest, if I were looking, I would choose her." He nodded towards Luella. "She is truly radiant."

Clara's breath caught in her throat while her face flushed. She composed herself. "My apologies. I was only trying to make polite conversation."

The doctor scoffed softly but said nothing else as Clara took Luella from his arms. "Her fever is gone, but she needs rest and to stay hydrated."

"We will see to her. Thank you again."

Once the door shut behind Tiernan, Clara pulled away, and Luella slumped to the floor as Aubrey walked in.

"Is she still sick?"

"No, but she must be exhausted from it. See to her while I enjoy my nightcap."

Aubrey opened her mouth to argue but promptly shut it when Clara gave her a sharp look. "Yes, Mother."

She helped Luella to her feet and into the washroom to clean up, before getting her ready for bed. They went into the sitting room so Luella could sleep on the sofa.

"You're worried about her, aren't you? Luella, I mean."

"Am I that obvious?"

Simon grinned. "Yes." He cleared his throat and turned serious. "You left the palace unprotected. Why?"

"I had a feeling something was wrong. You were all busy with Prince Seann and that whole debacle."

"Why they insist on hosting so many princes here, is beyond me. You put that many wolves together, from different regions, you are asking for trouble."

"Yes, but it helps keep the peace while aiding in finding them suitable mates."

"It makes me think of Prince Caspian."

"Why? That was ages ago." Remi's brow furrowed.

"I'm not sure. More importantly, why didn't you get me before you left? I would've followed you."

"I couldn't wait for an escort."

"Last time you left like that, you were attacked." Simon's voice trembled as he spoke, thinking of what might've happened, had Luella not intervened.

"You're right, my friend. I'm sorry. I won't do it again."

"Right. I've heard that before."

"I have no idea what you mean," Remi said with a chuckle.

"If I had a gold coin for every time you've slipped away, I would live like a prince myself."

They laughed for a moment, then Remi gripped Simon's shoulder. "I mean it. I promise I will find you, should I need to slip away again."

"You were hurt, and—"

"Hey, that was not your fault. Besides, I'm glad it happened. It showed me the kind of person Luella is, so I don't have to wonder if her feelings for me are genuine or if it's because I'm a fancy herald from the palace. You know, I smelled her scent before I saw her."

Simon choked on his laugh before his expression grew serious. "Wait, is that what you were pursuing, her scent?"

"Yes. I caught a whiff in the breeze and damn near went feral on the spot. I've never felt that way before."

"You really believe in destined mates, don't you?"

"What do you mean?"

"The way you describe it matches the legend. They find each other first by scent. Once their eyes meet, the mating bond locks into place, and there is no question. They are meant to be together."

"When did you get so romantic?"

"Oh, I'm not. I'm quoting what we learned in school. After all, not all of us had private tutors."

Remi nodded. "I never heard that. Father wouldn't let us learn about destined mates, since he doesn't believe in them. He said duty is more important than love."

"What are your thoughts on the subject?"

"I am unsure. Either way, I long to see her again. I'm sure she'll be fine."

Simon cocked his head. "Then why do you sound worried?"

Remi sighed. "She was sick and looked almost dead when I found her. Can you blame me?"

"Then let's go check on her."

"We can't, not yet, but I will soon enough."

"The king is most curious as to why you keep visiting that one colony in particular."

"Well, lucky for me, they tried to kill me. I am using that as my reason to go, saying I am keeping my eye on the colonists to ensure there is no threat of an uprising."

"Does he believe you when you tell him that?"

"Probably not, but at least it's a somewhat believable reason." The clock chimed. "We need to go. It's time for dinner. My father is expecting me."

Confused for a moment, Luella glanced around, curious to find herself in the drawing room. She went upstairs and changed before starting breakfast.

"Glad to see you are back to your tasks," Clara said as she entered the kitchen. "It was positively dreadful having to fend for ourselves."

Luella smiled, as if offering an inside joke. "I'm sorry, madam. Yes, I am much better. Thank you."

"Oh, I had nothing to do with it. That meddling herald found you in the woods and took you to the doctor."

"He did?"

"You don't remember?"

"No, it's all a bit of a blur."

"What matters is you are well enough to take care of us. We did have a fine time, and Henri seems intrigued with Madison. Perhaps they will begin courting soon."

"That is good news," Luella said softly, praying that was all the countess would say about it.

"I expect you to do all of your chores today, including what wasn't done yesterday. I do not want to hear any excuses, either."

"Yes, madam. I will start after breakfast."

"Very good."

Clara left, and Luella wondered about Remi. He saved her? How could she not remember? She shook her head to clear it, then began with eggs and bacon. Next, she placed the toast over the fire. Finally, fresh-squeezed orange juice. She filled the plates, loaded the tray, and went into the dining room.

A wave of exhaustion washed over her, and she barely made it to the table. She set down the tray and steadied herself before setting everything up. After she rang the bell, she rushed to the kitchen to sit and eat. Trying to regain her composure, Luella's hands trembled.

When she tried to mop, her strength nearly gave out, so she stepped outside for fresh air. The day was warm and sunny, so she decided to do laundry. She managed to gather everything and load up the cart, then clung to the donkey's harness as they walked.

At the pond, what little energy she had left abandoned her completely. Unable to do anything else, she sat against a tree trunk. Her eyes closed, and she had nearly nodded off when a familiar voice pulled her back.

"Hmm, this is pretty close to where I found you passed out. I wondered if you would return."

Luella looked up as Remi approached her. "The countess said you were the one who helped me. For that, I give you my thanks."

"I will accept it," he teased with a half-bow. "How are you feeling?"

"I am too tired to complete my chores, though I know I must."

Remi reached into the cart, removing the blanket on top along with the soap, and walked to the edge of the pond. "Then I shall do it for you."

"Why?" she asked as she attempted to stand.

He gestured for her to stay. "Please, sit and rest before you pass out again." There was no denying the insistence in his voice.

"Why are you helping me?"

"Because you are…" He cleared his throat. "Because you are beautiful and kind. You helped me when no one else would. Allow me to return the favor."

"And to prove to me you are more human than animal?" she asked, keeping her eyes low.

He chuckled. "I doubt washing a few blankets would convince you of that. No, because it's the right thing to do."

Her words failed her, so she watched while he continued to wash. He carefully hung each blanket, as though showing extra care in front of her. After hanging the last one, he stretched, then sat beside her.

"Thank you," she said softly while avoiding his gaze.

"What's the matter?"

Tears welled up in her eyes. "I'm embarrassed for how I spoke to you. I was scared and angry, and I took it out on you. I owe you an apology."

"I would expect nothing less from the daughter of a countess. After all, I am simply a herald, and a shifter at that, while you are from a house of nobility. Right?"

The anger in his voice penetrated her skin, finding its target, and piercing her heart. "I'm sorry," she said with a shaky voice. "I am worthy of your ire. Please, forgive me."

Remi was tired of humans looking down on shifters when all they did was try to protect humans. He also realized he had no right to react to her the way he did, to scare her. His hand clenched as a sigh blew from his lips.

"I apologize for losing my temper. After all, you did save me. I should not have shifted in front of you like that."

Her eyes squeezed shut. "I see that wolf every night in my dreams," she admitted, each word full of fear.

"Luella, I am so sorry."

"No, not you. It's the one who attacked us."

"Were you injured?"

"No, but… he killed someone dear to me."

"Oh. There are reports of feral shifters. Ones who stay in wolf form and attack without cause. We do what we can to contain them, even putting them down when necessary."

"You kill your own kind?"

"As if humans don't as well. But yes, if we must. Despite what you might think, we want to work with the humans. We want to protect you."

Luella scoffed, her voice laced with bitterness. "Your king's actions say otherwise. Corralling us into these colonies, heavy taxes, and for what?"

"There are monsters in the world, much worse than wolves. We keep them at bay."

"I've never seen the outside world."

"You've lived here your entire life?"

"From what I understand, I was born elsewhere. We came here when I was very young."

"I've traveled the whole of L'Evrope. I go wherever my king sends me."

"I'm sure you've seen some beautiful sights."

"None more so than the one before me."

Heat rose in her cheeks, and she could not speak or think for a moment. "I've been ill. Surely, I misheard you."

He let out another chuckle. "I assure you, you did not." The blankets fluttered as a gentle breeze passed by, catching his attention. "Any other tasks?"

"I need a few things from the market."

"I will accompany you there."

"Before we do that, I have a confession to make."

"Yes?"

"The countess, she isn't…" Luella trailed off, losing her nerve. "Um, she has forbidden me from seeing you."

"Forbidden, you say? I like the sound of that." He gave her a teasing smile.

"Remi, I'm serious. If we're seen together, I could get in a lot of trouble."

"Why does she forbid it? Because I'm a—"

"She didn't say."

Remi wanted to pursue it, but the pain expressed on her face confused him, and he decided to let it drop. "Fine. I'll take you to the market, we'll get what you need, then we'll return here. The countess won't know. If anyone tells her they saw us, tell her I ran into you there and helped you."

"Remi—"

"And the donkey will help you home, since you seem adamant to keep where you live a secret from me."

"There are so many things I long to tell you."

"What's stopping you?"

"I… It doesn't matter. I've rested enough, and I believe I can complete my shopping, with your help."

"Let's go."

Luella clung to Remi while they walked through the market, using what strength she had to keep herself upright. When they were purchasing her goods, Remi noticed a few odd looks from the merchants, but he said nothing.

They approached the last shop, and Luella stopped. "I'll only be a moment."

"Luella—"

"Please."

Reluctantly, he let her go. He stood outside, holding her goods and waiting. A young woman with strawberry-blonde hair walked out from the shop, giggling. Remi looked inside to see Luella, her face flush, while she argued with the merchant.

As he was considering going inside, Luella stepped out instead. "Are you all right?" he asked, noticing the dampness in her eyes.

She wiped her face. "I'm fine." The bag clutched tightly in her hands, she gave him a small smile. "That was the last purchase. We can return now."

He gripped her jawline and lifted her head, forcing her to meet his gaze. "What was that all about?" he asked, jutting his chin towards the shop.

"N… Nothing," she answered as she pulled away. "Please, we need to get back. I don't have much strength."

He kept his arm wrapped around her waist as they walked in silence through the woods. Her scent captivated him, and he became lost in thought.

"Thank you."

Her words brought him back. He helped her load up the cart. "How do you feel?"

"I wouldn't have been able to do this without you."

"Glad to be of service," he said as dark clouds rolled by overhead. "You need to get home before it rains."

"What about you?"

"Are you offering for me to join you?" He laughed when she became flustered in response. "I'm teasing. I'll be fine."

Grasping the donkey's harness, she gave Remi one last look. "Thank you for today."

"You are most welcome. May I see you again?"

Her smile was the only answer she gave before she turned to watch where she walked. Excitement washed over Remi as he stared at her, knowing he would meet with her again. He would tell her how he felt. Hope filled him that she would reciprocate his feelings.

Chapter 6

Playing Games

hursday, Luella hummed while she mopped, her mind drifting back to Remi and the market. Being so close to him, his warm, musky vanilla scent invaded her senses. She bit her lower lip as the memory of it consumed her.

"What is Cinderella smiling about today?" Aubrey asked.

"Perhaps the dormouse invited her over for tea," Madison teased as she passed through.

Aubrey giggled as she watched her sister leave. She turned back to Luella. "We were there yesterday, at the butcher shop."

Luella clutched the handle. "What do you mean?"

"I heard what the owner said, that he wouldn't sell you what you wanted, because you are nothing more than a servant. Madison had to leave before she drew attention with her fit of laughter."

Flushing with embarrassment, her grip loosened as she continued to mop. "I will be turning twenty-one soon."

"What does that have to do with anything?"

"Oh, only that I am excited for my birthday. Cake and presents."

"As if you've ever had any of that."

A painful lump formed in Luella's throat. "Still, I am looking forward to it."

"Why? Nothing will change for you." Aubrey's expression went from confusion to understanding. "Ah, you believe you will leave here, don't you?" She leaned in and lowered her voice. "I guess you aren't aware, then. Mother has ensured none of the merchants will hire you, nor will any of the men here court you."

"Why not?"

Aubrey shifted where she stood while avoiding Luella's gaze. "She may have spread the rumor around the colony that you are a liar and a thief."

"What?" Luella asked as the mop fell from her hands and landed with a clatter on the floor.

"She has been planting little stories here and there over the past year, knowing you would try to leave when you came of age. Now, you will have nowhere to go and no one to help you."

"But if I am what she says, why does she let me stay here?"

Aubrey sighed. "To her, that's the best part. It's because she feels an obligation to you, as you are her stepdaughter. Also, she has a 'big, caring heart and wants to try to change you for the better.' The colonists view her as the poor countess who has to deal with the likes of you."

"Why are you telling me this?"

"I thought you should be aware. Madison helped spread some of those lies, too. I wanted nothing to do with it. I'm sorry."

"Thank you," Luella said as the room began to shrink around her.

She spun around and hurried outside, paying no mind to her unfinished chores. The fresh air called to her, and she ran through the woods as tears streamed down her face. She paused by a tree to catch her breath.

Her mind raced as she tried to figure out what her next course of action could be. Putting up with her stepmother and stepsisters was only supposed to last until she turned twenty-one. She counted down the days until she would be free of them.

Between service as a maid, cooking, and other duties, she knew she'd acquired enough skills to work in the tavern or possibly in the manor of another noble. Still serving, but away from the countess and her daughters.

Despair pierced her heart. What would she do now? The countess had single-handedly destroyed Luella's dreams. Her plans fell apart around her. Her spine straightened as she lifted her head.

She would leave the colony and start fresh elsewhere. Remi said he had seen the country, surely he would recommend someplace for her. Her shoulders sagged. That meant she would have to tell him the truth.

Her mind battled her heart, knowing she cared for him, but she wasn't the right woman for him. He called himself a lowly herald, but she knew how much respect he and his position garnered. More than a few of the women colonists commented on how attractive he was. Plus, being in service to the king, he would surely have to marry someone of at least equal status. Not a servant girl like her.

His interest in her seemed genuine, and though she was loathe to do so, she would use that to her advantage. She would do whatever necessary to free herself. There must be a way to ask him about the different colonies, to learn where she might go, without revealing her true identity.

Of course, there would be the possibility he could still discover who she was. Anyone in the colony would tell him the truth, were he simply to ask. She had been fortunate so far, but she had a feeling her luck may be running out.

What if he fell in love with her? She knew for certain she could never be with a shifter. Regardless of his station or status. Still, better to take her chances in trying to earn her freedom, than to resign herself to a life of servitude.

Realization sank in, she needed to return to the manor and complete her chores. She buried all hope deep in her heart, so as not to arise any suspicion in the countess or her two daughters. Whatever lay ahead for Luella, she would be ready to face it.

"Henri will be here any time!" Madison exclaimed as she jumped up and down by the door.

"Calm yourself," Clara warned. "The fact that he wishes to have lunch with you, instead of tea with all of us, shows me his interest in you is more than friendship. This is the day we have waited for. Do not screw it up."

"Yes, Mother."

Luella went unnoticed, then finished setting up the table in the dining room. She had prepared quail, wheat rolls, steamed vegetables, and a sponge cake for dessert. Once everything was arranged, she returned to the kitchen to wait.

Clara walked in. Luella failed to hide her surprise. "Is everything all right, madam?"

"I am going out with Henri's mother, and Aubrey will be with us. I expect you to give them privacy and take care of whatever they need."

"Of course."

Clara stepped closer. "He informed me of his interest in you. We had a little talk the other day. I will not give you to him."

"Thank you, madam."

She scoffed. "Only because you are too valuable to me. However, you feign interest, play his game, and do what you must to help guarantee he chooses Madison. Am I understood?"

Tears pricked Luella's eyes. "Yes, madam."

"Good." She spun on her heel and left Luella alone.

The thought of flirting back, of trying to appease Henri, nearly made Luella gag. She would be polite and courteous, but that was the best she could offer. The realization sank in, if Madison married Henri and moved out, that would be at least one less person Luella would have to deal with. That alone made going along with Clara's plan worthwhile.

She continued around the kitchen, humming softly, until it happened. The bell rang. She collected herself and went into the dining room.

"Yes, Madison?"

"We are ready for dessert."

"Please," Henri said with a grin.

"Of course."

Luella fetched it from the kitchen and returned moments later. She set it on the table, served them their slices, then stepped back.

Madison stood. "Excuse me, I need to powder my nose."

Luella started to walk out with her. Henri cleared his throat. "Tell me about this cake."

Madison spun around. "Stay and answer any questions he may have. Keep him entertained," she hissed as she left the room.

Luella clasped her hands and slowly approached. "It's a traditional—"

"Yes, it sounds delicious. Hmm, not unlike you. I have to wonder…" He lowered his gaze to her apron before meeting her eyes. "Is all of your hair the same color?"

Luella's face flushed crimson as her mouth went dry. "What do you mean?"

He threw his linen on the table and swiftly approached her, grabbing her arms and pushing her against the wall.

"You know exactly what I mean. Now, tell me or I will look for myself."

Luella refused to answer him, her heart pounding in her ears and her breathing coming in shallow gasps. "Please, let me go," she finally managed to say.

"Answer my question, and I will."

"Never."

One hand remained firm around her wrists as his other trailed down to her waist.

"Please, don't," she begged.

"So, after dessert, would you like to tour our library?" Madison's voice called out as she walked down the hall towards the dining room.

Henri immediately dropped Luella's arms as he stepped back before returning to his seat. Luella smoothed over her hair and gown, calming herself as Madison entered.

"That sounds nice," Henri said with a smile.

Luella ran from the room, ignoring the glaring look from Madison. She fled the manor completely, running to the pond, where she dove in and swam around, attempting to cool her flush skin.

"Watch it, you stupid girl!" Clara's voice cut through the quiet of the room when Luella slopped water onto the floor.

"Yes, madam. It was an accident." Luella finished before retreating to the kitchen.

She wrung out the mop, then decided she would go outside and enjoy the pleasant weather. After taking care of the animals, she packed herself a small picnic. Waking up early, she completed most of her day's chores by breakfast.

A mild breeze blew past as she walked to the pond. It was a sunny day, and the scent of wildflowers filled the air. She sat down, about to spread everything out, when she heard a familiar voice.

"Hello, Luella."

Her heart skipped a beat as she scrambled to stand. "Hello, Remi," she responded. *Stick to the plan,* she reminded herself. *I need his help, if I am ever going to be free.*

"Fancy meeting you here."

"Meeting or stalking?" she teased with a smile. "After all, aren't you the hunter?" Her words gripped her heart like a vise, as regret filled her for the role she was forced to play.

"That depends, are you my prey?" he asked as he closed the gap between them.

He enveloped her in his arms, and his warmth consumed her. She could not remember ever being held in such a loving way.

His musky vanilla scent overtook her senses, and before she realized it, she clung to him in response. "I'm happy to see you," she admitted.

"Yes, that is apparent," he said with a quiet laugh. He glanced around. "No laundry?"

She stepped back and held up her pouch. "This has some cheese and bread, for a snack break. I do have enough to share."

"Well, I happen to have dessert." He pulled out a pouch of his own. After opening it, he poured the contents into the palm of his hand.

"What is that?" Luella asked, her nose crinkling at the sight of the small, brown lumps.

"Chocolate."

"Oh, that is an expensive treat! Is it any good?"

"You've never tried it before?"

"No, but I've heard how delicious it is."

"I'll let you decide that for yourself." He placed it back into the pouch.

They sat at the edge of the pond and spread everything out on an oversized table linen. "I'm curious, since you've traveled the country," she said as she straightened one of the corners. "What is your favorite colony to visit?"

"Thinking of going on an adventure?" he asked, biting into a dark, aged cheese.

The regret nearly gutted her, but she forced her smile and pressed on. "Of course not. I was merely curious, since I've never been anywhere else. Never mind." Her breath sucked in while she waited to see if he would take the bait.

"I have been to a few colonies that I quite enjoy. Lyouns is one of my favorites. It's nice, since it's prosperous. Between the annual solstice festival they throw, which draws in large crowds, and the mine nearby. The governor there is kind, and she seems to genuinely care for her people."

"Wait, a woman governor?"

"Yes. Her husband was the governor until he passed away unexpectedly. The people love her so much, they asked her to take over in his stead. She graciously accepted."

"Wow."

"The homes and businesses are very nice, dark and deep in color so as to blend in with the woods surrounding it."

"It sounds lovely."

"Lyndon is nice, as well. It is a small, quaint village to the north."

"To travel the way you do, to see so many wonderful places, it fills me with envy," she confessed as she enjoyed a bite of her oat bread.

"Maybe one day you will get to visit the world."

"Oh, I'm afraid this may be my whole world."

"It can be difficult to leave the comfort of home and try new things."

Luella bit her tongue. "Yes, it can."

"Well, here is a taste at least," he said as he handed her a piece of chocolate.

Though it looked unappealing, she did not wish to hurt his feelings. She took it from him and placed it delicately in her mouth. "Oh, this is divine!"

"It is a little hard to come by. This was a gift from the king for aiding him."

She nearly choked on her saliva. "Remi, I do not wish to take your reward."

"You aren't. I offered it, after all."

"But it is a treasure!"

"Why do you think I chose you to share this with?" He lifted another piece and held it to her mouth. Reluctantly, she parted her lips and accepted it.

"I don't deserve this," she said as her shoulders sagged. "You don't know anything about me."

"I know enough."

"What do you mean?"

"You are beautiful, both in appearance and heart. You are kind, compassionate, and caring. I care for you greatly, Luella."

She stood and turned away to hide the unshed tears forming in the corners of her eyes. "I… I need to return." Her guilt nearly swallowed her whole, creating an ache in her chest.

He jumped to his feet and clasped her hand. "Whatever is the matter?"

"I'm not who you think I am."

"Are any of us? You view me as a herald and a shifter, but I am more than that. You are the daughter of a countess, yet you carry yourself as someone who cares more for what's beneath the surface. That is truly rare." He took the chance, leaning down and placing a chaste kiss on her cheek.

She wiped her tears away and kept her head low. "This was a mistake. I'm sorry."

"We're young. We are supposed to make mistakes, to try new things. How else will we learn?"

"No, you don't understand."

Before she could continue, he pulled her to him, and his lips consumed hers. His tongue probed her mouth as his fingers caressed her neck, then gently gripped it. She fisted his hair as she met his kiss with every ounce of hunger and passion consuming her.

They broke apart, both panting for air. When her eyes met his, they kissed again. He enveloped her with one arm, keeping her tight against his torso.

"Remi, wait," she murmured.

"I've waited long enough."

"What? Remi—"

"I only meant, I have longed to taste your lips from the moment I first saw you."

"Really?"

"Yes. You feel the same. Do you deny it?"

She stumbled backward, her head shaking in disbelief. "I have to go."

"Luella—"

He watched as she ran away from him, wondering what he did or said wrong. It was obvious she enjoyed the kiss as much as he did. With a sigh, he scooped up the remaining chocolate, and carefully returned it to the pouch. He also took the linen, folding it up and placing it in his pocket.

Simon approached, and Remi held up his hand. "I don't want to hear it."

"Let's return. Watching you two eat, I'm getting hungry," Simon joked, attempting to lighten the mood. Remi smiled, though Simon could tell he wasn't happy. "I think running will help."

They hurried to the market and out the main gate. Away from the colony, they shifted and raced to the Loup Kingdom.

Once they arrived at the palace, Remi cleaned up and joined Simon in the dining hall.

Remi watched him eat for a few moments before breaking the silence. "You're awfully quiet," he said as he buttered his roll.

"Why did you give her chocolate?" Simon asked.

"Because I wanted to share it with her. You act like I did something wrong."

"You gave her food without telling her the significance."

"It's not as though I prepared a seven-course meal! It was only a few, small pieces."

"How did you feel while she was eating it?"

Remi averted his gaze. "Like my heart was going to explode in my chest."

Simon sighed. "This is why you have to tread carefully. What other wolf traditions have you done with her that she didn't understand?"

"None, I swear. I wasn't thinking. I was excited to share my treat with her, as rare as it is." Remi couldn't deny the look of concern on Simon's face. "You think I would take advantage, to use our methods to force her to select me as her chosen mate?"

"I didn't say that."

"You didn't have to. It's obvious! Yes, I care for her dearly, but I would never force her into anything she didn't want. Why do you think I am moving slowly with her?"

"If you call grabbing her to you and kissing her moving slow."

Remi's jaw clenched. "I couldn't help myself."

"Because you gave her food."

"I didn't mean it like that!" he shouted, ignoring the stares from the other diners as he wiped his mouth. He lowered his voice. "I'm sorry. I know you mean well. I am uncertain about what to do. It's not as though I have a lot of experience when it comes to courting a woman."

"Most of us don't. Since anymore, it seems our marriages are arranged for us. You are fortunate that is not quite the case."

"My father still has to approve whomever I marry."

"Of course."

Remi leaned back in his seat. "So, my friend, it's been awhile since I've asked. How are you doing?"

Simon's brow furrowed while he took a sip of his ale. "What do you mean? I'm fine."

"No, since you lost your mate."

Simon cleared his throat, nearly dropping his drink on the table. "I'm fine," he repeated.

"Look, I'm not going to push, but I do think you need to talk about her."

"What makes you think I don't?"

"Really, you spend most of your time with me. Who else would you talk to? You don't get to visit with your parents often, with their traveling post, visiting the other packs."

"Really, I'm okay. Do I miss her? Of course. I would give anything to have been able to save her, but her illness was sudden and..." He rubbed his eyes before he continued speaking. "She was gone before I could do anything. It is what it is. Will you please drop it now?"

"All right, but I mean it. I'm here if you ever want to talk about her."

"Thank you."

Luella stopped at the fence, holding onto it as if for dear life while consumed with guilt and anger. How could she be so cruel to him? Not only was it wrong to toy with his heart, but she would be punished if the countess saw them together.

"That will never happen again," she assured herself as she smoothed down her hair and made her way into the kitchen.

While cooking dinner, her thoughts were lost as she relived her first kiss. There was no denying the feelings his touch stirred in her, bringing her comfort. No one ever made her feel so alive.

The meat began to sizzle, bringing her back to the real world. She removed it from the fire and loaded up the tray. She set everything up in the dining room, then returned to the kitchen.

Her stomach churned, but she made herself eat. There was no choice. She would tell him exactly who and what she was the next time she saw him, revealing everything. Would he be done with her after learning the truth? It didn't matter. She knew it was for the best, especially because she knew what would happen if they were discovered.

The rest of the afternoon flew by as she completed her chores, cooked dinner, then went into the attic. Though the lighting in the drawing room was better, she needed privacy for the project she worked on.

She removed the loose floorboard and pulled out a square box containing her mother's gown. It was long and elegant, pale blue with satin ribbons and detailed embroidery.

Luella found it in her stepmother's closet a long time ago, along with the journal, and had hidden them away. When Clara discovered they were missing, she punished Luella by locking her in the attic without food or water for three days, until Clara could no longer take being without her servant. Luella never broke, refusing to say one word about either of her mother's belongings.

What little free time she had, she devoted to mending the gown. She didn't know if she would have an opportunity to wear it, as fancy balls and high tea were not meant for servant girls like her. She worked until she would not stop yawning, put everything away, and curled up on the ratty, torn blanket which served as her bed.

Chapter 7

The Festival

y sons were taken away because of you," Langdon called out from behind Luella. "How dare you betray your colony and your people? Especially for some dirty shifter you don't even know? My sons are good boys!"

Luella froze in her tracks, knowing they were far enough from the village no one would hear her if she called out for help.

"I am sorry about what happened, but I did not press charges."

"Regardless, you intervened when you were not needed. That stupid herald would never have said anything, if you had not saved him."

"You don't know that." She studied him for a moment, his eyes were wide and his breathing erratic. Nothing she said would calm him, as he was clearly out of his mind with grief over his sons and their punishment. "Governor, I can speak on their behalf. Perhaps—"

"Silence!"

Luella took the chance, closing her eyes, and focusing. *Remi, please.*

"Look at me, you horrible girl! You stole my sons away from me."

"I didn't, I swear."

He stormed towards her, and she fled into the woods as fast as she could.

Remi, please, he's chasing me.

Who?

I don't know what he's going to do. I was heading home from the market when he approached me. Now, he's after me.

I'm on my way.

Luella made a beeline for the stream, knowing several downed trees surrounding the area would be the perfect place for her to hide.

"I'm going to find you and make you pay!"

Her heart thudded in her ears as she moved swiftly, trying to avoid roots or other trip hazards. She stopped and listened, sighing in relief when the sounds of the babbling stream reached her.

The scent of damp earth mingled with the lingering fragrance of wildflowers, creating a bittersweet aroma that contrasted with the impending danger. The woods seemed to hold their breath, as if anticipating the governor's wrath.

A branch snapped, and she took off again. Luella's legs and lungs burned from the exertion as she sprinted through the undergrowth. Her muscles protested against the relentless chase. She was unsure of the governor's current location. Did he go quiet to hunt for her or did he give up already?

Either way, she wouldn't take the chance and found a small, downed tree. It had an opening that was covered with leaves. She climbed inside, then piled the leaves back on while quietly catching her breath.

The silence enveloped her, each moment threatening as she waited for the governor to discover her, to do whatever it was he planned. She kept her eyes closed and buried her face in her legs as the seconds ticked by. Her chest tightened, constricting her breathing as anxiety wrapped its icy fingers around her heart.

Footsteps approached, and her pulse raced as they drew closer. She froze in place, sitting as still as possible, then released a shrill scream when the leaves were kicked away.

"Are you hurt?"

Remi stood before her, offering his hand while he glanced around them. She willingly took it, and he pulled her out.

"What's wrong?"

"He… he was chasing me." Hoping to spare Remi the sight of an emotional breakdown, she fought back her tears.

"Who, Langdon?"

At his name, the dam broke, and her tears streamed down her cheeks. He pulled her against his chest. As Remi held her, she clung to him, desperately seeking solace from the nightmare she just escaped. Her bag of goods slipped to the ground.

"You're safe now," he assured her as his hand stroked gently through her hair.

"I'm filthy," she said with a small, nervous laugh.

"Come." He picked up her pack and led her to the stream. The cool water helped soothe her, as he helped rinse the mud off her arms and face. "Better?"

"Yes. You must think I'm crazy."

"Why would I think that?"

"Because I told you I was being chased, but there is no one else here."

"I can smell his scent, though it is weak. He must've lost you or he saw me. Either way, he's gone."

"I'm so grateful, but I still can't believe it."

"What's that?"

"You came for me."

"You called. I will always come for you. The king himself could not keep me from you."

She smiled at him as she kissed his cheek. "I was so scared."

"You're all right now," he said as they stood.

"Yes. I am not hurt. He didn't get the chance."

"What did he say?"

"He blames me for his sons being taken away." She bit her lip as she lowered her gaze. "I… I'm so sorry."

"For what?"

"It made him crazy, what happened to them. I put the blame on you, reminding him that I did not press charges. I'm a coward. I'm so sorry!"

"Luella, you did what you had to in order to survive. It's all right."

"No, it's not. You came all the way here to save me, and I couldn't even speak the truth. It is my fault."

"They chose to attack me, and you did the right thing by stopping them. This is their fault, not mine, not yours. You need to accept that. And so does their father."

"I don't think he ever will." Her eyes watered, but she didn't want him to see her crying again. She turned away and quickly wiped her face with the back of her hand.

"What's wrong?"

She smiled at him, but he saw through it. "I'm all right."

"No, you aren't."

When she didn't respond, he stepped up beside her and pressed her back against him, his arms wrapping around her waist. Her chest heaved as she fought the sobs threatening to escape once more.

"I was so scared," she confessed as she lowered her head.

He spun her around and gripped her chin, lifting gently until her gaze met his. "You had every right to be. He is dangerous."

Anger surged through her as she pulled away. "I told you he was, and you didn't believe me!"

"Yet, here I am, ready to defend and protect you."

"What happens next time?"

"I will speak to him. I assure you, there will not be a next time."

She shook her head. "Nothing you say, short of releasing his sons, will stop him. I know how determined he is to make me pay for what happened to them."

Remi stepped up and lowered his face until his mouth was inches from her own. "I will take care of this. You must trust me."

"Why?"

He sighed. "Because I mean it. I will do whatever I must to keep you safe. I will speak to him, then everything will be okay." He swept her hair from her face before kissing her softly. "I promise you, mon trésor."

"Thank you," she murmured softly.

"Are you all right to get home on your own?"

"Yes, thank you. I believe he is gone."

"Good. Never be afraid to call on me. I will come any time you do." Remi handed her the bag with her purchases.

He kissed her again before watching her go. Sure he was far enough behind her, he shifted into his wolf and followed quietly until she turned on the path that led to the manor. He then went into the village.

"What do you want?" Langdon asked from his desk.

Remi approached, eyeing him warily. "You will leave Luella alone."

Langdon gave a casual wave of his hand. "I have no idea what you are referring to." He flipped the page in his ledger and wrote something down.

Remi scoffed. "I'm not stupid. I smelled your foul stench all over those woods."

"I live here, so of course you would."

"No, it was fresh. I have no doubt you went after her."

"Is that what she said?" he asked with a burning gaze.

Remi thought carefully about his next words. "It doesn't matter what she said, it's what I know. Here is what matters, though. Leave. Her. Alone." The last three words were spoken through clenched teeth. "She is mine. If you hurt her, you may as well be hurting me."

"That does sound appealing," Langdon said with a smirk as he leaned back, attempting to appear at ease despite Remi's threat.

"Don't be coy. I am telling you now, you do not want to play these games with me."

"I don't have time to play games with anyone. I have a colony to run." He straightened, then as if to make his point, continued his writing.

"So you'll leave her alone?"

Langdon sighed before getting to his feet. "If it means I don't have to see you, except on days you have an announcement, then yes. I will leave her alone."

"Deal." Remi turned for the door but stopped to stare down Langdon. "Breathe a word of this to anyone, your sons will pay the price."

Langdon's eyes narrowed, his teeth gritting before he spoke next. "Not a word. I must say though, from one hunter to another, the chase is the best part. Isn't it?"

Remi left, slamming the door behind him as his response.

Luella attempted to keep her mind occupied on her tasks. Because when she didn't, she was in those woods, scared half to death, waiting for Langdon to find her.

"Oh!" she cried out when Clara gripped her elbow.

"My, you're a jumpy little thing. What has gotten into you?" Clara asked.

Luella's hands trembled as Clara's grip tightened, the touch sending a jolt of fear through her body. Her heart raced, and she struggled to regain her composure, her voice shaking as she explained her reaction.

"Nothing, madam. You startled me."

"Hmm, right. I am getting ready to turn in. Please, do try to keep it down?"

"Of course."

As soon as Clara left the kitchen, Luella made herself a cup of peppermint tea. Taking her time, she sat at the small table and savored each sip.

The aroma filled her nostrils, calming her racing mind. As her emotions swirled within, the warmth of the cup in her hands brought her a momentary peace.

Remi came for me. I shouldn't be surprised, but he seemed to be truly worried about me. Does he genuinely care for me or is this part of some alpha male claim? He clearly loathes Langdon, and I can't say I blame him.

Luella's heart raced, her mind filled with conflicting thoughts. Her feelings were a tangled mess, making it difficult for her to decide if she would truly open herself up to a shifter.

Regardless of what Clara said, telling her she was forbidden from seeing Remi, Luella was ready to fall in love and have her happily ever after. She deserved that, after so many years of mistreatment and pain.

I will find a way, and I will tell him. I'll tell him who I am, how I feel about him, and from there, I'll let him decide. If he rejects me, my life won't change much. If he accepts, who knows what wonderful possibilities might be in store?

For the first time in a long time, happiness radiated through her. Hope and the chance for a future were worth the risk, if it meant she would no longer be alone.

Remi looked himself over in the mirror once more. Today was an exciting day, and he couldn't wait. He hadn't seen Mia in nearly four months.

His black slacks and pale blue shirt fit snug. The color contrasted with his dark eyes. He ran a hand through his hair when the door opened, and Simon stepped inside.

"Are you ready for the festival?"

"I think so. How do I look?"

Simon glanced at him, assessing his appearance. "Like a proper gentleman. Which I guess answers my question."

Remi smiled as he walked to him, slapping him on the back and laughing heartily. "Mia is coming."

"Really? No wonder you're dressed to the nine! I am sure she will be happy to see you."

"Come, let's head on out. She should be here in about an hour."

"Luella, I am leaving with Aubrey and Madison shortly. We will be in Siennes, attending tea and watching a chess match, along with Henri and his mother. I expect you to fulfill your duties, as we will be gone for the better part of the day."

"Yes, madam."

While they dressed, Luella hurried to get most of her chores done. She waited until the countess and her daughters left in the carriage before she made her way to her stack of books beside the fireplace. Digging through them, she found the one she wanted and flipped through until she came across the map she needed. The Loup Kingdom was within riding distance.

She would go there, tell Remi everything, and when he rejected her as she was sure he would, she would finally be free of her guilt. The idea that he might still want her didn't even cross her mind.

In the attic, she searched through her sparce belongings. Then she remembered the pink gown Aubrey gave her, after Madison insisted she shouldn't wear it, saying it was tainted by Luella. She dressed and prepared her horse.

After checking the saddle and bridle, she mounted, then removed the map from the pocket of her cloak, along with a compass. There wouldn't be much of a view on the road to the kingdom, besides woods and plains. Still, with the wind whipping through her hair, the thought of traveling anywhere was exhilarating.

She rode fast and hard, knowing she had to return before the countess. Otherwise, there would be hell to pay. Going through the open field, she allowed herself a moment of vulnerability, silently questioning why she had fallen so deeply for Remi in such a brief time.

Her thoughts drifted to the excitement of seeing him again. His dark eyes seemed to stare into her very soul, looking at her in a way no one ever had before. The idea of kissing him, holding him, touching him made her heart race.

Luella closed her eyes and enjoyed the warm sun on her face, the gentle breeze whispering through the trees, as she imagined confessing her secret to Remi. Scared as she was, hope began to blossom within her. Would he still want her, after learning the truth?

A longing unlike any she had known before consumed her. Her face grew flush as her toes curled. Why did she crave him so? She barely knew him.

The thought of rejection stung, but she couldn't live with her guilt anymore. Its weight bore down on her, pressing her to the point it made it difficult to breathe. She would tell him the truth and live with whatever consequences.

She cleared the path from the woods and entered the open field, knowing she was nearing her destination when the palace came into view on the horizon. Once she arrived at the gate, a guard stepped forward, dressed in silver armor with red accents. He held up his hand.

"Halt! No visitors allowed in today."

"Why not?" Luella asked.

"There is a royal celebration going on. The city will be open as usual tomorrow. Come back then."

"Please, I am here to speak to a friend of mine. Perhaps you know him? His name is Remi?"

The guard scoffed. "Nice try, mi'lady. However, no one is allowed to enter, on the king's orders."

"I understand. Thank you."

She rode to the side, where she found an opening to look through. After dismounting, she approached the bars. Her jaw dropped at the beauty within.

The palace loomed in the background, tall and ivory with its spire reaching towards the heavens. Surrounding it were smaller buildings. Homes and businesses, no doubt. Music and laughter filled the air. Luella was lost in the sounds for a moment, until she saw a familiar sight.

"Remi!" she cried out, but he couldn't hear her.

Luella waved her arms in an attempt to catch his attention. She was about to try and reach out using their bargain but stopped when a woman approached him. The woman was dressed in fine silks with a silver circlet resting above her brow.

She flew into his arms, and he held her tight before kissing her softly on top of her head. He twirled her around. Her black hair flowed around them as he danced with her, spinning and moving to the music.

Remi was only using Luella. Her heart sank into her stomach at the realization, while her body grew ice cold. The irony of the situation was not lost on her. She realized this woman must be his betrothed, and Remi wanted one last fling before their wedding ceremony. Luella's heart shattered into a million pieces as she watched them. His betrayal hit her with a devastating force, leaving her utterly crushed.

Luella's tears fell fast as she mounted her steed and rode back to the manor. The thoughts racing inside her mind only made her sicker to her stomach, and she pushed them away. The cool wind did not bother her, as she was unable to feel anything in that moment, except her breaking heart.

She led the horse into the barn, removed the saddle and bridle, then headed for the manor. At the small fountain in the courtyard, Luella fell to her knees, weeping over the cold, hard stone.

"I'm sorry, Mother. You said not to let despair in, but I'm afraid it's too late. My heart is shattered and all hope is lost. I am numb to everything but this searing pain. I would give anything to make it stop."

When her tears at last ran dry, she gathered herself, and went inside. She tended to the fires before changing into her usual gown and cleaning her face.

Luella forced herself to focus on her chores. Sweeping and mopping did little to keep her mind occupied, and she kept seeing the image of them together. Remi looked so happy to see the unknown woman, and the way they held each other while they danced made Luella's chest ache.

She choked down her emotions, reminding herself that she had gone to tell him the truth, and he probably would've been done with her, anyway. So what did it matter? He deserved better than Luella.

The countess and her daughters returned home shortly after six, tired and ready for a hot meal. Luella set everything up, rang the bell, then went into the kitchen. She sat down, having taken her first bite, when the bell rang again. With a sigh, she stood and went into the dining room.

"Yes, madam?"

"I take it you have not heard the news?" Clara asked while buttering her bread.

"What news?"

"Stefan was attacked in the labor camp. They do not believe he will make it through the night, as his wounds are quite severe." Clara studied Luella, curious as to what her reaction would be. "We overheard this at the gate when we returned."

"I am sorry to hear that. Regardless of his actions, he does not deserve to die."

"Hmm, that is all."

Luella returned to the kitchen, glanced at her meal, but lost all appetite. She set the plate on the floor, and four curious mice slowly approached. Once the smell reached them, they dove in, clearly happy with the gift she had given them. Luella washed the plate before going upstairs, where she fell into a restless sleep.

Remi turned to see the woman he'd been waiting for. "Mia!" he called out.

She smiled as she approached him, then ran into his arms. He held her tightly before placing a gentle kiss on top of her head.

They spun around, laughing and enjoying the crowd around them. When the music stopped, he laced his arm around her waist then walked with her.

"I'm so glad you made it."

"Me, too," she replied. "I wasn't sure I would be able to get away."

"So," he said as he took her hand and spun her once more, looking her over. "Still human?"

She let out a small laugh. "Yes, I never shifted."

"I'm grateful for that."

Her expression grew serious as her gaze lowered. "I am, too. Because I could not be here with you if I was a shifter. But I feel terrible for the omegas."

"Believe me, a lot of us do. I'm trying to make changes, but it's slow going."

"Well, for now, let's enjoy the festival and each other's company."

"Race you to the food booths?"

"No," she said, laughing as she ran ahead of him.

"Cheater!" he called out as he joined her.

Luella watched her stepsisters and stepmother dining together, the sight serving as a painful reminder of her eternal outsider status. The contrast between their closeness and her perpetual solitude intensified her feelings of loneliness and longing.

Love would always be out of her grasp. She would never be the center of someone's attention. Remi pretended to care for her, but she must move past him. Even if it were one of the hardest things she would ever have to do.

She returned to the kitchen where she ate her meal alone, as she did three times a day, every day. The kitchen seemed larger, emptier, after seeing the family in the other room.

When she finished, she gathered all of the dishes, washed and put them away, then went to the small laundry room to gather the dirty clothing.

After loading everything up, she led the donkey to the pond. She longed to catch a glimpse of Remi once more, to see his smile, and listen to his laughter.

Pain ripped through her chest at the thought, and she didn't understand it. She barely knew him, so why was she so drawn to him? Why could she not resist his charm?

"Luella, why did you not answer me?"

She looked behind to see Clara approaching her. "Apologies, Countess. I was lost in my thoughts. What do you need?"

"I have heard talk that the governor is most displeased with you. It's all anyone at the market talked about today while we were there. Have you seen or heard from him since his sons were taken?"

Luella swallowed hard. "No, madam."

"Very well. If you do see him, you treat him with the respect he deserves. Do you hear me?"

"Of course."

"Also, the baroness and her son are coming over at three o'clock. Once you finish here, return and prepare for our company."

"Yes, madam."

Luella watched her leave before clutching the wet blanket to her chest. She knew Clara and Langdon associated at times, but they were never close, nor were they what Luella would consider friends.

She pushed the questions down as she continued in her task. Though her daily routine was dull, it brought her some comfort, a sense of familiarity.

Chapter 8

The Hunted

hank you for your purchase. I really appreciate your business," the candlemaker said as he wrapped the last of her order. He carefully placed everything in the bag before handing it to her. Luella smiled at him, the first to show her any kindness in months.

"You're welcome."

"I wouldn't speak to her, if I were you," said the older woman behind her. "After all, she's the reason for the governor's foul mood."

"No, it was his own sons who did that. You cannot blame Luella. If she hadn't stopped them, and they killed that poor, young man, there would be soldiers everywhere!"

Luella took her purchase, gave him a nod of gratitude, and left the market. Following her usual path home, thoughts of her upcoming birthday raced through her mind. There must be something she could do, some way to free herself of her stepmother's grasp.

The dusk approached, as Luella was at the market later than usual since Clara hosted the baroness. Luella was grateful Henri had not attended this time.

Lost in thought, the footsteps approaching behind her went unnoticed. Hands grabbed her shoulders, snatching her into the air before she could react. Her mouth opened to scream, but a gag was shoved in, cutting her off. She was dragged into the forest, then her arms and legs were bound with rough rope. She was forced to her knees.

"My son is dead because of you," Langdon said with a snarl.

Luella's head snapped up to see the governor himself standing before her. His face twisted into a grimace of pain and grief. The dagger in his hand caught her attention. She shook her head, her eyes wide with fear. Ice flowed through her veins as she struggled to breathe.

"I told you I would make you pay."

He slashed her arm, and as the crimson liquid gushed down her elbow, he smiled at her muffled cries. The pain tore through her, but she forced herself to close her eyes and focus. If she reached out to Remi, if he were nearby, perhaps he would find her, like before.

I am unsure if you can hear me. Please, Remi, help me. I'm in the woods, about a quarter of a mile south from the market. Please—

Her concentration broke when his blade sliced her leg open. Tears streamed down her cheeks.

"Please, stop," she cried, but it came out garbled by the fabric.

"Don't bother trying to speak. I am going to make you suffer for what you've done. My son died a slow, horrible death. So will you."

Lowering the dagger, he knelt beside her and wrapped his hand around her throat. He squeezed, lightly at first then going tighter, until the world around her began to dim. When he realized she was on the verge of losing consciousness, he released her.

He punched her in the eye before standing and sending a swift kick to her stomach. Another, then another, each one sending a sharp wave of pain through her, until she sobbed into the gag, begging Remi.

The silence cut as deeply as his dagger. Luella was abandoned. No one would come and save her. She grew cold as the realization seeped in.

The governor knelt before her once more, lifting his blade, and plunging it into her abdomen before he forcefully yanked it out. "I'll let you lay here, suffering and broken, the same as my beautiful boy." He jumped to his feet and fled from the scene.

Remi, please. I think I'm…

Then everything went black.

Remi took in a shuddered breath, then looked at Simon. "We have to leave. Now," he commanded.

"What's wrong?"

"It's Luella. She's in danger."

"Let's go."

Though his expression remained stoic, fear gripped Remi. Fear that he may be too late to save her.

He and Simon made their way through the palace, trying to avoid gaining attention. Once outside, they shifted and ran as fast as they could. Remi's heart hammered in his chest, every thought an attempt to reach out to Luella.

Receiving no response only made him move faster. Simon trailed behind, attempting to catch up. Remi didn't bother to look back to see if he was still behind him, only focusing on getting to her as soon as possible.

The sight of the colony brought him a small sense of relief. He shifted before approaching the gate, smiled and nodded at the guards as he walked through, then charged to the location Luella gave him.

He sniffed the air, immediately recognizing her jasmine scent, mixed with something coppery.

Blood.

His heart stopped for a moment, but he assured himself she would be all right. Simon still hadn't caught up to him, but at this point, he didn't care. He had to see Luella. He followed the scent into the woods.

The smell grew stronger, and he knew he was getting close. He nearly tripped over her body. Everything in him went ice cold at the sight, and he stared for a moment before collecting himself.

"Luella!" he called out as he fell to his knees beside her. He had never seen so much blood in all his life, even as violent and brutal as life at the palace could be. "Luella, please. Talk to me," he said as he gently shook her shoulder.

Her head lulled to the side, but he saw her chest rise and fall with each breath. Remi followed the blood and tried to see where it was coming from. He gripped the gash on her leg and the one on her stomach, attempting to keep pressure so the bleeding would stop, or at least, slow down.

"Is she… is she alive?" Simon asked.

Remi cut away the ropes and ripped out her gag. "Yes." One rope was long enough, he wrapped it around her leg, and formed a tourniquet. He stood and carried her in his arms. "There is a doctor in the colony."

Simon followed behind, glancing around them as they made their way, not sure if the person responsible lingered nearby. The woods cleared to the path, and they followed it into the market.

Remi held Luella tightly against his torso as they approached the doctor's office. Simon was right on his heels. The streets were empty, as it was now dark, and Remi prayed the doctor would be inside.

"Simon, stay out here."

"I will."

Remi didn't bother to knock, instead barging into the office. Even if the doctor were out, at least there were supplies, and he would do what he could to help her. Tiernan ran in, dressed for bed with a pipe in his hand.

"What is the meaning of this?" he demanded.

"Someone attacked her in the woods. Please, save her!"

"Follow me."

The doctor led him into the exam room. He placed his pipe in a bowl while Remi lay Luella on the table.

"Is this enough?" he asked, opening a pouch and dumping gold coins beside her. "I can get more."

"Calm down, son. First things first, let me take a look. Put those away."

"Where is your nurse?"

"Gone home for the evening. I'm afraid you will have to do." The doctor stripped away Luella's bloody gown. Remi dampened a rag and helped wipe her body clean.

"I tried to stop the bleeding as best I could before picking her up."

"You did a fine job." His hand paused over her stomach. "That's an unusual marking. What do you make of it?"

"She might start bleeding again any moment. We should focus on her wounds."

"Right, of course." Tiernan glanced at it once more before gathering his surgical tools and any other implements he would need.

"Hmm, where am I?" Luella mumbled as her eyelids fluttered.

"Luella, you're with me and the doctor. Everything will be all right. He'll fix you right up, good as new." Remi squeezed her hand, holding it tightly as the doctor stitched up her wounds. Luella moaned before losing consciousness again.

The doctor sighed when he finished suturing the one on her stomach. "I'm not sure how severe the internal damage is. There is a chance she may not survive."

Remi shook his head. "What can we do?"

Tiernan wiped his hands on a linen. "At this point, all we can do is pray." He collected his instruments in the bloody rag. "Excuse me," he said as he left the room.

Remi stroked Luella's hair and spoke softly. "You're going to be okay. I know you will. You have to be."

"Remi, is that you?" she asked through hooded lids. Her back arched as pain seared through her stomach.

"I'm right here."

"Please, don't." Her voice trailed off.

"I'm not going anywhere."

She sobbed quietly. "No, don't stay. I don't want you here."

"Luella, whatever has happened, you aren't thinking clearly. I'm right here, and I will not leave your side." He wiped her tears and kissed her forehead. "Save your strength. But first, tell me one thing."

"What?"

"Who did this to you?"

Luella carefully considered how to respond, knowing if she admitted it was Langdon, the entire colony would be after her. She was already on thin ice, and if the governor was arrested, she had no doubt the blame would fall on her.

"I was grabbed from behind and never saw his face."

"But it was a man? Did he say anything?"

"No," she murmured, closing her eyes as the pain swelled again within her. She squeezed Remi's hand. "Please, it hurts."

"I'm so sorry."

Tiernan walked in, carrying a syringe. "This will help." He looked down at Luella. "Besides the pain, how do you feel?"

"Woozy and like I'm going to be sick."

"That's to be expected." He injected her arm, then faced Remi. "She will probably sleep through this. How can I get in contact with you?"

"What do you mean?" Remi asked.

"So I can send you word on her condition."

Remi laughed. "I will be staying here tonight."

"But you aren't family."

"I don't care. Wild horses could not drag me from her side."

Tiernan opened his mouth to argue, but the determined look on Remi's face gave him pause. "Very well. I have sent word to the Countess Clara, though I doubt she will come here tonight."

"Why wouldn't she see her daughter?"

Luella launched into a coughing fit, and the doctor fetched her a glass of water. Remi held it while she took slow sips. When she finished, he set the glass on the table beside her, then helped her ease into a reclined position.

"There, rest now."

"I will turn in. My room is upstairs and to the left, should you need me."

"Thank you."

Tiernan stopped at the door. "Oh, and you need not worry about her bill."

"May I ask why not?"

"I know who you are. She saved your life. In doing so, she also saved the colony. Why the people here have turned against her, I am unsure. Allow me to do this for her, to show my gratitude."

"Thank you."

"Good night."

Remi watched him leave then stepped outside. Simon paced in the chilly night air. "How is she?" He looked Remi up and down, noting the blood covering his shirt and pants.

"Stable, but…" Remi cleared his throat. "We don't know if she's going to make it."

"Did she say who hurt her?"

Remi scoffed. "It was the governor, but she won't come right out and say so. I'd recognize his stench anywhere."

"What can I do?"

"Will you return for the night and bring me fresh clothes in the morning? I am staying here, and I assure you, it is perfectly safe."

Simon frowned. "Very well. I want it noted, I am not happy about this."

Remi chuckled. "Thank you." He went inside and rushed to Luella's side.

She slept peacefully, with her hair splayed across the pillow. Remi knew it was the medicine, but he was glad to see it.

He slipped out of his bloody shirt and threw it in a bin against the wall before climbing up beside her.

He wrapped his arm over her chest, breathing her in while saying a silent prayer. The notion of losing her created a void in his heart, but he comforted himself that she would be okay.

"I'm sorry to disturb you."

Remi bolted upright, quickly looking at Luella. Relief washed over him when he realized she was sound asleep, her chest rising and falling slowly. He turned to see Simon standing in the doorway.

"Is everything all right?"

Simon shook his head. He stepped forward and handed Remi a pack. "Here are the clothes you requested. We have to go. There was an incident at the palace."

Remi caressed Luella's face, not ready to leave her. "I have to wait until she wakes up, to be sure she's going to be all right."

"The king commands we return at once."

Reluctantly, Remi stood and faced him. "Fine, but give me some privacy. I'll be out shortly."

As soon as Simon left, Remi opened the pack and examined the contents. He stripped down completely and changed before checking on Luella again. Her wounds appeared to be clear of infection. He smiled at the sight before bending forward and placing a gentle kiss on her forehead.

"I will see you soon, mon trésor. I swear it."

Luella stirred as pain began to radiate down her chest and stomach. Her hands clenched until it eased slightly. She opened her eyes as Remi stepped out into the hallway.

"Remi," she called out. Given her poor condition, it was barely audible.

The door shut behind him, and he was gone. She wanted to go after him, but her body refused to cooperate. Her head pounded, and she tried to remember everything from the night before.

Tiernan walked in a few minutes later. "How are you?" he asked while checking her vitals.

"Everything hurts," she murmured.

"That's not surprising. You were in pretty bad shape. I'll be honest, I didn't think you would survive, given the severity of your injuries. It was kind of that man to bring you in here."

"Remi?"

"The herald, yes. He brought you in, saying you were attacked. Do you remember any of it?"

"No. I went to the market, and that's the last thing I recall."

"You were beaten and stabbed. I had to stitch you up."

Her fingers trailed over the sutures on her stomach. "So you saw my mark?"

"I did. I have sent word to the countess. Until we hear from her, you will stay here while you recover. You are in no shape to be moved right now."

"Thank you for your kindness. I don't know how, but I will find a way to pay you back."

"You needn't worry about that. I'll return shortly with breakfast."

Luella closed her eyes, her chest heaving as memories from the night before flooded her. Langdon was so angry, so distraught, he nearly killed her. *I called out for Remi, and he actually came. Why would he do that?*

"Are you all right?"

When she looked up, Tiernan stood before her, holding a tray with a bowl and a glass of juice.

"Yes," she responded as she arranged her pillows and sat up as best she could, wincing in pain. He set the tray beside her and helped her while she ate the beef broth. "You don't seem too surprised that the countess hasn't arrived yet."

He cleared his throat. "I'll be honest with you. I've overheard her speaking with your stepsisters. I have an inkling of what your life there is like. For now, stay here and focus on getting better."

"I will. Thank you."

She started to ask why Remi left but realized she was probably right. It was because he wanted to return to his beloved. After all, he only came to her because of the bargain.

As soon as the door closed behind the doctor, she lifted the blanket and traced over the mark on her stomach. There must be some way to remove it, and she would figure out how.

The nurse came in a few hours later to give her lunch, check her vitals, and gave her a book to read while she rested.

She lost herself in the story while trying to ignore the pain. The afternoon went by, and Tiernan came in with dinner and examined her.

"Hmm, odd."

"What?" Luella asked as she took a sip of her lemon and chamomile tea.

"Your wounds. Though you were only attacked last night, they look as though they are several days healed."

"What does that mean?"

He shook his head. "It's a good thing, and that's what matters."

Two days later, Tiernan helped Luella into his carriage and returned her to the manor. The countess greeted them at the door. He helped Luella into the drawing room, where he sat her on the couch before turning to the countess.

"She is healing well, but she needs at least one more week of full rest. Her wounds look good, but I want to be sure before she resumes normal activities. Let her get plenty of rest," he reiterated.

"I will," Clara assured him, approaching Luella and placing her hand gently on her arm. "My poor child, what happened?"

Luella ignored the false concern and kept her head down. "I was on my way home from the market when the attack occurred. I don't remember much else."

"Remi, one of the king's heralds, found her unconscious in the woods and brought her to me."

Clara sighed. "And dare I ask how much this bill is?"

"It is paid in full."

"By that boy?"

"No, ma'am. By her," he said as he nodded to Luella.

"I don't understand."

The doctor chuckled as he made his way to the door. "I'm sure she can explain. Now, she has enough medicine and antibiotics for a week. I will be by to check on her before that time is up."

"Thank you again."

"Of course."

As soon as he left, Clara marched up to Luella. "You explain yourself right now."

"For what?"

"The bill!"

Luella repeated what Tiernan said. "You haven't managed to turn everyone against me."

"I have no idea what you mean," Clara said, bringing her hand to her chest while feigning innocence.

"None of it matters. Come my twenty-first birthday, I will be free of you."

"Oh, and where will you enjoy this freedom?"

"I have a few places in mind. You will no longer own me."

"We shall see. In the meantime, your stepsisters will continue to take over your chores until you are recovered. Though, how on earth neither one can brew a proper cup of tea, I'll never understand."

"You spent your life spoiling them, teaching them nothing but manners and how to pursue nobility, then act surprised they cannot perform the simplest of tasks?" Luella laughed, causing her to cringe in pain. "Serves you right."

"If you weren't in your current state, I would teach you a thing or two about manners, you ungrateful wench. I heard the doctor, and I expect you to be back to your full duties at the end of the week."

Chapter 9

Luella's Confession

hat a week it was. Aubrey grabbed the bar of dye instead of soap and colored the sheets lavender while Madison nearly burnt down the kitchen. Clara was beside herself while trying to deal with her girls.

Tiernan examined Luella and gave her a clean bill of health, though he couldn't hide his surprise at how well she healed. He did warn her to rest from time to time, and if she felt any pain to sit down immediately.

"The external wounds have fully healed, but I am unsure how the internal ones are. I don't want you to overdo it."

"Thank you," she said.

Clara saw him out, and Luella went to the kitchen. She continued to clean Madison's mess before cooking lunch. The meals were set up in the dining room, then she ate her own.

Slowly, she gathered laundry and headed for the pond. Her pulse quickened at the thought Remi might be there, until she remembered the beautiful woman he danced with at the festival.

She arrived, grateful to see no trace of him. Her healing had been quicker than she expected, but it zapped her of her strength in exchange. Moving slowly, she managed to wash and hang a few blankets.

While reaching for the next one, a stab of pain passed through her abdomen. Apparently, she wasn't quite as healed as she thought. She gripped the cart while waiting for it to pass.

"Shouldn't you be resting?"

Her head hung as she refused to look at him. "I'm all right," she managed while another wave made its way through her.

"No, you aren't."

"Why are you here?" she demanded, ignoring the pain, and kneeling by the water to continue washing.

"I wanted to check on you."

"You could've reached out using this bargain between us. You didn't need to come all the way here."

"Luella, I came because I'm concerned about you. You nearly died. Why—"

"I never want to see you again." She realized just how ungrateful she sounded. Regardless of his betrayal, he did save her life. "Thank you for what you did. Now please, end the bargain and leave."

"No."

She stopped her work and made it to her feet, taking a moment before meeting his gaze. "What do you mean, no?"

"It is mine, and I will not release you from it."

"Why not?"

"Because you are still in danger."

"As if you care," she said with a scoff.

"I do care. I came for you, didn't I? Do you remember anything from the attack?"

She shook her head before picking up a blanket and carrying it to the line. Her hands trembled as she hung it up. "No, and you've done enough."

"I tell you what. You tell me the truth, tell me why you want to break the bargain. If I agree with you, I will do as you ask."

"I don't believe you."

"What if I swear?"

"Fine. I know now I am nothing to you. You needed to get one last fling out of your system."

"I have no idea what you are talking about."

Her glare caught him off guard. "I saw you with her! Don't lie to me."

"With who? What are you talking about?"

"A few weeks ago, I traveled to the palace to see you. The guards wouldn't let me in, saying there was a royal festival going on. I found an opening and peeked inside, only to see you dancing with a beautiful woman. She was well-dressed with long, black hair."

His laughter threw her for a moment, and she wondered what he found amusing. "Luella, the woman you saw me dancing with is none other than my cousin, Mia. She came to town for the festival, and I hadn't seen her in months."

"You… you're lying!"

"I swear on our bargain, it is the truth." He stepped up to her and gently gripped her chin, then tilted her face to him. Without another word, he kissed her.

Her eyes opened wide in surprise before closing as she gave in. The feelings of lust and passion were overtaken with guilt. "Remi—"

"There is no other woman. Never has been, and if I have my way, never will be. You are all I want."

"Wait, I have to tell you something."

"Tell me after."

"After what?"

He responded with his mouth on hers, his palm pressed against her spine as he pulled her closer to him. Part of her wanted to back away and run. She wasn't good enough for him, and she never would be. Her pounding heart broke at the thought, and pain radiated down her chest.

"What's wrong?" he asked, looking her over.

"Nothing."

He gripped her arm and helped her sit against the tree trunk. "No, something is the matter. I'm sure the doctor has been by. What did he say?"

"I'm fine."

"Stay and rest."

"But I need to get this done. Since you saved me, you aren't doing this again."

"I don't care. You are pale, and I can see how much pain you are in. I will finish these."

She wanted to argue, but the stoic look in his eyes stopped her. He was serious, and nothing she said would sway him. "Thank you."

He went to the cart and retrieved the last two blankets. After washing and hanging them up, he sat beside her.

"I was thinking, you said you came to the palace. Was it really only to see me?"

"I wanted to tell you something," she admitted, her fingers running through the grass by her feet.

"Oh?"

Spending time with him, growing close, she knew she had fooled herself that she could ever use him. Instead, she became attached and wasn't ready for whatever this was developing between them to end.

"I wanted to tell you that... I'm starting to have feelings for you."

"Really? What kind of feelings?"

"I care for you," she said, her eyes squeezing shut as her cheeks went flush. "I enjoy your company."

"Aren't you a natural-born romantic?"

Her eyes flew open, and anger surged through her at the sight of his smirking face. "This isn't easy for me," she snapped. "I've never said or done anything like this before."

He wrapped his arm around her shoulder and kissed her forehead. "I'm sorry. I should not have teased you. Thank you for having the courage to tell me how you feel."

She sighed. "It doesn't matter. I'm not enough for you."

"What do you mean?"

"I can't… I have obligations, and because of those, I won't always be available to you."

"Luella, I do, as well."

"Plus, the countess, she isn't—"

"We'll meet here every Wednesday."

"To do what? Wash bedding and talk?"

"I don't care what we're doing, as long as I get to see you and have you in my arms. You're already a part of my life, already staked your claim in my heart."

"We haven't known each other very long. How can you have such feelings for me so soon?"

"Because I am drawn to you, unable to resist your pull. You are amazing, beautiful, funny, and most importantly, you are mine."

"Remi, what are you saying?"

"I claim you, Luella. Your heart, your soul, all of you belongs to me. And in return, I belong to you. Will you do the same for me? Because I cannot go another day without knowing if you are mine or not. Will you take the chance?"

His words mended her heart, offering her the promise she never thought she would have. Nothing would make up for the lonely life she has led, but she would take the chance on him. A chance on a future. Though these violent delights may have violent ends, the price for passion would be worth every stolen moment.

"Yes."

"Do you willingly accept my claim on you?"

"I do."

Clara examined Luella's appearance thoroughly. "Hmm, I guess you are decent enough for company."

"Madam?"

"Henri and his mother will be here shortly."

"Yes, you said as much."

"I wish you would dress a little nicer for them."

Luella frowned. "And what would I wear, exactly?"

"Perhaps Aubrey or Madison have a gown to give you, something they no longer wear."

"If I am but a servant, what does it matter?"

"Do not give me lip," Clara snapped. "Go ask them right now."

"Yes, madam."

Luella went to Aubrey first, knowing she at least wouldn't be as cruel. She knocked softly and opened the door after Aubrey bade her to enter.

"Your mother wanted me to ask if you might have a gown you no longer wear? Something appropriate for me to wear today for her company."

Aubrey went to her closet and looked through her gowns before finding a pale blue day dress. "I think this would be fine."

"I thought you liked that one?" Luella asked as she took it.

"No, not since Mother told me—" Aubrey cleared her throat. "It doesn't matter. I'm sure it will look fine on you."

"Thank you."

Luella went to the nearest washroom and changed. She went into the kitchen to begin meal prep when Clara walked in.

"Much better."

"Thank you."

"Though, you still look like a peasant, but it's good enough, I suppose."

Luella nodded before continuing her work. She was used to such comments from her stepmother. The urge to point out that Clara had bought the gown herself for her own daughter nearly overtook Luella, but she bit her tongue.

"I will have everything ready shortly."

"Very good," Clara said on her way out.

Luella set the food up on the dining table before retreating to the kitchen, hoping she would not have to see Henri. She finished her own lunch and was washing the plate when the bell rang.

Her jaw clenched as she made herself enter the dining room. "Yes, madam?"

"We would like coffee and dessert."

Luella glanced at the buffet table against the wall behind her. "It's right here."

Clara's eyes went wide as the baroness attempted to avert her gaze. "Yes, and you will serve us," Clara said, doing her best to keep her anger at bay in front of company.

"Of course, madam."

Luella served everyone, then she made her way to the kitchen.

"Well, that was brazen of you."

She turned to face Henri, realizing he had come alone. "I only meant—"

He laughed as he shut the door behind him. "I know what you meant. Bravo! Clara can be a bit… snobbish at times. Don't get me wrong, my mother is the same way. It can be annoying. But you. I liked seeing this side of you."

"What do you want?"

Her eyes went wide when he approached her. "Why, to see you, of course. Clara has been somewhat stubborn in our negotiations, but that is to be expected. She is good at playing hardball, but I always get what I want."

"And what do you want?" Luella asked, licking her lips.

"You, of course. If I could, I would lift you onto this table and take you. Too bad we aren't alone here."

"The door is shut, and this is inappropriate," Luella said as she attempted to walk past him.

He grabbed her wrist and pulled her to him. One hand holding her in place, his other caressed down her cheek. "It's a shame you are but a servant. You are far lovelier than either of your stepsisters."

"Thank you," she said, trying to keep him calm. She knew if he became angry, he might explode and become far worse. "You're handsome yourself."

He laughed as he lowered his face to hers, his lips only a few inches away. She prayed for an interruption, for the bell to ring, anything that would stop him.

"I need to get back," he murmured into her mouth, "but we aren't through. No, we are just getting started."

In the blink of an eye, he was gone. Luella leaned against the counter and tried to calm her racing heart.

Luella, are you all right?

I'm fine.

Are you sure? I had the weirdest feeling and needed to hear it from you.

Yes, I mean it. I can't talk now. I promise I'll reach out this evening. We'll talk then.

All right, mon trésor.

Luella straightened up the kitchen and began some meal prep for dinner, knowing the bread would need to proof. After a while, the bell rang, and she entered the dining room.

Clara stood by herself at the table, as everyone else was gone. "The baroness and Henri had an enjoyable time. While she and Madison played cards in the corner, I had a nice chat with him. He seems almost enamored with you."

"I am sure it's nothing."

Clara scoffed. "Do not try that with me. He said he wants a package deal, you and Madison. I cannot afford to lose you, but I will play his game, for now. I will let him have you, to get it out of his system if need be, then you will be returned to me."

"Madam—"

"I do not want to hear it. I will do whatever I must to ensure my daughters are married off to nobility. Do you understand me?"

Luella raised her chin and refused to answer. Clara came up to her and grabbed her face.

"You will obey me, child."

"I will not give myself to him," she replied through gritted teeth.

Clara grabbed her wrist and pulled her to the closet. She opened it before shoving Luella inside.

"What are you doing?" she cried out as Clara slammed the door shut.

"Teaching you a lesson."

She pushed a chair up under the handle, effectively locking Luella in.

"I will see to dinner tonight. If I am in a charitable mood in the morning, I will let you out then."

"Please, let me out now!"

"You will stay in there and think about your position, the one you have that you cannot bargain with. I give the orders, you obey. That is your lot in life."

"Stepmother, please don't do this," Luella begged with a small whimper, keeping her arms wrapped around her stomach. "Do not leave me in here."

"Silence."

With that, Clara left the room. Luella collapsed to the ground and wiped away her streaming tears. She desperately wanted to reach out to Remi, if nothing else for comfort, but she was afraid he may try and find her if she did.

By the following Wednesday, Luella felt better. Her time in the closet had been unbearable, but Clara kept her word and released her the next morning. She reminded Luella that she belonged to her, and she could do whatever she wanted.

Luella was apprehensive about seeing Remi. He had been on her mind all week, as she replayed his words, and she wondered how serious it was. What did it mean to be claimed by a shifter? She researched a little in the evenings, but she didn't find any answers. She would ask him about it when she saw him.

Remi waited for her, leaning against the tree and smiling as she arrived. He rushed to her, taking her hands and looking her over.

"How do you feel?"

"I'm much better," she assured him. She bit her lower lip, about to ask her question regarding their words from the previous week, when he pulled her to him.

"And you're sure you don't know who did this to you?"

Her gaze lowered. "I don't wish to discuss it."

"Luella, you need to tell me."

"And what will you do about it?"

"Have him arrested, of course. Did you think I would kill him myself?"

"Yes," she admitted.

"I don't blame you for thinking that. I want nothing more than to take the life of the one who hurt you."

"Remi—"

"Why did you not reach out the other day? You said you would, but I never heard from you. I thought about reaching out to you instead, but I was worried I would interrupt something."

"Look, it was a difficult day. I'm sorry I didn't keep my word, but please. I am dealing with so much already."

"Then let me help you. Tell me who attacked you."

"No."

"Luella, you do not understand. No one touches what is mine. I need you to say his name so I can punish him."

"Remi, I can't. Besides, it's not your fight!"

"You accepted my claim, that means you are my responsibility."

"To what end?"

"To what… What do you think? Until we are nothing but dust. I will love you, own you, claim you, until my last breath, my last heartbeat. Time itself holds no meaning when you are in my arms."

He kissed her fiercely, his hand tracing down her jawline and neck, until he palmed her chest gently. She pressed into him, a silent reassurance she wanted everything he did for her.

He sat down and pulled her onto his lap. His fingers lifted the hem of her gown, until she went tense in response.

"What are you doing?" she asked.

"With your permission, I'll make you see stars."

"But I'm not… We aren't…"

"We aren't having sex. Not the way you're thinking. I need to feel you, to please you, until you cry out my name."

Heat pooled from her head to her core. With a ragged breath, she managed to say, "yes."

His hand continued, and she gasped when he brushed aside the lacy fabric covering her most tender spot. Her back arched when his fingers teased softly at first, gently stroking between her thighs.

"Remi," she said with a moan. "Please."

"Of course, mon trésor."

Her words died in her throat as he moved faster, building her up, and bringing her to the edge. She shuddered against him, panting for air, and cried out when pleasure consumed her body.

He removed his hand, licked his fingers, then brought them to her mouth. "Taste how deliciously sweet you are."

She sucked them clean, and he kissed her before helping her stand with him. Watching him wash his hands in the pond, her face reddened as she realized what she had just done.

"Are you recovered?" he asked as he began to load the blankets onto the cart.

When she shook her head, he chuckled. He approached her, and she surprised him by grabbing him by the back of his neck and kissing him.

"Thank you."

"You are positively glowing. Please, tell me what I need to hear," he implored.

"What is that?" she asked, worried he may ask her to tell him the truth.

"That you are mine."

"I already said yes last week."

"I need to hear the words. Please," he begged softly.

"I am yours. I belong to you, and you belong to me."

"Then without a single doubt, I will give you whatever you ask. I will protect you, honor you, cherish you."

She laughed softly. "Those sound like marriage vows."

"Would you say them back if they were?"

Luella realized it was only the two of them, and it's not as though they were actually getting married. If it reassured him what she felt, then she would say it. "Yes. I will protect you, honor you, cherish you."

"Until my spirit is no longer of this world."

"Until my spirit is no longer of this world," she repeated before kissing him again.

"I cannot tell you what that means to me. I love you, Luella. Things are a little rocky right now, with my obligation to the palace and yours to your mother, but we will make this work." He kissed her once more. "I'm sorry I can't stay longer, but I need to return to the palace."

"I can't wait to see you again. Every second will be eternity, every moment away from you, a dagger to my heart."

"For me as well. Parting is such sweet sorrow."

"You did what?" Simon asked with wide eyes.

"I will not lose her."

"You've only just met her. You don't know her well enough—"

"I know that she means everything to me."

Simon glanced around the dining hall to be sure no one listened in. "When you asked for privacy earlier, I thought it was so the two of you could kiss, not because you planned to—"

"I didn't plan it. I saw her, and I had to tell her."

"So you are determined to have her as your chosen mate?"

"Destined mate or chosen mate, I don't care what you call her, as long as I can call her mine."

"I've never seen you like this. Not even with Rosalyn."

"She was infatuated with me, but I never had those feelings for her. Besides, she is better suited for Tobias."

"How is your brother?"

Remi refrained from rolling his eyes. "Complaining about everything. What else is new?" They laughed as they took a drink of their ale.

"I thought you were going to take things slow with Luella?"

Remi turned serious in the blink of an eye. "I told you, it wasn't planned. You don't understand, these feelings I have for her, they are so deep. They are embedded in my very skin. She is all I think about, all that I long for."

Simon stared down into his empty pint. "I can understand that."

"Sorry. I forgot, it hasn't been a year since you lost Isabella."

A small, sad smile passed Simon's lips. "It's okay."

"No, it's not."

Simon nodded towards the door. "This doesn't look good." They sat up straight as the messenger reached the middle of the room.

"If I could have your attention, this is a sad day for our kingdom."

Chapter 10

Bitten

nable to sleep, Luella stared at the ceiling with the biggest smile plastered across her face. All she thought about was his hands on her flesh, the way he made her feel. Is this what love felt like? Could this be real? Or was she simply pretending, was she a scared little girl who fell for the first man to show her kindness?

No, it was very real. She knew this in her heart, he meant every word he said. When they made their vow, she would swear her soul was sewn onto his, stitched together with their love. They were now one body, one spirit, one heart.

Soon, she would have to tell him the truth. She would explain her position, both as a servant and as the stepdaughter of the countess. Her heart wrenched at the thought, but there was no choice. Love cannot be built on a lie, and he deserved to know everything.

She was unsure how to approach the situation with Henri. No matter what, he would not win. She would fight tooth and nail, and she would never give herself to the likes of him. The days passed, with Luella dreaming of her life outside the manor.

The clock chimed, and Luella decided to get an early start that morning in the kitchen. After changing into her work gown, she went downstairs. Yawning, she lit the fire before beginning her food prep.

Once breakfast was cooked and served, she went out to feed the animals.

Luella…

Remi, what's wrong?

Nothing, just… I need to see you.

I don't think I can today. Is something the matter? You sound distant. I don't mean literally, but—

Please. I need to hold you.

The hairs at the nape of her neck stood on end, and she was certain the countess watched from the parlor. She cleared her throat and resumed dropping meal for the chickens.

Give me half an hour and meet me at the pond.

I can't wait to see you.

Luella reacted with a flinch, as though the conversation's end was a door being slammed in her face. She normally mopped and did inside housework on Tuesdays. What excuse could she give Clara for slipping away, one that wouldn't arouse her suspicions?

Luella went inside and nearly ran into the countess. "I did not see you," she said, keeping her gaze low.

"Stupid girl. It doesn't matter. I am going to visit a friend and will not return until dinner. Aubrey and Madison are going to their dance lessons."

Luella started to ask how the countess afforded lessons but quickly thought better of it. "Yes, madam."

She grabbed the mop bucket, filled it from the pump outside, then began to clean while waiting for them to leave. Once gone, she slipped into Madison's room and borrowed a lavender gown to wear. She glanced at the clock, realizing Remi must be waiting on her, and rushed to the pond.

When she arrived, her heart sank at the sight of him. He leaned against the tree with his head buried in his hands. She did not know what was the matter, only that she would do whatever she must to help him.

"I'm here," she said softly as she approached him from behind.

She yelped when he reached around and gripped her arm, pulling her to him, and holding her tightly as he wept into the crook of her neck. She stroked his hair as she whispered reassurances.

"Please, you have me worried sick! What is wrong?" she asked when he at last wiped his tears.

"I guess news hasn't reached here, yet."

"What news?"

"Prince Marc passed away."

Luella gasped. "I am so sorry. Were you close with the prince?"

"Yes," he murmured as his eyes watered again. "I am sorry you are seeing me like this."

"I care not, I only wish to bring you some reprieve. I'm sorry for your grief."

"Thank you." He sniffled into his kerchief before folding it up and placing back in his pocket.

Luella expressed her sympathy by gently touching his shoulder. "What do you need? What can I do?"

He took her hand and led her to the pond, sitting together on a fallen tree. "Sit here with me?"

"Anything. Do you want to talk about him?"

"A little. He was my… he was a good friend, and I still can't believe he's gone."

"What happened?"

Remi cleared his throat as he lifted a rock and tossed it into the pond. "You know the hierarchy with shifters?"

"That you are above us humans, yes."

"Well, besides that I mean… No, but within the packs themselves."

"Oh, not really."

"As the king becomes older, it is expected for one of his sons to kill him, to remove him from the pack and take over himself."

"Is that what happened with Marc?"

"No. He agrees with me, the practice is outdated and needs to stop. One of the other princes sent an assassin after the king, instead of trying to kill him himself. This is frowned upon, and it only makes him look weaker for not fighting himself. Marc tried to stop the assassin, to save the king, and was wounded in the process."

"I am so sorry."

"It's why I had to return to the palace, but we thought his healing would work, and he would be fine. I don't know what happened, if it was another assassin or if his wounds were more serious than we had been led to believe, but either way, he's gone."

They sat in silence a little while longer, until Remi stood and turned away.

"I need to get back. They are planning for his…" His voice cracked. "Anyway, thank you for meeting me here."

"Anything for you." She stood and reached for him, but before she could, he shifted and took off. "It's his grief," she assured herself as she returned to the manor.

The clock chimed, and Luella quickly dressed before going into the kitchen. Despite his abrupt departure the day before, she couldn't wait to see Remi again.

"My, you're chipper today," Clara commented while Luella loaded the cart.

"Did you need something, madam?"

"Only to sate my curiosity. Tell me, why are you in such a good mood?"

"It's a beautiful day, that's all," Luella answered.

"Of course." Clara glanced at her once more before going inside the manor.

Luella patted the donkey on the shoulder, and they made their way to the pond. Disappointment flooded her when she realized she was alone. She had been certain Remi would be waiting for her.

The first blanket washed and hung, she reached for the second when the voice she had waited for called out.

"Do you know how radiant you are in the afternoon light? For here is the east, and Luella is the sun."

She let the blanket slip from her hands and ran to him, jumping into his arms and kissing him passionately. Being enveloped by him sent waves of desire flowing through her.

"I'm guessing you missed me?" he asked as he placed her on her feet.

"I did," she admitted. "Did you miss me?" she asked, biting her lower lip.

"Of course. I apologize, I was delayed at the palace. I ran nearly the whole way here to see you."

"Faster than your steed?" she teased.

"Only at some things," he responded with a wink.

"That is most inappropriate."

"Hmm, so is this." His lips met hers, then he gently parted them with his tongue. She moaned in response as she gripped his arms. He stared at her for a moment. "I am sorry for how I left yesterday."

"You were dealing with a lot. It's all right."

"No, after you risked yourself to come to me, for me to simply leave you that way. It was rude. I am truly sorry."

"I'm glad to be with you now. Being away from you is torture."

"For both of us," he agreed.

"I have a question, but I'm not sure how to ask."

"Luella, there is no reason for you to worry about something like that. Speak freely."

"Where do you see this going? Us, I mean. I know it's not just a summer fling, but—"

"Did our vows mean nothing to you?"

The anger in his voice sent a shiver down her spine. She shrank back, her eyes wide and mouth agape. "I… I didn't mean to offend you. Please, I—"

"I'm sorry." He gripped her hand and pulled her to him, kissing her tenderly on her forehead. "As you said, all of this is new to you. I apologize for my anger. As far as what I want, I thought I had made that abundantly clear."

"You're right, you did. Still, I'm afraid."

"Of what?"

"The future. Our future."

"How so?"

"We are forbidden by the countess. You live at the palace, and I live here. How are we going to make this work?"

"Look, I will be coming here in a few weeks to make an official announcement on behalf of the king. It is very good news and will be beneficial to us."

"Can you tell me what it is?"

"Not yet."

"I can understand."

"What do you mean?"

She sighed. "Only that there are things I wish I could tell you. Things about me you don't know."

"I will learn them in time, when you are ready to open up. For now, is this not enough, what we have?"

"It is."

He helped her with laundry, smiling and laughing as she told him stories about taking care of the animals and the mice that live in the kitchen.

When they finished hanging the last one, they sat under the nearest tree. She rested in his lap, with her back against his chest. His fingers trailed down her arm to her stomach.

"Remi, as much as I enjoyed that before, being with you like this means everything to me."

"Are you sure?"

"What do you want?" she asked.

"I wish to see all of you."

Without a word, she stood and faced him. He joined her, helping her remove her gown. He admired every curve. Wearing only her corset, underwear, and a glass pendant, a surge of warmth coursed through his veins. It was as if his blood had transformed into a symphony of desire, each note playing an intoxicating melody. His hand teased along her chest and stomach before moving between her thighs.

He trailed soft, wet kisses along her neck, and she moaned when his tongue flicked at her collar bone. Instincts kicked in, and he could not stop himself.

Before he knew what was happening, he bared his teeth, then sank them into the smooth flesh of her shoulder. A cry of pain flew from her lips, and she fell backwards, landing hard on the ground while clutching the wound.

"What are you doing?" she yelled while trembling with fear.

He knelt beside her, his touch feather-light as his fingertips traced the contours of her arm, a gesture to express his remorse. "I am so sorry. It's part of our mating instinct, to bite the one we claim. I didn't know it was going to happen so soon, or I would've warned you."

"You bit me," she murmured in disbelief as he led her to the pond.

"If you knew what it means to me," he said as he washed away the blood. "If you knew what it means to my kind—"

"But I don't, because I'm a human. I am not a shifter, and right now, all I know is you hurt me!"

"I didn't mean to," he said as she lifted her gown.

"I don't care," she snapped as she slipped it on. "How could you do that to me? First, this mark on my stomach. Now this. Do you want the countess to find out? Was that your plan all along?"

"Of course not. I love you, Luella. I would never hurt you intentionally."

"Tell that to my shoulder." Her eyes went wide. "Oh, gods. Will I turn into a wolf now?"

Remi couldn't stop the bark of laughter. "That is lycanthropy. Werewolves are a myth, along with vampyrs. They don't exist. As a shifter, I do not have venom, nor do we turn people. You are either born a shifter or you aren't."

"That's a little reassuring, I guess."

He leaned down and gently kissed her wound. "How can I make this right?"

She pulled back and shook her head. "I am unsure, but I need to leave."

"Please, not yet."

"I have to go to the market, then finish here."

"I wish I could go with you."

"You bit her?"

"Simon—"

"Remi, what is it going to take for you to see what's right in front of you? She isn't your chosen mate, she must be your destined one! Biting rarely occurs now, with humans and shifters mating."

"Wait, what?"

"It was more common when both partners were shifters."

"The book I read—"

"Is outdated. I'm telling you."

"No, destined mates don't exist. Not anymore, not if they ever did. I don't believe I love her because I have to, but because I choose to. She is my *chosen* mate, and that's that."

Simon started to argue, but the determination etched on Remi's face held him back. "Very well. Now, about the upcoming ball."

"I don't want to talk about it."

"I thought you were excited?"

"After what happened today, I'm not even sure Luella will speak to me again."

"I am sure she will."

"I can only pray. I'm grateful for us to have a joyous occasion to plan for, after the loss we sustained. Everyone puts on a smile, but I can see the pain in their eyes."

Chapter 11

The Choice

ednesday could not come fast enough. Luella's shoulder healed, and with it, her anger dissipated. She desired to see Remi again. Her waking thoughts were consumed by him. Disappointment flooded her when she arrived at the pond.

He was not there, but she reminded herself he may be running late, like before. Her work kept her occupied, until she heard what she longed for.

"There you are."

With every ounce of self-control she could muster, she kept herself calm as she faced him. She smiled when he approached her, and he gripped her arm but kept his distance.

"Please, kiss me," she begged softly. His lips landed on hers, and his grip on her arm tightened.

"I missed you this past week," he said as he pulled back.

"So have I."

"I've been thinking about what happened. I'm so sorry."

"No, you've already apologized. I did a little reading up on shifters, and I see now. It truly is a symbol of love from your kind. Even if it did hurt," she teased.

He lifted one of the blankets and spread it on the ground. She said nothing, only watched, until he guided her to it. They sat together, with her in between his legs, as his hand caressed her neck.

"I long to taste you."

She pulled away. "I realize I forgave you, but that doesn't mean I want to be bitten again."

He crawled around her and gripped her legs. "No, that is not what I mean. Not with my teeth, but with my tongue." His mouth opened, and he placed wet kisses along her knee and moved upward.

"Oh, gods. Yes."

She shimmied as he reached up and removed her underwear. His warm breath blew over the exposed skin, sending a shiver of anticipation running down her spine. Her back arched when his tongue ran the length of her.

With a moan, she grasped his hair as he held her steady by gripping her thighs with both hands. As he devoured every sensitive inch of her, she writhed against him.

"Oh, please!" she cried out as she came.

He smiled as he wiped his mouth. "You taste like fine honey and sweet amber."

Fire rose in her cheeks as she shook her head. "I don't believe you."

"Taste for yourself, then." He kissed her fiercely, his tongue penetrating every corner of her mouth.

"I… I want to do the same for you," she said, biting her lower lip and keeping her eyes down.

"Are you sure?"

She met his gaze and offered a shy smile. "More than anything. Please, let me?"

To hear her beg for him, he could hardly keep himself restrained. His pants tightened as his lust for her grew, and he grunted as he undid them. She slowly pulled them down, and his eyes squeezed shut as the longing became almost painful.

She froze at the full sight of him, both in admiration and fear. From under her lashes, she glanced up at him, swallowing hard.

"I don't know if I'm able to. You're so…"

"Luella, it's all right. You don't have to."

"I want to try."

"If it's too much for you, or if you need to stop, then do so. I only want you to be comfortable."

"I've never done this before," she admitted as she positioned herself before him.

"Here." He grasped her hand and used it to stroke him. "Take in a little at a time. You may feel like you are choking or need to cough. If that happens, pull back, and take a break to catch your breath."

Her hand gripped him gently, and he was sure he would spill out right at her touch. He stilled himself and focused. Her lips curled around the tip, and he nearly fell when her tongue swirled over him. She opened her mouth wider to take him in. He groaned again, his hands clenched tightly, as the pleasure ravaged him.

Taking this as her sign, she sucked harder while her hand continued to stroke. Each moan and gasp from him encouraged her, and she teased him. His length grew harder and trembled the more she worked. He knew what was about to happen and tried to back away, but she kept him firmly in her mouth, swallowing every last drop of him.

He tangled his fingers in her hair and bent down to kiss the top of her head. "Good girl," he murmured as he pulled her to her feet. "For your first time, you were absolutely perfect." His lips brushed hers before kissing her softly.

"Really?"

"Yes," he said as he dressed.

She shifted where she stood, unable to face him. "How many women… I mean…"

"How many women have I done this with?" he asked as he adjusted his shirt.

"Yes," she whispered.

"None."

At that single word, her head snapped up. "What?"

"As shifters, we take mating seriously, including any and all acts that lead up to it. We do not do this with just anyone, and we mate for life."

"For life? What does that mean for us? What are you saying?"

His hand brushed gently over the bite mark on her shoulder. "Luella, I have already claimed you. You are mine. Don't ever doubt that."

"But we hardly know each other."

"Do you not feel this? My heart burns for you, my very soul aches when I am away from you."

She swallowed hard. "I shouldn't say this, because I am so afraid."

Remi stepped closer, taking her hand and kissing between her knuckles. "You have no reason to be. I never want you to be afraid, not of me, nor anything you wish to say to me."

Luella's mind raced with fear and vulnerability as she mustered the courage to make her confession. Her thoughts were consumed by the longing for acceptance. As she stared into his eyes, her lungs seized. She choked in air before saying what she needed to say.

"Remi, I love you."

He froze, and for a moment, she wondered if he did not hear her, that perhaps she hadn't spoken aloud like she thought she did. She opened her mouth to repeat herself. Instead, their lips collided in a storm of passion, a tempest of emotions and desires that surged through their bodies, leaving them breathless and consumed by the intensity of their connection.

"I love you, too."

The relief was apparent on her face. "But if we're caught—"

"We won't be. I have a few guards with me." He chuckled when her face grew red. "Luella, they face away to give us privacy, I assure you. However, we have a signal in place to alert me if someone is coming."

"Really?"

"I promise you." His brow furrowed. "Though I am curious, what would happen if we were caught? Why are you so afraid of your mother?"

Luella released a shuddered breath. "I don't want to talk about her. Not right now." She kissed him again. "Not after you've made me so happy."

"I would say the same for you, mon trésor. How you are perfect, fit and molded for me in every way, as if made for me, I will never understand."

She bit her lower lip as she met his gaze. "How can we feel like this when we've only known each other a fleeting time? I swore I would never be with a shifter, but it is as though I cannot control myself. I need to be with you, ache for you, long for you."

Remi straightened and took a step back. "What do you mean?" His voice was emotionless with a slight chill to his tone.

She reached for him, frowning when he recoiled from her touch. Remi's sudden withdrawal and coldness sent shockwaves through Luella's heart, her confusion and desperation mounting as she fought to salvage their relationship "I don't understand. Please tell me, what did I do?"

"I choose you, Luella, because I fell for you the moment we met. It was difficult at first, since I frightened you. I thought you wanted to be with me, too. I see how wrong I was. Perhaps we were too hasty with our vows."

Luella's knees weakened, threatening to buckle as Remi's words pierced her heart. "Remi, I don't understand what is going on? What are you talking about?"

"You cannot control yourself with me?"

"I only meant—"

"I have no doubts about what you meant."

She shook her head as tears streamed down. "I thought I made you happy. What did I do wrong?"

"I have to go. I need to think about this."

"Please, at least tell me!" she begged.

"I thought we were chosen mates, but now I wonder. I will not force myself on you."

Her hands clenched then opened towards him to express her exasperation. "You never have! Yes, you bit me. Everything else we have done together, I have wanted to happen. I let you claim me, and I gave myself willingly to that claim. Why are you pulling away now?" With wide eyes and opened mouth, she lowered her gaze to the ground. "I didn't please you the way you wanted, did I?"

Remi's mind flooded with memories of their few moments of intimacy, each memory a testament to the depth of his love for her. He rushed to her and wrapped her in his arms. "That is not what I speak of. You are perfect in every way." He pulled back. "I never want to hurt you."

"You just did! I've never been so confused in my entire life."

He sighed. "You said you have done some research on wolf shifters?"

"Yes."

"Did you read anything about mates?"

"A little. A shifter may choose a mate or they may have one destined for them. I think that's what the book said. It didn't go into detail. What does it mean?"

"A chosen mate is when a shifter and either another shifter or a human agree to be together. A destined mate is selected by our moon Goddess, Luna, but there hasn't been a destined mate in centuries. So it doesn't make sense to have one now!"

"Why are you so angry?"

He took a breath to collect himself. "Because I want you to choose me. I don't want it to be something you have to do."

"I do choose you! I lay awake the night we met, fighting my feelings. I was attracted to you, but I promised myself I would never be with a shifter, not after one killed my father. But in the time we have spent together, you have saved my life, protected me, been there for me in a way no one else ever has."

"That's twice you've mentioned you would never be with a shifter."

She pulled herself to him, gripping his chin and meeting his eyes. "Yet, here I am. What does that tell you?"

"I'm genuinely confused," he responded honestly. "Because if you hate shifters so much—"

"I don't hate them. I've been scared of them my whole life, but how can I hate them all?"

"But you said—"

"Because I was angry. And I was confused, especially about my feelings for you. Listen to me when I tell you, I have thought long and hard about this. We should not be together, for so many reasons. Whether it is destiny or by our own choice, here we are. I don't care why! I only care to have you in my life. Please, don't reject me now. I can't bear it." Her lips trembled as her confession tumbled out.

"Reject you?"

"I read about rejected mates, and I was afraid that was what you were going to do next. My heart wouldn't be able to bear it if you did." She hated how pathetic the words sounded, but her whole life had been without love. The thought of having it ripped away from her made her chest ache.

"I am not going anywhere," he assured her before pressing his lips softly to her temple. "And I am sorry you thought I was. You're right. I chose you as my mate, claimed you, and accepted you. Whatever the reason, I love you, and I couldn't imagine my life without you."

Remi gently wiped away Luella's tears with his thumb. His touch acted as a soothing balm against her pain, and a silent reassurance that he was there for her, no matter what.

"Thank you. I love you, too." A gentle breeze brushed their skin, and Luella stared lovingly into his eyes. "Please, whatever the issue is, don't turn away from me. Talk to me, so we can take it on together. I have been alone enough in my life. With you, I feel ready to take on the world."

"I promise to do better. I know I apologized, but I will show you as well. I will be whoever you deserve, because you are the sweetest, most incredible woman I've ever met." He cleared his throat as he threw his shoulders back. "There will come a time when we will have to tell your mother. Did she forbid it solely because I am a shifter or is there some other reason?" He looked down when she trembled in his arms.

"Remi, I'm not ready to talk about it."

"We need to if we want to plan for our future. You asked me, how will this work? It will, but not without both of us."

She pulled away and stepped back, glancing behind him. He turned to look, seeing nothing, then faced her, only to see her running through the woods.

Remi tilted his head. "So much for the two of us facing anything together."

Remi returned to his quarters after dinner. He didn't intend to push Luella about her mother, but he couldn't help wondering what she kept hidden from him. He hadn't meant to risk pushing her away, and yet that was exactly what happened when he pursued it further.

Standing in the shower, eyes closed, as he remembered Luella's lips, her touch, and her taste. The thought of waiting another week to see her became too much to bear.

A thought flickered for a moment. What if he went to see her on Friday? Surprising her at the market, they could then find privacy on the path to talk without being noticed. He knew she visited on Wednesdays and Fridays, and seeing her again so soon brought a smile to his face.

Two days sounded more bearable than a week. He finished in the washroom and climbed into bed. The excitement kept him tossing and turning, hardly allowing him to sleep. Then he remembered the announcement he would make soon, and his excitement only grew.

He thought of her blue eyes staring into his, her small laugh that made his heart feel as though it would explode. Every beautiful part of her belonged to him. He finally drifted off to sleep.

"You haven't seen that boy again, have you, Luella? Not since the day he found you after you were attacked?"

Luella bit her tongue and collected herself. "No, madam. I told you I wouldn't see him."

"There was a rumor today that you were seen in the woods with him. I will not tolerate deceitfulness, not in this house. If you are found with him, you will be punished."

"I am not afraid of you."

Clara stalked across the room, stopping only a few inches from Luella. "You should be. You thought being locked in the closet was bad? What if I had you thrown into the stocks? Or perhaps—"

"You don't have that kind of power."

"No, but my good friend Langdon does. Oh, by the way, he will be joining us for tea one day soon. You will treat him with respect, do you understand me?"

Luella's jaw ticked, but it was the only sign of distress she would allow. "Of course, madam."

"Good."

Luella made her last purchase and headed for the path home when she froze in her tracks. Remi waited for her on the edge of town. She quickly glanced around to see if anyone noticed him.

She walked past him without looking at him. "What are you doing here?" she whispered.

"I had to see you."

"Why? What's wrong?"

"Everything," he answered, taking her hand once they were out of sight. "I missed you and couldn't wait to see you again."

She set her bag down and faced him, her demeanor more serious than he anticipated. "We agreed to meet every Wednesday."

"Luella—"

"Look, I missed you, too. I did. But this is dangerous."

"I don't care."

"Well, I do!"

He debated once more, curious about her home life while afraid of pushing her too hard. "I'm sure it's not that bad. Are you really upset because I came to see you?"

Luella's mind drifted back to the night when Clara realized the gown and journal were gone. Tears threatened to escape, and she'd had enough.

"Do not try to make me feel guilty because of something you did." She snatched up her pack. "We will discuss this on Wednesday," she said, walking away without so much as a glance in his direction.

"Luella, please. Stop."

He stepped forward to follow her, but the hairs on the back of his neck stood on end. Something was wrong. Regardless of what she said, he followed her. He kept to the shadows in the woods to be sure she made it home unharmed.

Simon joined him as he made his way back. "Want to tell me what that was all about?"

Remi's jaw clenched. "She wasn't exactly thrilled to see me."

"That was pretty obvious. I told you this was a bad idea."

Remi stopped walking. "I need your help with something."

"That's ominous."

Chapter 12

A Threat

onday afternoon, Luella swept and hummed while the stew simmered over the fire. Moving back and forth, she meticulously cleaned the kitchen floor. Startled, Luella jumped when she bumped into Clara.

"Apologies, madam. I did not see you!"

When Clara smiled at Luella, it sent a shiver coursing through her. "It's quite all right."

Luella had never heard her use such a gentle tone with her. "Did you need something?"

"Well, I've noticed over the past few weeks that you seem to be… happy. So naturally, I'm curious."

Luella cleared her throat as she set the broom aside, rinsed her hands in the sink, then stirred the stew. "I am usually upbeat, am I not?"

Clara sighed. "You are hiding something from me. And I don't mean the gown or journal, either. Though I am sure it was you who took them."

The lie stuck in her throat, nearly choking her before forcing it out. "I promise you, I'm not."

"And the herald?"

"What about him?"

"You saw him the other day but failed to mention it."

"He stopped me on my way home to thank me once more, that is all. I assure you. There is nothing else."

"We'll see." Clara leaned down and whispered into Luella's ear, making her threat very clear. Luella's color faded at her words.

Clara abruptly left before Luella could respond. Luella's hand shook as she prepared each plate. Her heart sank as she realized she was right to tell Remi, it is too dangerous for them. She forced herself steady as she carried the tray and set everything up in the dining room.

Once she returned to the kitchen, she made herself a bowl and carried it outside. She sat on the edge of the fountain. As Clara's words echoed in Luella's mind, her chest tightened with the realization that her actions not only endangered her own happiness, but also Remi's safety. She would put Remi first, protecting him, regardless if it cost her the very happiness she had been desperately longing for.

Remi, I don't know if you can hear me. A moment went by, then a few more. Her body tingled as though on pins and needles. *Remi, are you there?*

Luella, what's wrong? Are you hurt?

No, but there is something I must tell you. It can't wait another moment longer. The thick tension nearly snapped as she gathered her courage. *I'm sorry, but it's over.*

What is?

Us.

Silence. Tears formed as she made herself eat. She knew he would never understand. How could she convince him?

You don't mean that.

Remi—

I own you. I claimed you, and you claimed me in return. We said our vows, and my heart is yours. Why would you do this?

I don't have a choice.

Then tell me why, damn it! You said rejection would break your heart, so there must be something more to it. Not only would rejection break your heart, but my own as well. You must tell me!

His anger flowed into her, piercing her chest. She wiped the tears away and took a deep breath.

I love you, but we were only fooling ourselves. It's too dangerous. I'm sorry.

She mustered up all her strength to shut herself off. She locked away her heart, and she shuttered her mind from him.

"I'm sorry," she said once more before returning to the kitchen to continue her chores.

Remi fell from the chair, landing with a thud on the floor. Simon raced to his side.

"Are you all right?"

Remi shook his head as he stood and dusted himself off. "No, and I have no idea what is going on. We're going to the colony."

"We can't. The Duchess Amelia arrives later this evening. Remember your orders."

"Remember your place," Remi snapped.

Simon stood straight. "Yes, sir."

"Simon—"

He ignored Remi and walked away.

"Great, I'm losing people left and right."

He returned to his quarters to change for the reception. While he understood his duty to the king came first, would they even notice his absence?

Despite the circumstances, he would at least admit his admiration for her ability to shut him out. Usually, that sort of mental strength took months, sometimes even years to build up.

His shoulders sagged. It also told him that whatever happened must be quite serious. Torn between love and duty, he said to hell with it and decided to sneak away from the palace. The consequences be damned.

Seeing her and reassuring her was all that mattered. He would take physical pain any day over whatever it was that consumed him whole, leaving him as though he were drowning, and she were his oxygen. His love for Luella was a wildfire, burning fiercely within him. It consumed everything in its path, unstoppable and unyielding.

He knew everyone would be focused on the arrival of the duchess, so he used that as his distraction. Smiling and nodding, he milled around a bit, then walked down the hallway. Once out of sight, he ducked through a side exit.

"And where do you think you're going?"

"To get some air," Remi answered as he faced Simon.

"Right."

"I'll be inside momentarily."

Laughter erupted from Simon. "I wasn't born yesterday. Whatever it is you're up to, I'm right there with you."

"I have to see Luella. I don't understand why she is pushing me away now. Something is wrong."

Simon pursed his lips. "Promise me I won't get dismissed from my position?"

"For what? I slipped out, you saw me, and you had no time to alert anyone. Otherwise, you would've lost me."

"Well, I've enjoyed being employed by the king. Don't know what I'll do after."

"Didn't you hear me?" Remi clapped his shoulder. "But can you keep up?" He shifted and took off.

They ran through the trees and across the plains, stopping before approaching the wall to the colony. Simon shifted first, from a red wolf to his human form. Remi joined him a moment later.

"I have a bad feeling about this."

Simon nodded in agreement. They entered the town, and Remi led the way to the path. Trying not to catch anyone's attention, they strolled through the village until they were out of sight. They sped up and walked to the manor. Once it came into view, they went around back, staying hidden in the trees.

Luella fed the animals, humming softly as she did. Simon's face lit up as they watched her. "I can see why it's hard for you to stay away. She really is quite lovely."

Remi only gave a slight nod, so enamored in watching her every move. A woman Luella's age approached, though a tad shorter. Her strawberry blonde hair was plaited down her back. Remi gestured for Simon to follow as he moved closer so they could hear.

"Did you need something, Aubrey?" Luella asked as she spread out more feed for the chickens.

"Mother asked me to check on you."

"I beg your pardon?"

"She said… she said you are up to no good."

Luella gave a shrug of her shoulder. "Ask the chickens if that is true."

Remi stifled the laughter threatening to escape. Simon didn't try to hide his smile.

"Why is she so suspicious of you lately?"

Before Luella responded, her body stiffened, and she looked in Remi's direction.

"Shit!" he whispered in panic, grabbing Simon's shoulder, and pulling him to the ground. "Did she see us?"

Simon risked a glance. "No."

They slowly stood and watched as Luella continued to feed the animals. Remi shook his head. "I need to speak to her, but I can't. Not with her sister out here."

Simon winked then stalked towards them. Remi reached for his arm but missed. Simon approached the two women.

"Good afternoon."

They both startled and gave him a questioning look. Luella steadied herself and offered him a polite smile. "Good afternoon."

"I was on my way to the market, and somehow, I ended up all turned around. Would one of you be able to help me?"

Luella glanced over his shoulder and saw Remi before he ducked down. "Aubrey, I think you should go with him."

"What?" she cried out, clearly indignant at the suggestion.

"Do you not see his uniform? He is from the palace. Why, I bet he could give you all sorts of useful information about the prince and life as a royal on your way."

Aubrey broke into a smile. "That's not a bad idea. Yes, I'll take you there."

"I'm Simon," he said as she laced her arm with his.

"Nice to meet you."

Luella watched as they made their way to the path. She sighed before turning to the woods, dropped the last of the feed, and went into the trees.

Remi met her by a large, fallen pine. "Hello, mon trésor."

Luella kept her gaze to the ground. "I told you, we're through. You need to go." Remi didn't move, and Luella took a chance. She glimpsed his hurt expression. "Why are you here?"

"Because I don't believe you. Because I refuse your rejection." Remi watched in concern as Luella's breaths came in rapid succession, her body visibly trembling with fear. "What's wrong?"

"We can't do this," she said, her voice barely a wisp in the breeze.

"We claimed each other. Why are you turning your back on us now? At least tell me what I did."

"It's… it's complicated."

"Do you not understand? It is killing me, that I don't know what to do, how to fix this." He took her hand, kissing along her palm and wrist. "Please, tell me what you need. I will do anything."

"Luella!"

Upon hearing her name, she looked and saw the countess in the backyard. "Stay here," she demanded before running towards her stepmother. "I'm here, madam. I thought a chicken had wandered off."

"Where is Aubrey?"

"At the market."

Clara sighed. "That girl never listens." She scanned the woods. "Are you sure that's all you were doing?"

"Whatever do you mean?"

"You weren't with that boy, were you?"

"No, of course not."

"Good! Because I told you exactly what would happen if you did. The governor already has hard feelings for him, so it would take nothing to convince him that the herald did something to me. He would gladly chain him up like the dog he is!"

Remi's blood boiled at her words. He stepped forward, ready to defend himself and Luella.

Please, stay there.

His hands clenched, but he respected her request.

"I assure you, he knows it is dangerous to come around here. You don't have to worry about him."

"Good. Now, I am going to the market to find your sister." The countess didn't realize her slip of tongue, but Luella was grateful for it.

Luella watched her leave, pretending to tighten a hinge on the gate until she was sure Clara was gone. Then she made her way to Remi.

"I thought you were worried about your own punishment. It never occurred to me you were protecting me." He grabbed her to him and kissed her hard, his lips attacking hers as his tongue probed her mouth. "Gods, I am grateful, but please, never do that again. Don't shut me out."

"I never wanted to hurt you, Remi," Luella choked out, her voice cracking with the weight of her guilt.

"But I was hurt because of you." He wondered if she understood the depth of his pain.

"What? Where?" Luella interrupted, her voice filled with concern as she scanned Remi for any signs of injury.

His hand rested on his heart. "Here. When you reached out and told me we were through. It nearly killed me. Do you even care about what you did?" Remi's eyes burned with a fiery intensity, filled with a desperate longing that pierced through Luella's soul.

Her breath sucked in as she wiped her tears while trying to avoid his gaze. "I only did it to protect you."

"You gave into your fear, instead of trusting me."

"What would you have me do? Clara and Langdon are two peas in a pod. They hate shifters, and they will use any excuse to punish one."

"Then why didn't you tell me?" he asked, every word filled with his exasperation.

"Because you're right, I was afraid. From our first moment together, I have been so scared. Scared that either I would give you my heart, just for you to abandon me," his body tensed against hers, "or that you would be taken from me. You are the first person to ever love me, and it terrified me."

"Luella—"

"So I did what I must to protect you from them. But please, don't hate me for the choices I had to make."

He pulled her tightly into his warm embrace. "Luella, of course I don't hate you. I was angry and hurt, but I love you. You belong with me, and I can't think of living without you. Please, promise me you will never do anything like that again."

"I swear, I won't." She kissed him softly. "I have to go. Madison is here, and I don't want her to find us. Plus, I still have chores to do."

"I will see you Wednesday at our pond."

"I can't wait."

Simon and Aubrey walked in silence for a few moments. She kept her gaze down, unsure of how to start a conversation with him.

She cleared her throat. "How long have you been a guard?" Her hands clasped tightly in front of her, and there was a small waver in her voice.

Simon smiled. "Almost four years."

"Ah."

He chuckled when she fidgeted with her hair. "What do you do?"

She stopped walking. "Do?"

"Yes. Are you a governess? Or perhaps a seamstress?"

A frog formed in her throat, and it hurt to swallow it down. "Well, I… My mother and I…" She continued moving forward. "We visit with friends, while my sister and I are trying to find partners." Her cheeks went crimson.

"Aubrey, may I ask, why are you so nervous talking to me?"

"I think you're handsome," she blurted out.

Simon laughed, shaking his head. "Well, I appreciate your honesty."

"Um, thanks." They walked in silence a few more minutes. Aubrey built up her courage. "So, what is life like at the palace?"

"Well, for the royals, it's probably about as luxurious as you imagine. For us guards, heralds, and so on, it's not too bad. The food is good. It can get a little violent, when one wolf decides to challenge another."

"Oh, right. I didn't think, if you work at the palace as a guard, it makes sense you would be a shifter."

Simon noted the extra space she put between them. "Yes, but we really aren't so different from humans."

"That's not what Mother says. She told us shifters are evil and not to be trusted." Her mouth slammed shut as a look of uneasiness crept over her. "I'm sorry."

"For what? Telling me how you feel?"

She peeked up at him. "Honestly, I'm not sure how to feel. I've never met a shifter, before you, I mean. As far as I know, they've never hurt me. Mother says we are to be afraid of them, but I…" She trailed off for a moment. "I have dreams where I am playing with a large black wolf."

"Interesting."

"She says it's my vivid imagination."

Simon chuckled. "What do you think?"

"I think it's a memory."

"Then that's what it is."

"Thank you."

"Whatever for?"

"Being so nice. Be honest, you weren't really lost, were you?"

Simon immediately went stiff. "I beg your pardon?"

"I saw you at the town hall the last time the herald made his announcements. I thought perhaps you noticed me."

Simon smiled at her. "I did notice you."

She blushed again, biting her lip. "Really?"

"I did. Are you…" He cleared his throat. "Is this okay?"

A small, pleasant laugh escaped her. "Would I still be walking with you if it wasn't? After all, you admitted you aren't lost."

His smile grew before he turned serious. "Though you put some space between us—"

"I apologize. Not only because it is how I was brought up, to be proper around a man, but also because I am…" She bit her lip and looked down for a moment. "I am not the most comfortable around new people."

"That's understandable."

"Why are you really here?" she blurted out. "You had no idea I would be in the backyard, where Luella usually is. Something isn't right."

He sighed. "You caught me. I wanted to scope you out, first. I am enamored and curious at the same time."

She stopped in her tracks. "I beg your pardon?"

"I am aware that is being forward, but you are a lovely young woman. I lost my mate last year, and I hadn't even considered courting anyone. However, one look at you, and I lost my train of thought." Simon laid it on thick, but he knew he must to help Remi and Luella.

Her smile grew as her cheeks flushed. "Will you tell me more about yourself?"

"Of course."

"Ready to face the music?" Simon asked as they approached the palace.

"Hey, I know she still loves me. Nothing else matters," Remi replied with a smile.

Simon chuckled. "That is good."

"What about you? You seem to be in good spirits, after visiting with her sister."

"Well, I did enjoy her company. Perhaps there could be something there. Remi—"

"You two! His Majesty is looking for you," a young guard announced as they entered.

Remi nodded. "Lead the way."

Simon and Remi exchanged a knowing look. Together, they entered the throne room.

"There you are! You are fortunate, that the Duchess's caravan is delayed. Hurry and get dressed, immediately."

"Yes, Your Majesty," they said in unison with a bow.

Remi smirked at Simon as they entered the corridor, and he chuckled in return.

Chapter 13

The Royal Announcement

ervousness settled in Luella's stomach as she approached the pond. Would Remi be waiting for her? And had he truly forgiven her for what she did? She let her fear take control, and in doing so, nearly destroyed the first relationship she'd ever had. She would have to be more careful.

The countess announced after breakfast they would be at lunch with the baroness and her son, and would probably be gone for most of the afternoon. This news thrilled Luella. Once they left, she slipped into one of Madison's lavender day dresses before tying a ribbon in her hair. Her reflection lifted her spirits, as she was excited about seeing Remi.

Except he wasn't there. She kept herself upbeat, humming softly while she washed and hung blankets. She was on the third blanket, and had built up her courage to reach out, when he joined her.

"By the gods. Is that the most beautiful woman standing before me?"

His voice sent a shudder through her body, and she regained her composure before turning to face him. She offered him a smile. "Remi, I am sorry."

"You've already apologized."

"No, for Friday, when you surprised me. I had no right to get so angry. It's not you." Her eyes watered, but she swallowed her tears. "I am so scared what may happen if we are discovered. I took that out on you. I cannot apologize enough."

He stepped up to her and pulled her to him, kissing her fiercely as she clung to him. His hand tangled in her hair. Her lips remained firm on his, as she wrapped herself tighter around him.

"Luella, I forgive you. I saw the fear in your eyes. And after what happened with the countess and her threat, I understand now why you are so afraid." He kissed her again. Then he pulled back, gasping air. "What's wrong?" he finally managed.

"I needed you," she said.

He held her chin and caressed her jawline with his thumb. "Luella, I always need you."

"There's something I have to tell you."

"Then please, do so."

"I was so scared for you, so angry at Clara and Langdon, I…" Her voice cracked. "I shouldn't even say it."

"Tell me."

"I thought it might be better for everyone if I wasn't here anymore."

"You mean you thought about running away from the colony?"

"No, as in, my life."

Remi's eyes went wide as his breath shuddered. "Luella, I will tell you right now. A world where you no longer exist is not a world I wish to live in. Promise me you won't think like that again. Promise me!"

She buried her face in his shirt as her tears fell fast. "I'm sorry. I was terrified and thought such awful things."

"We will be together soon, I promise. I will be making an announcement, and it is wonderful news." He pulled her back to meet her gaze. "Something else is bothering you, isn't it?"

Despite her turning away, he grabbed her wrist and brought her closer to him. Pain was etched across her face. "There is so much I wish to tell you. That I need to tell you. But I'm a coward."

"Luella, you aren't. And I already know about your family."

She gasped in surprise. "You… What?"

"It's all right. I understand why you didn't tell me. I had no idea."

"But you… I…" A lump swelled in her throat.

He kissed her fiercely, holding her with everything he had while trying to be gentle as well. When they broke apart, she smiled at him.

"I love you, Luella. You. Not who you are to them or to the colony. I love you for you."

"I love you, too," she said as her face eased into an expression of relief that she didn't have to keep secrets from him anymore.

"Soon, everything will change. We will no longer have to hide."

"Really?"

"I swear it on my very life."

"It will be wonderful, to be free together. Can you picture it?"

He kissed her hand. "We stroll together, smiling at familiar faces. We can visit here, any time you wish."

"It all sounds nice."

She walked to the basket and picked up the next blanket to wash. After rinsing it, she hung it with care before looking at him.

"What?" he asked.

"Thinking of the future."

"Our future."

"Yes!" she said, practically bursting with enthusiasm.

"I do have to warn you, life at the palace isn't all wine and roses. It can be dangerous, with shifters fighting for domination and power."

"What do you mean?" she asked, hanging the blanket, then approaching him.

"Though we are born into ranks, such as alpha or omega, we still fight for power. Some wolves are cunning and work behind the scenes while others are violent and cutthroat."

"What sort of life is that?" she asked as she stepped back.

"It's the way things are."

"I never agreed to that."

"You accepted my claim. We have said our vows. We are inseparable now."

"All I want is to live a quiet, peaceful life. One with love and joy."

"We will have that."

Luella scoffed. "How? What, I'll sit in our quarters, waiting for you to return, hoping you do?" She shook her head. "No. What if we moved away? We could start over together."

"I'm afraid that's not possible for me. My life is at that palace."

Her heart pounded heavily in her chest. "You would willingly subject me to that sort of life?"

"All right, I think I made it sound worse than it is. You saw us at the festival. Were people killing each other in the streets?"

"Well… No."

"There you are. Yes, it can be dangerous, but it's not all the time. Only as the king grows old and weak, and other wolves are prime to claim the throne. Otherwise, it really isn't so bad. I swear it to you."

"I've waited my whole life to be loved, to be safe and cared for. Am I asking for so much?"

"Absolutely not. I will give you everything you desire. We will live together, we will have a family, if you want to. I am consumed by you, and I will do anything, give anything, to keep you by my side. You are my life, and without you…" He stammered for a moment. "I can't even think of it. My heart would turn to stone without you, would no longer beat if you were gone. How can I get this through to you, how much I love you, and how much I need you?"

"You say these words, make these promises, but I need you to prove it to me. I do by taking the chance of being seen with you. But what are you risking, what are you giving me to prove your love?"

"I could swear by the moon."

"She changes too often. I would not believe such a swear."

"Then by the sun."

"No. What else?"

"Our bargain. I swear to you, if our love were not real, you would be free of your bargain this instant."

Luella stood still for a moment before she spoke. "Nothing happened."

"Then there is your answer." He kissed the top of her head. "I swear this to you. I will always be here for you. I will always come for you. And you never have to question if my love for you is real or not. Please, tell me you believe that."

"I do. I do believe you. And on our bargain, I swear my love to you is as real as your own."

"That is a relief to hear."

Luella continued with the laundry when he stepped up beside her.

"I have to go, but I cannot wait to see you again." He kissed her softly.

"I've made arrangements for you and Henri. Once he signs the marriage contract with Madison, you will belong to him, one day a week, until he is tired of you. Madison is not to know, and she is only to be told you are there to help settle them into their marital home."

"I will be of age by then and long gone," Luella argued. "You can promise him whatever you want, but I will not be here for it."

"I've thought about that."

"What do you mean?"

"Agree to his terms, lead him on, until they sign the contract. Once they are officially married, do as you please. Since you are intent to leave, anyway."

"You said I was too valuable for you to lose."

"Once you are of age, it will be out of my hands."

Luella could see the wheels turning, realizing the countess had something up her sleeve. She decided not to push, that she would discover it for herself. "Of course. Very well, as long as you will stop spreading rumors about me and try to repair some of the damage you have done to my reputation, I will play your game."

Clara's jaw dropped, and she wanted to argue, but she realized Luella had her where she wanted her. "Fine," she snapped before leaving the room.

Monday morning, Luella returned from feeding the animals when Aubrey ran in. Her face was red, and she was huffing and puffing for air.

"Have you heard?"

"Heard what?" Luella asked.

"Of course you haven't. A herald from the palace is calling for an assembly, and all colonists are to go at once. Even you. Come on!"

Luella removed her apron, then followed the countess with her stepsisters. They went straight to the town hall, which was nearly full to the brim with people. Remi passed Luella, giving her a sly smile before approaching the governor.

He stayed back while Langdon spoke. "Attention, citizens. The king has sent his herald with a particularly important announcement." He gestured Remi forward. "All yours," he said, low enough for only Remi to hear.

"Good afternoon. I am Remi, and as Langdon said, I am here on behalf of your king." He removed a rolled-up piece of parchment. "One month from Saturday, on the thirteenth, the youngest prince, Prince Sebastian..." He cleared his throat. "Prince Sebastian Montague shall celebrate his twenty-first birthday.

As per tradition, a royal ball will be held in his honor. The king commands all women who are twenty or older and eligible attend, so the prince may select his bride."

The crowd erupted into murmurs and gasps. "I don't want to marry a shifter. You can't make me!" a woman cried out.

The governor stepped forward, gesturing with both hands for the crowd to settle down. "Ladies and gentlemen, please. Let him continue his announcement."

Remi waited a moment for everything to calm down. "As I was saying, so Prince Sebastian may select his bride. Other members of nobility and lower members of the house will also be looking, so be in your finest apparel. The events begin at 8 o'clock. Thank you."

He rolled up the parchment, returned it to his pocket, then left without another word. Luella's cheeks flushed, and her heart sank, as she yearned to touch him again. The fog in her head cleared.

Other members of nobility and lower members of the house will also be looking. She smiled at the thought.

"Oh, dear. I am about to be swamped for the next four weeks!"

Luella turned to see Camille, the garment maker, tugging on her sleeve. "Whatever is the matter?"

"My assistant just had her baby. I'm sure I will have lots of orders to fill. I can't do this on my own. Whatever will I do?"

Clara stepped up beside Luella. "I couldn't help but overhear your predicament. I would love to help you."

Luella's eyes narrowed as she tried to figure out the countess's game. "How so?" she asked, noting the glint of anger in Clara's eyes.

"Why, you, my dear. You repair and fix Aubrey and Madison's gowns quite well. You are exceptionally good at what you do."

"I am unable to pay her, I'm afraid. Not until after, because I will have to restock my fabric and—"

"You needn't pay her at all." Clara's words sent Luella reeling. "All I ask, is she help you make a dress for Aubrey and Madison in exchange."

Luella nodded, the true motive revealed. She glanced at Camille, praying she would see right through Clara's supposed kindness. Instead, she smiled. "Oh, mi'lady. That would be wonderful! Yes, Luella and I could make their dresses."

"When would you need her? Wednesdays and Fridays, perhaps?"

Luella's heart sank. She bit her tongue and waited for Camille's response. "No, what about Monday, Tuesday, and if needed, Saturday?"

"Perfect! Then it's all arranged. She will be there shortly to start."

"I need to do a few things, make preparations. Luella, would you come to the shop at five?"

"Of course."

"Thank you."

Luella perused the gowns while Camille helped her last client of the evening. Once they finished, she approached.

"Thank you for coming. I deeply appreciate your help."

"I'm happy to do it," Luella said as Camille locked the door and flipped the sign to show the store was now closed.

"Are you?"

Luella cleared her throat. "I enjoy working with fabrics and garments. I've been mending a dress myself."

"Well, I wasn't going to ask."

"What do you mean?"

Camille gestured Luella to follow her to her workshop in the back. "That the countess only asked for two dresses."

"Oh, right. I have one I plan to wear."

"I see."

"Where do we start?" Luella asked, hoping to change the topic.

Camille showed her a small workstation in the corner. "This should have everything you need, but if not, let me know."

"Thank you."

Luella took the first pattern and fabric, then she began to mark her cuts. Camille watched for a few minutes until she was satisfied Luella knew what she was doing.

"I'll be out front to finish a few things for closing."

"Yes, madam."

"Luella, please, call me Camille."

"Thank you."

Luella continued her work until the clock struck nine. Camille yawned as she walked in. "I didn't realize it was so late! I will see you tomorrow morning at eight."

"So early?" Luella asked.

"Yes. That is the agreement I made with the countess. Mondays and Tuesdays, you will work here from eight until six, taking an hour break to return home for your lunch."

Luella forced a small smile. "Then I will see you in the morning."

As she left the shop, she clenched and unclenched her hands, knowing they will be sore from cutting and stitching. She glanced around to be sure no one followed her as she made her way home.

The moon helped provide some light, and she let out a sigh of relief as she approached the manor. She stepped in, shut the door, and nearly ran into Clara.

"How did it go?" she demanded.

"Fine."

"Just fine? What did she say?"

"Camille said I am doing an excellent job. She also said I am to work Monday and Tuesday all day? But who will take care of things around here? Are Madison and Aubrey going to help?"

Clara laughed at the notion. "Absolutely not. You will get up at 4 in the morning, do as much as you can here, then return here every day at noon to fix our lunch. After you are finished for the day at the shop, you will complete your chores before turning in."

"Yes, madam." Luella knew there was no point in arguing. "I will turn in now."

"Oh, no. You need to mop the kitchen and straighten up in the dining room."

"I did that before I left."

"Yes, and I had company. Now don't argue!"

"Yes, madam."

Luella completed her final chore for Tuesday at one in the morning on Wednesday. She didn't even try to climb the stairs and instead fell asleep beside the fire.

She awoke at five, groggy and sore, and rushed as best she could to get breakfast going. Every muscle ached with each movement. Sleep called to her, but she forced herself to complete her chores.

After lunch, she gathered the laundry and went to the pond. She knew it was early, but she would rather get it out of the way and try to rest at the same time. She lifted the first blanket, and as the sun streamed through the trees, she was unable to fight it.

She curled up with the dirty blanket at the base of a tree and fell into a heavy slumber. The approaching footsteps went unnoticed by her, as she remained sound asleep.

Chapter 14

The Visitor

uella, are you sick?" Remi knelt beside her, checking her forehead and her pulse. "Can you hear me?" He shook her gently when she didn't respond. "Are you hurt?" When she remained unresponsive, he nearly scooped her up to rush her to the doctor.

"Hmm, no. I need more sleep," she finally said with a yawn, keeping her eyes closed.

"What's wrong?"

She clumsily waved him away, until he lifted her onto his lap. Her eyes flew open. "What are you doing?" she murmured.

"Checking you for injuries."

"I'm not hurt. Only tired."

"You don't have a fever, so that's good. Why are you so tired?"

"I… Yesterday, I didn't sleep well. That's all."

"What do you need?"

"To get these blankets washed so I can go to the market."

Remi waved a guard over. "Luella, do you have a list of what you need?"

She slowly removed it from her pocket. "Here."

Remi took it and held it up to the man as he approached. "Go to the market and get everything on this list." Remi then proceeded to pull out a small pouch and hand him as well. "This should cover it."

"Yes, sire."

The guard turned and left. Remi shook his head when he realized Luella drifted off again. He carefully placed her on the blanket, then began to wash the laundry. Glancing over from time to time, he watched her sleep in peace. Doubt crept in, that it was more than she let on.

He hung the last blanket, then sat beside her, lifting her onto his lap and holding her. Looking up under hooded eyes, she met his gaze.

"Remi, what are you doing here?" she asked as she jumped to her feet. She looked around, surprised to see the blankets hanging up. "What happened?"

"I would ask you that. You were quite out of it when I arrived, and you said you needed sleep."

"Thank you. I can't tell you what this means to me, that you would help me like this." She glanced upward and gasped softly. "But it is getting late. I need to go to the market and—"

He nodded towards the cart. She spun around, surprised to see the packages.

"You did that, too?"

"Well, a guard did."

"Still. I don't know what to say."

"Tell me the truth. Why are you so tired? Is something wrong?"

"No. I didn't sleep much last night. I'll be better Friday, you'll see," she assured him.

"Friday?"

"You'll come see me, won't you? Since I missed today."

Remi smiled. "I'll try."

"I'm so sorry."

"Whatever for?"

"Today."

He gripped her chin and kissed her as he clasped her in his arms. "You owe no apology. Promise me, you're all right?"

"I am, but I need to get back."

"Be safe."

"Well, you look like you're back to normal."

Luella laughed softly. "I told you, just a bad night. I hoped you were going to make it." Her face turned scarlet.

"What's wrong?"

She glanced back before meeting Remi's gaze. "This is why I don't have you come on Fridays. I forgot it's our clothing today."

He barked with laughter. "Luella, I think I can handle a few gowns and corsets. I promise."

She bit her lower lip as she approached him. "It nearly killed me on Monday to see you and not even be able to speak with you."

"That will be changing soon."

Would he be formally announcing their courtship at the ball? Would he then ask for her hand in marriage? Because if he did it in public, what could the countess do? Her heart skipped a beat, but she thought it best not to ask.

"I pray that is the case."

"Hmm, then let us pray together," he said, taking her hand.

"How do you mean?"

He placed his palm flat with hers. "Our hands meet in prayer, and so should our lips."

Her eyes lit up. The last bit of self-restraint melted away, and her mouth tasted his. Every inch of her ached to be near him, to have him and touch him.

"I'm right here," he assured her. "I want to ask, have your mother and sisters always been so cruel to you?"

Luella's heart pounded furiously in her ears. "But, I thought you said you knew? They are not—"

"I know how cruel they are. I have heard a few stories in the market. Do not pretend otherwise. I only wish to know if they have always behaved that way."

"Then you truly don't know," she murmured. After what he'd said, she was sure he knew who she really was. Her chest ached as she fought the tears threatening to escape. She swallowed them down and collected herself. She stood tall before meeting his gaze. "I will tell you everything."

Simon approached them and caught their attention. "Apologies, Remi, but we need to go."

"This is important," Luella argued.

Remi kissed her jawline. "I promise you, Wednesday I will return. We will discuss whatever you want."

"What I want is more time with you."

"As do I. Soon, mon trésor. We will have all the time in the world."

She caressed his face as she peered into his eyes. "I feel like a lovesick schoolgirl."

"You look like one," he teased. "If your face were any redder, I would worry you were going to pass out." He kissed the top of her head. "You are everything to me."

"We haven't been together long, but you mean everything to me, too."

"You are what I have been searching for my entire life, even if I didn't realize it at the time." He kissed her again. "Be safe. I will see you soon."

She watched him leave while her heart returned to its normal beat. Once she hung the last gown, she went to the market. It would be grueling to countdown the days until she saw him again, but there wasn't any choice. She had to wait.

The shop resonated with laughter as several young women tried on gowns in an assortment of colors and styles. Luella watched a pair of friends, plotting to meet the prince, dance with him, and get him to fall in love.

"I'm sure he will choose me, Reana," the blonde said as she twirled around with her dress.

"What if he's hideous?" her brunette friend teased. "Would you still dance with him?"

"Who cares what he looks like? Though I have heard he is quite handsome. But it doesn't matter. Any chance to marry and live at the palace, I'll take."

"What if he chooses me?" Reana asked, teasingly.

Her friend laughed. "Then I will have to look better than you."

"You can try."

They giggled as they ran into the dressing room together. Luella smiled to hide the ache in her heart. She never had a best friend, and her stepsisters never spoke with her in such a way. She longed for acceptance.

Thoughts of approaching the girls and introducing herself flew out the window when Aubrey and Madison walked in, accompanied by their mother. Luella cleared her throat and approached them.

"Here to pick out your gown?" she asked, keeping her gaze low.

"No, we came to say hi. We missed you," Madison replied in a high pitch voice. She burst into laughter when Luella's face turned crimson. "Move, little cinder girl. We will only be dealing with Camille. This is too important."

They brushed past her, ignoring her, and making their way towards the middle of the shop, where Camille currently helped a young woman into a pale pink gown.

Taking a quick glance upwards, she then directed her focus back to her customer. "I will be with you ladies in a moment."

"No rush," Clara said sweetly. "Please, take your time."

Luella never understood how she pulled it off, being so kind and polite in public while barking orders at Luella in private.

She swallowed down her emotions and continued to help the two women. Once they decided on their gowns, she rang them up and told them to enjoy the ball.

Camille helped Aubrey first, who went through the book of samples with fabrics and colors to choose from. While she did that, Madison insisted on trying on a gown much too expensive for Camille to part with.

Clara cleared her throat. "Madison, darling, it is a lovely gown. However, the neckline is unflattering to you, and the waist would only hide your natural features. Let us find something more suited to you."

Luella shook her head, knowing Clara always had an answer for everything. They continued to look while she put away the dresses that were tried on but not purchased.

Occasionally, she glanced over to see Aubrey and Madison smiling together as they admired the gowns. Another ache went through her chest, a longing for friendship, for family, to belong, ripped through her.

"Luella, are you all right?" Camille asked as she appeared beside her.

"Yes, I'm fine. I need to check on the…" Luella didn't finish as tears flooded her eyes. She ran to the stockroom so no one would see her in such a state.

She cleaned herself up and returned to her work station, where Camille joined her.

"I must say, Luella, you have quite a natural skill. I've done this work for fifteen years, yet you can mend three gowns in the time I do one."

Luella didn't have the heart to explain she learned at an early age, how to be fast and efficient to avoid Clara's rage. "Thank you," she offered instead.

"You've been quiet today."

"Sorry, just focusing, I guess."

Camille sat beside Luella, taking the gown she worked on and setting it on the table. "We don't know each other that well, but I sense you are carrying more than you let on."

"What do you mean?"

"You smile and have a kind heart, but there is such an emptiness in your eyes. Sorry, I don't mean to sound rude."

"No, it's all right. I'd really like to finish, if you don't mind?"

"Of course." She handed the gown to Luella before walking towards the showroom. "I am here if you ever need someone to talk to."

"Thank you."

"Especially about your stepmother and the horrible rumors she started about you."

The gown nearly fell from Luella's grip. "I beg your pardon?"

"I live here, and I am a merchant. Of course I know of the things she said. Obviously, I don't believe them, or you wouldn't be here."

"Why bring it up?"

"Because you seem like you need a friend."

"I don't have time for friends," Luella admitted as she resumed her sewing.

"We are here for several hours together. When I am not with customers, feel free to discuss anything with me."

"I'll keep that in mind, thank you."

"Did you have a good lunch?" Camille asked.

"It was nice," Luella answered as she resumed at her workstation.

She concentrated on mending and sewing gowns well into the evening, until she realized Camille stood behind her. After finishing the final stitch, she lay the gown on the table, then turned to face her.

"Do you need something?"

"No, I'm watching you work."

"Did I do something wrong? I didn't mean to. I'm so sorry—"

"No, Luella. I watch because your fingers are so nimble, I can hardly see the movements. It's soothing to watch."

Luella stifled the laugh as her expression turned to one of confusion. "Soothing?"

"It's nothing. It's getting late, why don't you head home?"

"I still have a half an hour. Are you sure I didn't do something wrong?"

"No, but you've yawned five times in the last two minutes," Camille said with a giggle. "I think you need to get some rest. I'll see you Monday."

"Of course. Thank you."

Luella gathered her things and made her way to the manor. Her nerves were on edge every time she walked home, thinking about the night Langdon nearly killed her. Remi asked a time or two for her to open up, but she didn't want to talk about it.

She focused on her surroundings, after realizing she nearly lost herself in her thoughts again.

Luella, are you all right?

Yes, why do you ask?

I'm not really sure. I'm sitting with Simon, and I had the strangest sensation. Are you sure everything is fine?

I am about to start dinner, then I will get ready to turn in. Even lying through the bargain made her ache in her chest. *I'll see you Wednesday at the pond.*

Hmm, all right. I miss you, mon trésor.

I miss you, too.

She smiled as she entered the back door and began food prep for dinner. The countess walked in.

"Oh, I'm glad you are early. We are having company tonight, so please prepare extra for one more."

"Yes, madam."

Luella didn't ask but instead focused on getting everything ready. While the stew simmered over the heat, she went to her room and changed into a fresh gown. Unsure who was coming for dinner, she at least wanted to look presentable.

She returned downstairs and set everything up in the dining room. After ringing the bell, she went into the kitchen to eat. She looked up to see the countess watching her.

"Is everything all right?"

"I summoned you, but here you sit and eat?" Clara stormed up to her and pointed her finger in Luella's face. "Why didn't you come?"

"I am so sorry. I truly did not hear it."

"Well, we are ready for dessert and a night cap. Get a move on, good for nothing…" Clara continued to grumble as she left the room.

Luella gathered her dishes, placed them in the sink, then set the blackberry tarts on the tray. She kept her eyes low as she entered the dining room. Once the dessert was set up, she turned to leave, when a hand gripped her wrist, ironclad.

To her surprise, she realized that Langdon was keeping Clara company for the night. Her breath hitched as tears pricked her eyes. She cleared her throat.

"Did you need anything else?" she asked as she attempted to pull away from him.

"I just wanted to say hello."

"Hello," she managed as she freed herself. "Excuse me."

She fled the room, going into the kitchen and gripping the counter.

Remi, he's here. I can't…

Who's there? What's wrong?

She bit back tears as she composed herself. *I'm sorry. False alarm. Everything is all right.*

No, it's not. You're terrified! What's going on?

How do you know that? You told me this only opened a channel to communicate, not to let you into my personal thoughts or feelings.

That is all it does. I swear. I could hear your panic. Please, don't shut me out. Are you all right?

The bell rang, and Luella's heart sank at the thought of seeing Langdon again.

I'm fine, but I have to go.

Luella—

Goodbye, Remi.

If I have to come there, I will.

Please, don't.

She closed her eyes, forcing herself to shut down, to close off from him, before she walked back into the dining room.

"Did you need something, madam?"

"The governor is leaving. Please see to this, then I wish to speak with you shortly."

"Of course."

Luella gathered dishes, as Langdon's heated gaze burned its way into her. Without looking at him, she knew he watched her every movement before finally following Clara out.

She swept the rest of the dishes into her arms and rushed to the kitchen. Focusing on washing and drying kept the tears at bay, until Clara walked in.

"Luella?"

She wiped her eyes before facing Clara. "Yes, madam?"

"The governor will be coming over more to visit, so I expect you to treat him better than you did tonight."

Luella debated but figured she had nothing to lose. "After what he did to me? Or perhaps you are unaware it was him?"

Clara gave her a sympathetic look, until she burst out laughing. "Oh, pathetic child. Of course I know it was him! I scolded him. After all, we had to make up for your absence. Other than that, do you think I care?"

Luella bit her tongue as her chest heaved with each breath. "I didn't know what to think."

"It is irrelevant. What matters, you need to treat him with respect when he is here. I have given up on Aubrey finding a noble to court, but perhaps she and Anthony could, once he is released back to the governor."

"Does Aubrey know?" Luella asked, her voice low and steady though her nerves were on edge.

"No, and you will not tell her."

"Yes, madam."

"Now, you need to finish all of your chores."

"The countess is getting closer to agreeing to my terms," Henri whispered in Luella's ear while it was the two of them in the parlor.

"So I've heard," Luella said in response.

"Are you going to come willingly, or will you fight me every step of the way?"

"The countess would have me tell you I am coming willingly. That, however, is not the truth. I will fight it until my last breath, if need be."

He released a groan as he stepped back. "That's what I hoped to hear. Your stepsister will be pliant enough. I need someone to challenge me. To—"

Clara and Madison entered. "Is everything all right?" Madison asked as she looked between Luella and Henri.

"Of course. I was asking Luella which she preferred, the lemon bars or carrot cake, though both look scrumptious."

"I recommend the lemon bars," Luella said as she plated the dessert. She served everyone, then left the parlor and went outside for some fresh air.

She would never give in to someone like Henri. A small part of her actually felt pity for Madison, knowing the life that lay ahead of her. Luella was merely a servant to her, but she would be no better once married off to him. He would display her in public in fine gowns and jewels, but behind closed doors…

The thought made Luella shudder. She did not hear Clara as she approached from behind.

"Do you want to tell me what that was about? With you and Henri?"

"Only that he is happy I am part of the deal. He cannot wait to have both of us."

"He said that?"

Luella forced a small smile as she faced her. "Oh, yes. He is absolutely enamored with Madison."

"That is good news! Well, perhaps I will let him wait for a bit, to know what he wants is just out of reach." Clara grinned before heading back to the manor. She stopped and faced Luella. "Oh, and I believe I will sign the deal the day of the ball. Let them enjoy each other's company that night. Then we will officially announce their engagement on Monday. I believe that will be perfect!"

Luella watched her go inside. Maybe everything would work in her favor. That Remi will ask her to marry him, as well. Surely, if they are engaged, she would not be obligated to fulfill Clara's deal, to be a part of Henri and Madison's engagement.

As before, she buried all hope deep inside her heart, knowing she had to keep her plans a secret. Otherwise, it would all be for naught.

Remi did not show up Wednesday. Her body flooded with mixed emotions, anger and worry. As she hung blankets, she would try to reach out to him.

Remi, are you all right? Where are you?

Though she could barely stand, she forced herself to wash and hang the laundry before making the trip to the market. Thankfully, she did not need much on this visit. It seemed Clara kept her promise, as several of the merchants seemed kinder to her than they had in a long time.

She returned and began to load laundry on the cart. There was still no response. She prayed he was safe and realized he may be making announcements at other colonies. Perhaps that was why he didn't show up or answer her.

Downtrodden, she returned to the manor. After finishing dinner and the last of her daily chores, she went to her room. She retrieved the box from under her floorboard.

The gown was nearly complete, only needing a few final changes. Luckily, her stepsisters had thrown out some older gowns to make room for the new ones they would wear to the ball. Luella salvaged a sash from one and ribbons from the other.

She knew her gown wouldn't be nearly as fancy as theirs, but she thought it good enough to attend and dance with Remi. The thought of them going public with their courtship made her glow, but she had to push down her worries at the same time.

How would the countess react? And more importantly, what will she do?

"Luella, we will be gone to Borgouse today. Please see to the drawing room, as it needs to be clean for our guests tomorrow."

As soon as they left, she hurried and cleaned up, then decided to take a bath. She was not allowed to use the tub in Clara's private washroom, but she would enjoy it while they were gone.

She fetched the water while the copper warmed up. After a few rounds, she had enough she could rest comfortably in it. Checking once more to be sure the manor was indeed empty, she then stripped down and stepped into the nice, hot water.

Her muscles eased as steam swirled around her. Finally able to relax, she laid her head back on the folded towel. Her stepmother would punish her for this if she were caught, but it was rare for her to be alone in the house.

She allowed herself the small indulgence and continued to relax until the water was lukewarm. About to pull the drain, a knock at the door startled her. Clara would've simply come inside.

"Who... Who is it?" she called out.

"Remi."

Her heart nearly stopped in her chest. "What?"

The door opened, and he walked in. She grabbed the towel and threw it to cover herself.

"Luella—"

"What are you doing here?" she demanded.

"I was coming in through the gate as your family exited. I heard the countess tell the guard they were going to be gone all day, so I decided to visit you. I knocked and walked around, but I didn't see you. I was worried and decided to come inside. If I didn't find you, then I would use the bargain to reach out to you." He stopped for a moment and watched her with concern etched on his face. "You're shivering."

"The water has turned cold."

He removed a towel from the rack on the wall and approached her. "Here, allow me to help you."

"What? Why?"

"Because you are mine. I want to take care of you. Will you let me?"

She pulled the drain and stood up. He extended his hand and helped her step out before wrapping the towel around her. Gripping the ends, he pulled her to him and kissed her fiercely.

"I missed you, mon trésor."

"Where were you?"

"I am sorry I couldn't come. I really wanted to, please believe me."

"You didn't answer my question."

"I had business on behalf of the king."

"What kind of business?"

He sighed. "I can't really discuss it."

"I'll dry off and be out in a moment," she said as she attempted to step back.

His grip on the towel tightened. "Luella, please. I assure you, it was not a big deal. I will tell you everything, once we are together at the palace."

"You keep saying you will tell me what is going on, but you do not keep your word."

"What about you?"

"What about me?"

"You called out to me, remember? What happened?"

"While you have your secrets, I will have mine. If you had been there Wednesday, perhaps I would've told you."

Remi debated for a moment, wanting to ask, but again fearful of pushing her away. "For now, let me enjoy you? Let me please you. Seeing you like this, I can hardly stand it."

"Stand what?"

"How badly I need you."

She trembled in his arms. "Need what from me?"

"To take care of you," he offered, as his lips brushed hers. "Please, Luella?"

She led him from the room. They entered a small parlor, and he helped her onto the sofa. He kissed her softly as his hand caressed her chest and stomach. He leaned back, smiling as his fingers traced over her mark.

"I realize it's from our bargain, but I like to think of this as my claim on you."

"We did swear on it, so you aren't totally wrong," she admitted.

He kissed around her navel softly, his tongue teasing as he went lower. Her back arched as he sucked and licked, sending her into waves of pleasure with each tantalizing movement.

"Oh, Remi," she moaned as his fingers stroked in and out.

When she came, she trembled as she cried out, her breaths coming in gasps before she collapsed onto the sofa.

He undid his pants and slowly lowered them down, ready to claim her, to own her, to possess her in every way he could.

"Good girl," he said in a low, sultry tone before claiming her mouth.

The taste of her arousal only urged her on, as she slowly began to tease along his length, smiling as he went stiff against her, his breath ragged and a slight sheen of sweat washed over his face. After he finished, she cleaned him up using the towel, then they dressed.

"Are you all right?" she asked.

He gave a small smile. "Well, that wasn't exactly what I had planned."

"Did I do something wrong?"

Regret filled him. "No, you were perfect. I enjoyed every moment of this with you."

"Even as dangerous as it was?"

"Are you telling me you didn't?"

She giggled as she finished buttoning up her gown. "Yes, of course I did. But we have to be more careful."

"Do you forget? I don't come alone. Simon would've distracted them, had they returned home early."

"Would you like a cup of tea?"

His laughter startled her. "Really?"

"What?"

"After what we did, you can be so casual with me. Don't get me wrong, I am happy to see this, instead of you blushing and keeping your eyes averted from mine."

She gave him a smile before turning away and going into the kitchen. After filling the kettle and placing it over the fire, she reached for the teacups when his hand brushed hers. One touch, and he was on fire for her again. He pulled her to him and kissed her hard, his tongue probing her mouth as his fingers tangled in her soft tresses.

He lifted her onto the counter as he trailed her body and his lips devoured hers. With one hand, he began to unbutton the front of her gown.

Without a word, she jumped down, forcing Remi back, and began to place the cups on the saucers. He watched her intently, wondering what happened in that moment. Finally, he had to know.

"Are you all right?"

"I'm fine."

"Then why did you stop?"

The glass clanked as she set the cup and saucer down. "Is this… Are we just…" She shook her head. "Is this only physical with you?" she asked as her eyes met his, the pain drawn across her face at the thought of it.

"Luella, absolutely not! Am I attracted to you? Of course! You are the most beautiful woman I have ever laid eyes on. I'll be honest. Yes, there is a part of me, my primal desire, to bed you for a week until you cannot even walk." Her cheeks turned crimson as she swallowed hard at his words. "Yet, I also want to know everything about you. I want to know your dreams and desires, what keeps you awake at night, what you think about when I'm not around."

"Then why not ask that? Why kiss me as though your life depended on it?"

"Perhaps in that moment, it did. You are my breath, my heartbeat, my life. Why do you not understand this yet? What must I do to prove it?"

"You already did, we did. I'm sorry I doubted!"

"Hey, there's no need to be upset over this." He took her hand and kissed her palm before kissing his way up her arm and to her neck. Her sweet amber scent rushed into him, and it took everything he had to keep his wolf at bay. "I want you to feel like you can ask me anything or tell me whatever you must, and understand I will not be upset. After all, isn't that what a husband and wife are supposed to do?"

"Husband and wife? But we—" Before she could finish, the kettle screamed from the heat, and she rushed to it.

While she poured the tea, he set the table with linens and lemon scones. They sat together in silence for a few moments. She sipped her tea slowly before broaching the subject.

"What plans do you have for our future?"

"Wonderful ones. We will settle down, raise a family, and live happily ever after."

"It sounds wonderful, yes. But I mean, how will this work? When will we tell Clara and everyone about us?"

"I could stay here and tell her myself."

Luella nearly choked on her tea, her anger growing as he laughed. "It isn't funny, Remi. You do not understand."

"But I do. Please, be patient. Everything will come together soon enough."

"The night of the ball?" she asked, biting her lower lip as hope filled her eyes.

"Yes," he responded, brushing away crumbs from his lap. "I will take care of you, and you will spend the rest of your life knowing exactly how loved you are. I promise you."

She set the cup down before she landed in his lap, kissing him as her arms latched around his neck. He returned her passion.

Chapter 15

The Winning Hand

hy were you really here?" Aubrey asked as she approached Simon. "Yesterday, I was excited to see you, while you almost looked startled, as if you weren't expecting us. Don't get me wrong, I was happy to see you. Still, I have to ask. Why were you here?"

"What do you mean?

"You told my mother you wished to speak with me, and she told you basically to get lost. I think there was more to it."

"I don't know what you mean."

"No, I saw the look on your face. Who are you protecting? You raised your horn and blew, as if to announce our arrival." Her jaw dropped. "That's exactly what you were doing!"

"Aubrey, I can explain."

"Save it! Is Luella with that herald, the one she rescued from the governor's sons?"

"I can't speak of it."

"Simon, tell me the truth, or I will leave now and never speak to you again!"

"I cannot betray my… my friend. I'm sorry. Believe me, to watch you leave will shatter my heart in ways I cannot express."

Aubrey stopped and went rigid at his words. "I beg your pardon?"

"While I may be protecting someone, I meant everything I told you. I did have a mate, Isabella, whom I lost last year. I have not had feelings for anyone else, until I met you. I may do some questionable things, working in the ranks that I do, but I would never toy with someone's emotions."

"Then tell me the truth, please."

"What I can tell you, yes. I was helping someone."

Aubrey began to walk away from him. Simon hung his head, debating whether to run after her or give her time, knowing the truth hurt her.

"He was protecting me."

They both turned to see Remi enter the path. Aubrey approached him. "Are you with Luella?"

He studied her for a moment, wondering how much he could divulge to her. "I guess my answer depends on you. If I say we are together, will you run to your mother and get her in trouble?"

"Do I look like Madison to you?"

"You did not answer my question."

"No, I will not rat her out." She lifted her chin, and Simon stifled his laugh at the sight. "I am better than that."

"Not much, from what I've heard in the market."

"Do you want to gossip or do you want to tell me what is going on?" Aubrey demanded.

Simon and Remi exchanged a glance before Remi stepped forward. "Luella and I are together. I plan to announce it at the ball and make it official. We are holding off, because of your mother."

"I don't understand? Why don't you take her now and whisk her away to your palace?"

Remi ran his hand through his hair and let out a sigh. "It's not that easy. We have customs and traditions to uphold."

Aubrey dared to glance at Simon. "So, if we decided to court?"

"It would be a slow process, like them. I would not just say, 'you are my mate, let's go' then take you to the palace, either."

"Wait, how long have you two been together?" she asked as she spun on her heel to face Remi.

"A while now."

"No wonder she has been so secretive. Mother was sure she was hiding something, but she had no idea."

"And it will stay that way." Remi stepped closer and gripped Aubrey by the chin, firm but so as not to hurt her. Simon stiffened in his stance but kept back. "You are not to say a word. Do you understand?"

"I promise, I won't say a word."

Remi nodded as he released her. "Very well." He looked at Simon. "Did you two want to speak before we return to the palace?"

"Yes, give us a few minutes?"

"Of course."

Simon took Aubrey's hand and walked with her. When his eyes met hers, there was no denying the pain she saw in them.

"I did have a mate. We courted for about six months. I was ready to ask her to become mine, when she died from a sudden illness. I swore I would never love another, not even open myself up to the possibility."

"So, you're saying I should ignore everything you said to me?"

"No, quite the opposite. I wasn't finished. I swore I would remain closed off, until I met you. Yes, I took you to the market so Luella and Remi could be alone. And yes, I laid it on thick to keep your focus on me. Here is the truth of it, that every word I said, I meant. You are beautiful and full of fire, and I do wish to claim you for myself."

"Simon—"

"But I understand you are reluctant to take a chance on a shifter, and I don't blame you. Since it is a bit scary for us both, we will take this slow. You dictate what you want from me, how you want this to go, and I will follow."

"You would allow a human to have such power over you?"

"If that human is you, yes."

Her heart hammered in her chest as she considered what he proposed. "I will give you my answer the next time I see you."

"Very well."

The bell rang, and Luella went to the drawing room. She froze in her tracks in the doorway, seeing Clara and Langdon sitting together on the sofa and speaking quietly.

She turned on her heel and went to gather blankets for laundry, when the bell rang again. Without a care or fear of being punished, she fled the manor and rushed to the pond.

The tears fell fast as she leaned against the tree, holding her head in her hands. Why were they together? Were they planning something more, besides handing Aubrey off to Anthony?

"Hmm, kind of hard to do laundry without the laundry, isn't it?" Remi teased as he approached her from behind. When she turned to him, his expression became deadly serious. He rushed to her and gathered her in his arms. "Luella, whatever is the matter?"

She said nothing as she buried her face in his chest. He continued to hold her as she sobbed quietly, her cries muffled by his shirt. Deciding he would give her a few minutes, he did not push, but let her continue to get out whatever she was going through.

When Luella was calm enough, she pulled away and dried her face on her apron before glancing up at Remi. His concern was apparent, but she didn't know what to say.

"Thank you," she managed as she kept her head low.

"Are you hurt? Or sick? What happened?"

She clasped her hands together. "I was overwhelmed, but I am much better now. I—"

A loud whistle blew through the trees. "I am not leaving," Remi said as he rushed into the woods.

Aubrey came into sight and approached Luella. She had the donkey, cart, and blankets with her.

"I saw mother with her company in the drawing room and watched you run out. It wasn't hard to piece together what happened. I thought if I brought you the laundry, you could say that is why you did not hear the bell ring, when she asks later."

"Aubrey, thank you. I do not know why the change in you, but I am grateful for it."

"You are most welcome. Mother and the governor are still talking, and I am unsure how long he plans to stay. He may be there when you return for dinner. I wanted to inform you."

"Thank you," Luella said.

"You're welcome," Aubrey replied as she turned and walked towards the manor.

Even without glancing his way, she could feel the intensity of Remi's heated gaze as he came near. "The governor?" he asked, his voice low and almost coming out more of a growl than a question.

"He is visiting with the countess today," Luella said, trying to sound casual as she reached for the first blanket.

She jumped with a start when his hand landed on hers. "And what else?"

"I don't know what you mean." She pulled away and began to wash.

"Is that why you were so upset? Because the man who nearly killed you is in your home right now?"

Luella said nothing as she continued, only fighting back tears and trying not to relive the night she almost died. Remi knelt beside her and placed his hand gently on her arm.

"I'm sorry. I'm sure it must be difficult to talk about, but I really wish you would tell me the truth. I have a right to know."

"What right do you have?"

"Because I promised to protect you, and instead, you were nearly killed. Tell me it was him, let me see justice done, then you will no longer be afraid of him."

"It isn't so simple," she said softly. She stood to hang the blanket before grabbing the next one. "Things may work like that at the palace, but out here, we are on our own. All of us. There are other factors at work, too."

"What do you mean?"

Luella thought of her stepmother and Langdon, plotting Aubrey's future. "I can't."

"Luella—"

"I also am not ready to face the horrors of that night. It was the worst night of my life. Why are you pushing?"

"It was the worst night of my life, as well. I lay with you on the exam table, holding you close, not knowing if you would be alive in the morning. I couldn't bear the thought of losing you."

"You… you stayed with me the whole time?"

"I did."

"I thought perhaps you dropped me off, then returned the next morning to check on me. As you were leaving, I remember regaining consciousness. I tried calling out to you, running to you, but my body wouldn't respond. I was too groggy from the shock and the medicine."

"Departing from your side was the last thing I wanted to do, but the king commanded us back to the palace. I did not want to obey, believe me."

"At the time, I thought you helped me only because of our bargain, and that you were returning to your betrothed." His laughter forced her to meet his gaze. "Why is that funny?"

"Because I love seeing you jealous, though I probably should not admit that," he teased as he kissed her forehead. "Knowing how much you were, it reassures me."

"Jealousy is not a good thing."

"No, you're right. It's not jealousy. It's being protective. You own me and want to protect me from anyone else. Believe me, I feel the same way about you."

"Remi, I think that sounds worse than jealousy."

His laughter grew louder until he could scarcely breathe. "That is not how I meant it. Hmm, as a wolf shifter, of course I am protective and possessive of my mate. It's part of who we are."

"And because I am a human, I couldn't possibly feel that way?" Luella teased back.

His canines gleamed like polished ivory, a predator's hunger burning in his eyes as he devoured her lips. He pulled her to him so there was no space at all between them.

"So, ever gone skinny dipping?" Remi asked as he nodded toward the pond.

"What? No!"

"Come on. Live a little."

"Remi, I have to get this done, then go to the market."

He whistled and a guard approached. "Tell him what you need, he will get it and bring it here."

As she anxiously nibbled her lower lip, her shoulders slouched. "I don't know about this."

"I do, because you are not used to asking for help. He will get what you need, so you and I can enjoy ourselves today." Noticing the conflicting desire in her eyes, he took her hand, and kissed it softly. "Please."

"Clara and Langdon are at the manor. This is far too dangerous."

"I assure you, we are protected here. I give you my word."

Luella relented, giving a nod, and turning to the guard. She removed her list and pouch of coin from her apron pocket, then she handed it to the man. He gave a stiff bow and left for the market.

Remi let out a shrill whistle before he began to untie her apron. "That lets the guards know to give us privacy. I assure you, I don't want anyone to look upon you. You are mine."

She arched against him as he unbuttoned her gown, then she began to undress him as well. They joined hands and walked side by side into the water.

Remi couldn't help but be impressed as he watched her swim. They splashed and floated, enjoying the afternoon sun. The warmth helped them dry on the edge of the pond, and she smiled as she slipped her gown back on.

"You were right, that was fun."

"I knew you would enjoy it. I assume it wasn't your first time?"

Her face went crimson. Did he know she bathed in the pond once a week? Had he seen her? "I... well—"

"Why are you embarrassed to admit you've swam in here before?" His expression eased as the realization set in. "You've gone skinny dipping here before? With who?"

"No, it wasn't like that," she said as she pulled away.

"Then why were you so embarrassed?"

"I have returned," the guard said as he approached them.

Remi gestured to the cart, where the guard set down the purchases, then he retreated. Luella inspected everything, hoping Remi would let it go.

As she checked the blankets to see if they were dry yet, he stepped up beside her.

"I'm sorry. You don't have to tell me anything you don't want to. I don't mean to push or seem possessive."

"You don't seem possessive, you are."

"I can't help it. It's in my nature. Even so, I really am trying. Please, forgive me."

"Do you realize, this was the first time we spent together where we were undressed, but it was innocent? For fun. I really liked seeing that side of you."

"I enjoyed the time with you as well."

Clara stared across the table at Langdon, smiling at the cards in her hand.

"So, the bet is simple. If you win, Aubrey marries Anthony once he is released from the labor camp. If I win, I get Luella for one week, to punish her."

Clara lowered her eyes to her cards as her brow arched. "Yes, but how will you get away with it? You said it yourself, you received a message from the king about the incident, and that there is to be no more violence."

Langdon's mouth twitched, one corner raising slightly. "I have a fairly good idea. You don't need to worry about the details. Just confirm what I said."

"Yes, if I win, Aubrey marries Anthony. It is not my ideal partner for her, but no one else has expressed any interest. At least with him, she will be with a future governor."

"And?"

"If you win, you get Luella for one week. Though I am concerned for what state she will be in once you return her to me."

"Do not worry, she will still be able to perform her chores for you. Though, she may need a day or two to recover before so." He noticed the grimace on Clara's face, though she tried to hide it behind her cards. "Countess, I believe I have made it clear. I have no interest in her that way. Instead, I only wish to inflict pain on her for what she did."

"I care little for what you do to her. Though, if I am being honest, I am glad to hear that. As you and I may come to some… arrangement as well." She smiled at him. Hook, line, and sinker.

"That sounds like music to my ears."

Luella rang the bell but remained in the dining room. Clara didn't hide her surprise to find her waiting.

"What do you want?" she demanded as she sat.

"How was your visit?"

"Very nice, even if you were nowhere to be found."

"I was tending to laundry."

"Right. Now, do you need anything else?" Clara asked as she buttered her bread.

"I wish to speak with you about the ball."

Aubrey and Madison joined their mother at the table. Madison giggled. "Oh, do you wish to dance with the chimney sweep?"

"Silence," Clara commanded before returning her attention to Luella. "What about the ball, exactly?"

"I wish to attend." Luella kept her head high when Clara scoffed at her. "It is, after all, by the king's decree that all eligible ladies attend. Would you defy your king?"

Clara pondered her words for a moment before saying something that sent her daughters reeling. "Very well, you may come with us."

"What?" Madison yelled, dropping her fork with a clatter. "You can't be serious!" Aubrey only watched, her mouth agape in confusion.

Clara held up one hand to silence her while never breaking Luella's gaze. "On one condition. You must have all your chores for that day completed on time."

"Oh, I will. Thank you!" Luella turned and ran from the room, unable to contain her joy.

"Mother, what are you thinking?" Aubrey asked.

"We can't possibly be seen with her," Madison said with a pout.

Clara took a sip of her lemon and honey tea. "I said she may come *if* she completed her chores. I will have a list of at least a hundred things for her to do. She will never finish in time." Devious laughter blew from her lips as her mouth contorted into a wicked grin. "And to see her defeated will be the icing on the cake. I promise you, she will not attend this ball."

"I must say, Luella, you have done an excellent job. I almost hate to see you go."

"Thank you. Are you sure you do not need me here on Saturday? With last minute alterations and such, I'm sure it will be busy."

"My assistant, Sophie, is coming to help. She said she needs to get out of the house," Camille said with a laugh. "Besides, you've gone above and beyond what I could ask for. I really appreciate your help. Gods know, I never would've finished in time."

"I am happy to help."

Camille hugged her. "I guess I'll see you at the ball."

Luella forced a smile. "I'll see you then."

She left the shop and started for the manor. Images of the night of the ball floated before her vision. She could see herself arriving at the palace, walking into the ballroom, and dancing with Remi. Lost in thought, she made it home in no time.

Luella prepared dinner, set up the dining room, then quickly ate. Eager to attend to her own dress, she hurried her tasks and rushed up to her room. She removed the box and lifted out its contents.

Seeing the silver-blue gown with the matching sash tied around the middle, ribbons accenting the U-neck, and the billowing skirt lifted Luella's spirits. It turned out better than she pictured, and she knew it would be good enough for the ball.

She hummed to herself as she pretended to dance with Remi, imagining his arms around her as the orchestra played.

"Another dance? Oh, I suppose I could," she said to herself as she bowed to her pretend partner. Her arms extended out, and she twirled around the attic.

Unbeknownst to her, Clara stood at the edge of the steps, only visible from her chin up, and she watched the entire interaction. Her mind spun with ideas, as she knew she would do whatever she must to ensure Luella did not attend.

Luella did not hear her retreat as she went downstairs. Instead, she changed into her nightgown, returned the dress to its box, and curled up on the floor, excited for the upcoming ball.

Chapter 16

Preparations

riday, Luella mopped every floor, being extra careful so as not to add to her worklist for Saturday. She wasn't sure what Clara might have in store, but she would do whatever she must in order to see Remi at the ball.

She helped her stepsisters with their final fittings. As soon as they were finished, she prepared lunch, then gathered laundry, murmuring a quiet prayer Remi would be at the pond. Part of her doubted he would be, since he had the upcoming ball to help prepare for. Still, she held onto hope.

As she unharnessed the donkey, she heard a low growl, but she ignored it. She went to the water and began to wash and hang the blankets. A sound startled her, and she turned as Remi approached, except he was in wolf form.

She stood still as he sniffed around her before shifting back. Her eyes went wide and her mouth agape. "Why did you do that?" she asked as she pinned the blanket on the line.

"My apologies. I thought I smelled another scent here, and my protective nature kicked in."

Luella shook her head. "No one here but me. Do you seriously think I would bring a man here?"

"Of course not. However, I wouldn't be surprised if the governor sent someone after you."

Luella gasped as her eyes lowered. "I… I didn't think of that."

"I still fear for you, that he may be planning something else."

"Something else?"

"Though you deny it, I know it was him who hurt you. Did you think I wouldn't recognize his scent?"

"Then why didn't you do something about it?"

Remi's hands clenched. "I appealed to my king, but he refused. He said the governor was too important. He is more concerned about the upcoming ball and celebrating the prince's birthday. If we can get through tomorrow night—"

"I pray I can come."

Remi stared at her for a full minute, his head tilted. He licked his lips. "And why wouldn't you?"

"The countess said I could, but I must have all of my chores completed. I can't make any promises, though."

In the blink of an eye, Remi stood before Luella, his hand laced in her hair as he stared into her eyes. "I need you there. Do you understand?"

"I will do everything I can—"

"Not good enough."

"What? Remi, you know how she is."

"I don't care if you have to sneak out. This is one of the most important nights of our life. You must attend." His voice wavered with desperation, nearly demanding in his last line.

"Believe me, I need this to happen as much as you. But I must ask. What will happen tomorrow night?"

"Everything you've been waiting for," Remi responded.

"Please, stop with the vague responses and tell me!" she cried out.

"You do not give me orders," he growled. "I am the wolf, I am in charge. You are my mate, not my master."

"Right now, I don't know if I even want to be your mate," Luella declared, ignoring the tears that began to stream down her cheeks.

"You don't mean that," he said sharply, his eyes narrowing. "Why won't you leave this one thing up to me?"

"I hate this, not knowing. My whole life has been one of rules, and discipline, and planning out each task each day. To not know what you are thinking, what you are planning, how my life is going to change, is driving me crazy! Please, why will you not talk to me?" she cried out in frustration.

"You're afraid of the unknown and too proud to admit it. The truth is, I'm afraid, too," he confessed, his voice so low she nearly didn't hear him.

"Why?"

"Because nothing about tomorrow is guaranteed. But having you on my arm, introducing you to my father and family, gaining their blessing, is what I want more than anything."

"Why did you not tell me this sooner?"

"I didn't want to add to your worries," he said softly.

"That's a lie."

"What? First you question me, now you call me a liar? As if you've been completely honest with me from the start."

Her lower lip quivered as her gaze hardened. "Please go now. I have work to do."

"Your work will wait. We need to discuss this."

She walked to the blankets and reached for the next one when he growled at her. Her posture straightened as she held her chin high. She ignored the sound as she washed.

Remi appeared beside her. "Fine. I understand if you cannot make a promise to come. I guess it's not as important to you as I thought."

She almost replied for him not to do that but decided she was done. If this is how he would treat her, would speak to her, she had no desire to take part.

"Luella, please. I'm sorry, but I am under so much pressure right now. You can't begin to imagine what it's like for me. Everyone is on edge about tomorrow night, wondering who the prince will select. We are attempting to keep spirits high, with our recent loss. Because of this, we are all putting in extra effort around the palace to make sure everything is perfect. All I am asking, is for you to attend."

"You say that as though it were so easy."

"Why would your mother refuse to let you come? The king ordered it, after all."

"That is what I said when I asked if I could attend."

"I don't understand that. Why did you have to ask at all?"

"Because it's how it is. I'm not favored in our house, and I have to put in extra effort all the time, every day, all day. So what you have been doing this past week or so, is what my entire life has been like, as far as I can remember."

"Why is that?"

"I don't know," she answered honestly. "I have done everything I can to prove myself, to earn their love, only to remain the outsider. Because of my hair? Because of my father? I doubt if I'll ever learn the reason."

"Is this why you wouldn't show me your room? Were you embarrassed?"

"Yes," she said as she hung the blanket before facing him, her gaze remaining on the ground. "As I said, I do not know what your life is like at the palace, but my life has not been easy. Even so, I am determined not to let it break me."

"You haven't. You are the kindest, most compassionate woman I have ever met. Perhaps if there were more people like you in this world, it wouldn't be in the state it's in."

"Do you mean that?"

He kissed her softly. "Absolutely. I'm sorry, about earlier. I never meant to take my frustrations out on you. I understand you are bound with obligations as well."

"Thank you for that."

"You weren't lying."

They turned to see Aubrey, with Simon rushing behind and trying to catch up to her.

"Aubrey—"

"So this is why you asked to attend the ball."

Luella ran to her and took her hand. "Please, please don't tell the countess! I beg of you!"

"You needn't worry. I've known for a while."

"She has," Remi confirmed.

Aubrey released Luella's hand and clasped Simon's instead. "You aren't the only one."

Luella's face went from serious to happy in a flash. "Oh, thank you!"

"I don't know what Mother has in store, but I will do what I can to help you attend."

"Thank you."

Simon and Aubrey walked back onto the path and out of sight. Luella returned to Remi.

"I see now how truly afraid you are. What has your mother done to you? Both of you? I could see it on Aubrey's face, as well."

Luella bit back tears. "I don't want to talk about it. I hope she means it, because I am sure if I have her help, I will be there tomorrow night. I apologize in advance, however."

"For what?"

"My gown won't be nearly as fancy as theirs. My... mother has gone all out for them, trying to snag them a noble husband."

"What will she do when she finds out about Aubrey and Simon?"

"I cannot say for sure, only that I know she will not be pleased." She took a deep breath and built up her courage. "Is that part of tomorrow? That official announcements will be made, and couples will be made public?"

He cocked his eyebrow. "Are you worried that your mother will embarrass you in front of everyone, if I choose to announce it?"

"No, of course not, but—"

"Luella, of all things for you to be worried about. I think part of you doesn't even want to attend." She opened her mouth to argue, but he cut her off. "You said it yourself, everything has been planned for you. Perhaps you can't handle the possibility of change and would rather shut yourself off to me?"

"That is not the case at all," she shot back with clenched hands.

"If you make it to the ball, I will be most pleased. If not, I honestly would not be surprised."

"How can you even say these things?"

"Then prove me wrong by showing up."

"If I do come, it would be because I want to see you!"

"If you come at all."

Before she could retort, he shifted and took off into the woods. Her shoulders sagged, her heart sank, and she couldn't decide if she were more hurt or angry. Everything felt off, and she did her best to push it away while continuing in her tasks.

Luella sat to eat breakfast when the bell rang. She hurried into the dining room.

"Yes, madam?"

Clara smiled and held up a sheet of paper. "I need all of this done. If you are to attend the ball tonight, that is."

"Of course." Luella took the paper and returned to the kitchen, where she skimmed over the list while she ate. "There must be at least a hundred chores on here! How will I ever get all of this finished in time?"

"Because I will help you, like I said I would."

Luella turned to see Aubrey beside her. "If she catches you—"

"She won't." Aubrey nodded toward the sheet of paper in Luella's hand. "Let me see?" She read the list, then handed it back. "I can handle a few of the upstairs tasks, after breakfast. She and Madison will retire to the drawing room to discuss the ball."

"Thank you. I appreciate it."

Luella ate, cleaned the kitchen, then hurried to get started. With determination in her heart and on her face, she set to work on her first task. She emptied the ash from every fireplace, replaced the logs, then cleaned her hands. She dusted every corner of the manor, beat every rug outside until no more dirt blew off, then fixed lunch.

She had only seven hours until they would leave, and she barely made a dent so far in her list. The thought of Clara gloating in the dining room riled her up and gave her a second wind. She continued to move through the list, checking off each task as soon as it was completed.

At dinner, the bell rang. Reluctantly, she approached the countess. "Yes, madam?"

"How many items have you checked off?" Clara asked while wiping her mouth.

Luella hated to lie, but she knew if she told the truth, the countess would only add to her list. "A little more than half."

"Hmm, so you might not finish in time?"

"Possibly not."

"That is too bad," Clara said with a smile. "You are dismissed."

Luella went into the kitchen, finished her meal, and continued in her tasks. At six-thirty, she marked her final chore complete. She found her stepmother in the drawing room.

"Madam, I have completed my list."

The embroidery fell from Clara's hand as her jaw dropped. "I beg your pardon?"

Beaming with pride, Luella approached. "I have completed every task you asked of me."

Clara snatched the paper and studied it closely. "How?" she muttered in disbelief.

"I can go with you, right?" Luella asked.

Clara glanced at her daughters, knowing exactly how to handle this unexpected setback. "We did make an agreement, and you have upheld your end. Of course you may come with us."

Madison began to complain, insisting Luella couldn't possibly go. Clara held up her hand to silence her protests.

"Thank you," Luella said with a half-bow. "I am most excited to attend."

"First, help your stepsisters. Once they are ready for the ball, then you may get dressed yourself."

"Yes, madam."

Luella walked with Aubrey into her room. She held up her teal dress. "Do you think Simon will like it?" Aubrey asked.

"Of course. You two seem like a good match."

Aubrey smiled. "Yes. When we walked to the market, we talked more about him than the court, if you can believe it. He is extremely sweet and handsome."

Luella sat Aubrey in front of the vanity and began to fix her hair. "I believe the two of you will have a wonderful time tonight."

"I only hope he accepts me. I'm terrified of mother handing me off to Anthony."

Luella gasped softly. "So you know?"

"Mother isn't as subtle as she thinks she is. The day you ran to the pond, when she entertained Langdon, I overheard some of their conversation. I would run away before marrying someone like him!"

"I think Simon would be a good choice, and I pray it works out for you."

Aubrey opened her mouth but shut it when Madison walked in. "Aren't you done yet?"

Luella gave her a polite smile. "Just about." She finished Aubrey's hair, then followed Madison into her room to get ready. Her gown was a bright, garish pink. Luella said nothing about it.

She braided Madison's hair, pinned it in place, and she tightened the corset bodice as the finishing touch.

"Are you excited to attend with Henri?" Luella asked, in an attempt to fill the void between them.

"Yes and no. He was supposed to sign the nuptial agreement with Mother, but he gave some excuse. He claims he will sign it tomorrow. She told me to flirt with every duke and prince I can, in case things fall through." Madison laughed. "Also, to make Henri jealous."

"Is he riding with us?"

"He said he'll meet us there," Madison muttered, the words spitting from her mouth with anger. "This was not how tonight was supposed to go." She shot a look of disdain at Luella. "Especially having to go with the likes of you."

Luella hid the hurt as best she could before she went upstairs. She adorned herself in her blue gown and shoes.

Time was running out, so she hurried downstairs, not used to wearing heels. Aubrey was going to throw the pair away, saying they were no longer in style, but she gave them to Luella instead. She dyed them in the pond to match her gown.

Her stepmother and stepsisters were at the entrance, about to go out the door, when Luella made it down the final staircase.

"Wait," she called out. "Please, wait. I'm coming."

Aubrey stared in disbelief at her gown, before giving Madison a look of sheer envy. They turned to their mother, who smiled in response.

"Don't worry. We haven't left yet," Clara assured Luella. "After all, I didn't want to miss the best part."

"Mother, please, she can't come with us!" Madison begged.

"But doesn't she look lovely? Especially with that sash tied around her waist. Don't you agree, Madison?"

"Why would I care about… Oh, that is *my* sash, you thief!" Madison charged at Luella and violently ripped it away.

"What do you think of the ribbons?" Clara asked Aubrey.

"They were mine, but I threw them away."

Clara stomped her foot. "Help your sister, or you don't get to attend the ball tonight."

Aubrey faced Luella with a horrified expression. Luella's shoulders sagged when Aubrey approached. "Those are my ribbons," she said as she pulled them so hard, the gown tattered around Luella. She gave her a sympathetic look before she joined her mother and sister.

"Oh, dear. It looks as though you couldn't possibly go with us now. What a shame!" Clara said as she ushered her daughters from the manor. "Farewell, Luella. Enjoy your evening. I know we will." She laughed as the door shut behind them.

Luella ran out the back and into the courtyard. She collapsed against the fountain, knowing whatever chance she had of dancing with Remi was as destroyed as the very dress she wore. And their courtship? Would that have to remain a secret, or what would they do?

Oh, no. She realized, if Henri did sign the marriage contract, the countess would announce Madison and Henri's engagement on Monday. If she doesn't know about Luella and Remi by then…

Her fingers trailed over the damaged fabric, and pain tore through Luella at the thought of so many hours wasted.

I'm so sorry, Remi. I wish I could be there tonight, to hold you and dance with you. How did this go so wrong?

Luella pushed away the negative thoughts as she wept into her hands.

Chapter 17

The Ball

'm sorry to bother you, miss. Could you spare some bread and perhaps a small cup of milk? If it's not too much trouble." The voice pulled Luella from her thoughts, and she wiped her tears as she looked up.

An old, gnarled woman approached her. Most of her face was hidden under the dark blue cloak she wore, but her eyes appeared kind.

"Of course. One moment, and I shall fetch that for you." Luella went into the kitchen, fixed up a tray, and brought it to the woman, who sat at the edge of the fountain. "Here you are."

"Thank you, my dear. So sweet of you." The woman drank a sip of milk. "May I ask why you are crying?"

"Oh, it's nothing," Luella said as she wiped her tears away.

"Won't you indulge an old woman while she eats?"

"Very well. I was invited to a ball tonight, and I wanted to spend the evening with the man I love. Alas, it was not meant to be."

The woman finished her bread, then took another sip. "One should not lose hope. For you never know when a miracle might happen."

"I used to believe that, but I don't know if I can anymore."

Gripping Luella's arm, the woman stood and faced her. "You will believe again. For I wish to repay your kindness." A bright light encompassed her, and her façade fell away, leaving a beautiful, blonde woman standing before her. "After all, I am Alyssa, your faery godmother."

Luella's mouth dropped open, and she needed a moment to take in the sight before her. "You're my… What?" She couldn't help but stare at the shimmering wings upon her back.

"I am here to help you, child. I will see to it that you go to the ball."

"But how?"

"First, I require a pumpkin. Do you grow those here?"

Luella's brow furrowed in confusion, but she thought it better not to ask. "Yes, in fact. We have a few over here."

"Let's pick one out, shall we?"

They walked to the small patch in the back corner. "Is this what you are looking for?"

"It is," Alyssa said as she decided on a large, white pumpkin. "This one is perfect."

With a flick of her wrist, a silver wand appeared in her hand. She murmured softly, and Luella stepped back in surprise as the pumpkin creaked and groaned while growing in size. A burst of light, and a white shimmering carriage stood where the pumpkin had been.

"This is impossible!"

Alyssa laughed softly before glancing around the garden. "Perchance, are there any mice nearby?"

"There are."

Luella ran into the kitchen to fetch a small wheel of cheese. She returned to Alyssa and set it on the ground. Within a minute, four mice appeared and began to feast on it.

Alyssa pointed her wand at them, and they grew into four large horses, harnessed, and attached to the carriage.

"Let's see. Something is missing. Oh, yes. You need a driver and a footman."

At that moment, two lizards scurried across the wall. Another flick, and they grew into men, each wearing a dark blue suit. One sat in the driver's seat while the other waited by the door of the carriage.

"Oh, this is amazing!"

"Now, my dear. We have already lost so much time. Let's get you on your way."

"But my dress!"

"Yes, yes. Your dress is lovely! Now, come along."

"Faery godmother, please. My dress is torn."

Alyssa stopped and looked her over. "Oh, dear. So it is. One moment." She lifted her wand.

"Wait!" Luella cried out. "This was my mother's gown."

"And so it will remain." Alyssa aimed her wand at her, and the magic glowed as it wrapped around Luella, mending her gown and adding a shimmer that reflected in the light. The shoes she wore disappeared, only to be replaced by clear heels with faery wings attached at the back. "They look like glass, but they are much stronger while still comfortable, as well."

"It's all stunning," Luella said as she admired her reflection in the water at the base of the fountain.

"Off you go."

The coachmen gripped Luella's arm and helped her into the carriage. After he shut the door, she turned to Alyssa. "Thank you, Faery Godmother. This is a dream come true."

"I'm happy to help, my dear." The carriage started to move. "Oh, wait. I almost forgot! At the last stroke of midnight, the magic will fade, and everything will return to the way it was.

You must promise me you will leave the ball before that happens. Otherwise, the consequences may be dire!"

"I promise I will. Thank you again."

The carriage lurched forward and began its journey to the palace, moving at an almost unnatural speed. Conflict swirled in Luella. On one hand, she was excited to see Remi again, while another part of her was angry he had ignored her. More than anything, she hoped she would get the answers she needed.

The world breezed by, but she noticed very little of it. Her heart battled her mind, telling her what she felt for him was more important than whatever happened to keep them apart. Could she let go of her anger and enjoy the evening with him? After all, that was what she desired more than anything else.

They approached the gate, and the guards let them pass. Her heart thudded in her ribcage as the carriage pulled up to the stairs of the palace.

Luella stepped out, and she couldn't help but stare. She had never seen such a large, magnificent structure. Slowly, she made her way up to the entrance.

Excitement flowed through her veins, and she paused for a moment. A guard approached and escorted her to the grand ballroom.

He opened the door, and she drew in a breath, reminding herself to have courage. She walked inside, finding herself standing on a small balcony and looking at the crowd below. Everyone in attendance was dressed in decadent clothing. Nobles and commoners mixed as they ate, drank, and danced.

She slowly made her way down the stairs, taking in the sights and sounds. People laughed and enjoyed the merriment as the music played on. Until she saw Remi. The sight of him caused her to stop in her tracks. Leaving immediately entered her mind.

Remi laughed with the woman Luella had seen him with at the festival. They stood close together, and Luella would swear they were flirting. Her chest ached as she realized this was why he wanted her to come, to see him with this other woman so he wouldn't have to tell her himself. Other nonsensical thoughts wove through her mind as she watched them.

She turned to run up the stairs when a hand gripped hers and pulled her towards the dance floor. The man escorting her was a few inches taller than her, with short black hair and bright green eyes. She smiled at him.

"I am Sir Tybalt. Will you honor me with a dance?"

"I will," she responded before introducing herself.

The song was fast and animated, and she used the opportunity to keep herself close to him as they spun on the dance floor. When she glanced at Remi, his eyes narrowed and darkened with jealousy. She shot him a shy grin before giving her attention back to her dance partner. In a flash, Remi yanked Tybalt away, then took her hands.

"Do not touch what is mine," he growled to the lord, who immediately retreated from them.

Luella tried to free herself of his grasp, but he was too strong. Causing a scene was the last thing she wanted, so when a slow song began to play, she let herself ease against his chest.

"What the hell was that about?" he demanded once they were out of earshot of the other dancers.

"I don't know what you mean," Luella said as she studied him with wide eyes. "You were otherwise occupied, and a gentleman asked me to dance."

"Occupied?"

"Well, you and that beautiful woman—"

"My cousin, Mia."

"That's what you've told me. Though the two of you looked quite cozy together."

"Her parents died when she was young, and she was raised here in the palace with me. Most of my family ignores her, but she adores me and sees me as the older brother she always wanted, because I am protective of her and spend time with her."

Humiliation crept in, and Luella's cheeks reddened. "I'm so sorry. I started to believe I was right. I thought you were using me." Her voice trembled.

"After the words we've spoken, after we have claimed each other, you still have doubts about me?"

"Can you blame me? I tried to reach out to you last night, to see what I did that was so wrong. You never responded! Where were you?"

"I didn't want to leave you hanging, believe me. I was acting on behalf of the king."

"Then why not tell me so? To not even hear back from you…" she added softly.

"That is entirely my fault. Growing up here, we learn to shut ourselves off. I didn't mean to do that to you, and in the process, violate our bargain. For that, I offer my sincerest of apologies."

"I have been looking forward to this ball. To seeing you, dancing with you, being with you. Though I am still hurt and angry, too."

"You have every right to be. I never meant for you to feel this way. What can I do? How can I make this up to you?"

"Be with me now," she begged as her lower lip quivered.

"I promise." He took her hands and stepped back while taking her all in. "You are ravishing in this gown."

"Thank you."

"We will dance the evening away, then I will make the announcement on behalf of the prince. Once he has chosen his bride."

Luella glanced around the grand ballroom, taking in the opulent decorations and the murmurs of conversation filling the air. "Where is the prince?" she asked.

"He is speaking with a potential bride at the moment. Typically, he is expected to meet with quite a few before making a decision. It's been tradition for hundreds of years."

"And you?" she asked, daring to meet his gaze.

"What about me?"

"How do you choose your bride?" Her own boldness surprised her, but she did her best not to let it show.

Remi's voice softened as he answered. "Well, I would find a woman who is kind, beautiful, compassionate, and worthy."

She failed to hide the hurt written across her face. "Worthy? What makes her so?"

He laughed softly. "You think I am referring to wealth and nobility?" When she nodded, he became serious. "Those things may be important to some people, but for me, I care more about the person than the title. Don't you?"

She swallowed hard. "Yes, I do. I do not believe we are defined by title alone."

"That is good to hear."

The song ended. Luella and Remi offered each other a small bow before the next song began. He took her hand, and they moved together along the dance floor. Luella realized everyone was staring at them. She told herself it was him they were focusing on, that or her gown. Self-doubt crept in, telling her they were staring at her because she didn't belong there.

Her face flushed. "I apologize, but I am getting warm. Would you get me something to drink?"

"Of course. Don't go far," he teased with a wink as he spun away, leaving her at the edge of the dance floor.

She watched as he approached the bar and lifted a glass of champagne while speaking to the bartender. He sipped slowly while her own drink was made.

Henri approached Luella, placing his hand on her waist and leaning down. "Good evening."

"To you as well," Luella said in response while attempting to appear calm. She glanced over to see Madison staring daggers at them. "It looks as though your betrothed is waiting for you."

"She is not the one who has my attention."

"Neither do I."

He laughed. "That is what you think. You come in here, dressed in this fantastic gown, with all eyes on you. How could I refrain from paying you any attention?"

She opened her mouth to respond, but Sir Tybalt grabbed Henri by the elbow. "You need to come with me."

Henri tried to shake free of his grip. "Leave us be."

"I assure you, you need to hear this. Now."

Henri sighed before stepping away. Luella was grateful to be left alone. Her heart sank into her stomach when Madison approached Remi. She placed her hand on his arm while speaking with him. They spoke for a few moments, appearing to have a polite conversation. Then his spine straightened, and he turned to Luella.

When their eyes met, she knew she had been found out. She forced a small smile until his attention went back to Madison, then she fled from the ballroom.

The cool night air helped soothe her heated skin. As she ran around the corner, she saw the fountain, lit up with clear, crisp water. She rushed to it before splashing some on her face and neck while panting for air.

"Luella, are you ill?" Remi asked as he knelt beside her.

"I'm not sure. Everything feels… off." She glanced up at him. "Madison told you, didn't she? Who I really am, I mean." The thought of facing the truth threatened to suffocate her. Fear of rejection overtook her.

"She said you are her stepsister and a servant in their household. Is that the truth?"

Bile rose in the back of her throat as her eyes squeezed shut. "Yes, it's the truth. I have tried so many times to tell you. When I came here before, to see you, that was why I came. If you never want to see me again, I understand completely." Despite her best efforts, she couldn't conceal the sadness overwhelming her.

"Why did you not tell me this sooner? How dare you keep this from me, after we agreed to be honest?" His voice raised with each word.

Luella's chest ached, and she knew she deserved the pain for lying to him. She prayed he would forgive her, that all was not lost between them. Before she could beg him to hear her out, a voice cut through the air.

"Don't speak to her that way!"

They turned to see Aubrey storming up to Remi.

"What?" he asked in disbelief.

"Do you have any idea what hell she went through, just to come here tonight?" Her finger waggled in front of his face as she spoke. "I am surprised she even had the energy to dance with you, let alone run out here. She has been working two to three days a week at the dressmakers, in addition to all of her chores."

Remi looked at Luella. "That's why you fell asleep at the pond?"

Before Luella could answer, Aubrey continued. "My mother put her through the ringer. The least you can do is be grateful she is here at all!"

"You're right," Remi said as he stepped back, then knelt beside Luella. "You are mine. Regardless of who or what you are, we belong to each other." His words soothed her.

"Good," Aubrey exclaimed before returning to the ball.

"We said our vows, and no title will change that."

"Really?" Luella asked, her eyes glistening with unshed tears. Her heartache eased.

His lips brushed softly over hers. "Really. I only hope, when the time comes, you will have the same—"

She fell to the ground, clutching her abdomen and crying out in pain. "Oh," she whimpered.

He moved closer and took her hand. "What's wrong?"

"I'm hot, my skin is crawling, and I can barely catch my breath." Her mouth opened as her inner thighs rubbed together. Desire pooled in her stomach. "I can't…"

Remi sniffed the air, and his pupils dilated. "Luella, you are going into heat."

"What, no!" she cried out angrily as she sat up. "I am a human. Humans don't do that."

"I have been around enough omegas to recognize the scent. I assure you, it is why you are feeling this way."

"You're wrong. I'm a human," she protested once more.

When he examined her, he noticed the pendant which had fallen over her chest. "What is that?"

Her eyes lowered, and she lifted it up. "This? My stepmother gave it to me when I was very young. She made me swear to never take it off, saying it would protect me from shifters."

"No, she gave it to you to prevent you from shifting."

"What?" Luella asked in utter disbelief.

"It's made of moonstone, which hampers our ability. As shifters, we begin to change around five years of age. Your body is finally realizing it never did. Between that and going into heat, you will shut down completely if you do not change soon."

"I am a human!" she screamed as he lifted her off the ground. She buried her face in his chest as tears streamed down her face. "I'm not a wolf!"

"Then prove it to me. Take off the necklace and toss it away."

"No." Her hand clutched it tightly.

"Fine, then I will."

"Don't you dare—" Before she could finish, he wrapped his hand around hers, squeezing with a slight enough pressure to force her to release it. He tore it away and flung it as far from her as possible. "Give it back!" she demanded.

"I'm sorry. You have to do this. Otherwise, you might go insane or die."

"Please. Please, don't."

He gave her one last look of regret, then he clasped her hands. She held her breath, but after several moments passed with no change, her body eased.

"I told you, I'm not—"

Her hair grew longer, wrapping over her as her face and body stretched, and her canines elongated. Each muscle corded together, shifting and changing shape until she stood on all fours as a snow-white wolf.

"Gods, you are beautiful."

She collapsed to the ground, her eyes staring forward. Remi knelt beside her. He gently stroked between her ears.

"Luella?"

No response, nor did she acknowledge his presence. She stayed still, the only movement was the rapid up and down of her chest as she struggled to breathe, struggled to understand what just happened to her.

"Luella, you're all right," Remi assured her.

What did you do to me? she asked through their bond.

"What I had to. I showed you who and what you really are."

She rested her chin on her paw and let out a mournful whimper. *Please, change me back. I don't want this. I'm not a shifter. You did this to me, when you bit me!* Fear ravaged her emotions, causing her to tremble uncontrollably.

"I promise you, I did not. I meant it when I told you that you are either born a shifter or you aren't. You were not made into one."

I don't believe you.

"It's the truth. I'm going to shift as well, then we will run through the woods together. Having gone as long as you did, you need to stretch and let your inner wolf out."

She responded with a low growl.

"Luella, I mean it."

A moment later, he appeared next to her, transformed into a magnificent, dark brown wolf. He nuzzled her side with his snout, encouraging her to get up. She let out another whimper.

Luella, please. Stand up. Not for me, but for yourself. You need to. No! I don't want this!

I'll make you a deal. If you get up and run through the woods with me for at least five minutes, we will return here, and I will change you back. Otherwise, you are on your own.

You promised to stay with me.

And I will. Even like this, he said as he nestled beside her, *I am with you, am I not? But if you want to go back to your human form, you have to work with me.*

I want to wake up from this nightmare. Please.

Luella, that's not going to happen. I can show you how wonderful this is, if you'll let me. All I am asking for is five measly minutes. Please, give me that.

With a sigh, she reluctantly stood. He joined her, then took a few steps forward. She watched him intently before trying for herself.

Her feet moved on their own, as if they knew what to do, and she stepped up beside him. He let out a howl, and they took off for the woods. She stumbled and nearly fell but caught herself.

As they ran through the trees, the wind whipped through their fur, the earth beneath their paws hummed with wild energy. Her despair and confusion gave way to happiness as a sense of freedom unlike any she'd ever known washed over her.

When they approached the edge of the forest, he stopped to wait for her. The moonlight filtered through the trees, casting a silvery glow on their figures. Luella nuzzled her head along his neck.

This is the sign of ultimate trust, letting your mate so near your throat.

Really?

Yes.

Thank you, but I don't deserve it.

Luella—

She took off running, and he was impressed by her speed. Instinct kicked in, and he gave chase. They ran through the forest, weaving in and out of trees, jumping over fallen logs, and enjoying the evening together.

Are you ready to return?

Yes.

Chapter 18

Midnight

e caught up to her at the fountain. After shifting back, he approached her. His hand gripped the scruff of her neck, and she returned to her human form as well. She stood before him, collecting herself before she would meet his gaze.

"My dress?" she asked, looking herself over. Her hands patted down her skirt and corset to ensure nothing was damaged.

"Everything is fine. It's from the fae magic I told you about. Our clothing is not destroyed when we shift."

"I'm grateful for that." She shook her head as her breathing came in rasps. "How could my stepmother keep this from me? I never knew. Wait, how did she know I would be a wolf?" She glanced at Remi. "You said we typically shift around the age of five. I've had that pendant for as long as I can remember."

"She didn't want to take the chance. If she were hiding you in a colony, the last thing she needed was for you to randomly turn into a wolf in the middle of the market."

"All these years, she raised us to hate shifters."

"Why?"

"She said they attacked us when I was about two years old. That's when my father was killed. She said he died protecting us." The memory of her father's sacrifice tugged at her heart.

"I'm sorry." Remi cocked his head. "Wait, you were told what happened?"

Pushing back her tears, she cleared her throat. "Because I don't really remember it. I keep seeing a large, black wolf lunging at me, but that's all. Clara made it clear, shifters are dangerous, and we are to keep away from them. Though, if one of her daughters has a chance to marry a prince, I guess that is more important to her."

"And you? Were you really raised as a servant in your own home?"

"I was, and I still am. I do not turn twenty-one for a few more weeks." Her shoulders sagged. "I planned to find a new job and move out. Then I discovered she poisoned the merchants against me by spreading horrible lies. Some merchants have been kinder lately, but I am unsure if anyone will hire me. I fear I am trapped with her."

"No, you aren't. That's the other thing we need to talk about. Come, let's return to the ballroom."

Her feet refused to budge, as though she were rooted to the ground itself. "I can't."

"What's wrong?"

"Please, go inside without me. I need a few minutes to myself, after discovering all of this."

Gently, he gripped her arm. His words were laced with tenderness as he whispered, "You're not alone, Luella. I'm here for you, no matter what."

In her mind, she screamed at her limbs to obey, but an invisible force held her captive. Her eyes squeezed shut. A rush of humiliation stained her cheeks a deep, burning crimson. Lust and longing unlike anything she'd experienced before consumed her.

"I… I can't move."

He glanced down and noticed her hands rubbing her hips. "Right. You were going into heat. I will help you with that."

"Remi!"

He lifted her up, throwing her over his shoulder, and carrying her into a side entrance of the palace. Thankfully, with everyone at the ball, the corridor was empty. He took her into a bedroom and placed her on her feet.

"Where are we?"

"My private quarters."

She immediately took notice of the fine furnishings and silk bedding. "It's nicer than I expected. It must be nice to have your own bed, too."

"What do you mean?"

"Is it as soft as it looks?" she asked, staring at it with envy in her eyes.

"You do have one of your own, right?" His heart sank when she shook her head.

"I sleep on the floor in the attic. The closest to being in a bed was the exam table at the doctor's office."

"Luella, why didn't you tell me?"

"It's humiliating. I don't know why I was never allowed my own bed."

Remi released a small gasp. "Part of Clara keeping your wolf at bay."

"What do you mean?"

"Your stepmother must've known that having your own bed would help your nesting instincts kick in. Were you allowed blankets?"

"One small, tattered blanket." She collapsed against him. He led her to the bed, but she pulled away from him. "Please, I am hurting, but I don't want our first time together to be like this. You deserve better."

"We will have that, I promise you. I also promise not to do anything unless you tell me I can. I want to take care of you, the way I did by the pond. Will you let me?"

As soon as she nodded, he stripped out of his jacket and shoes. She climbed onto the bed, where he joined her. He gently gripped her legs until she was in a reclined position, her head resting against his pillows. After lifting the hem of her dress, he slowly removed her underwear. The pleasant sensation caused her to moan and writhe in response.

"So sensitive. I will see to all of your needs, mon trésor."

He lowered his face between her thighs and lapped gently. Every inch of her burned with need, her desire flickering as if his touch was fuel to her fire. He stoked her passion and devoured her.

Each time she came, she breathed in shallow pants. Sure she was finished, her jaw dropped open as he penetrated her with his tongue, ravaging her. The pleasure caused her to scream, and her heat finally began to ease. Her back arched as she cried out his name. Her honeyed taste lingered on his lips after he drank every last drop.

"Thank you," she murmured as she struggled to sit up. He lifted her gently and adjusted the pillow behind her.

"Rest now, after everything you have endured tonight." He kissed her softly, but it grew in hunger. Tasting herself on his lips rekindled her desire.

"Remi, please—"

"I feel it as well."

His hand slid up her leg, and he caressed between her thighs, teasing her until she begged for release. When she finished once more, she fell back, her body spent.

"I need a shower," he said with a chuckle.

"It's getting late," she said as she sat up slowly. "I need to leave soon."

"No, you can't. We will return to the ball, and I will make the announcement. This is of the utmost importance. I've been waiting a long time for this."

She smiled as he slipped away after kissing her forehead. The door shut behind him, and the thought didn't occur to her, that how could he know the prince was ready to make an announcement? He had spent the entire evening with her, after all.

Lost in bliss, she almost didn't hear the first chime of the clock. Realization sank in. It was midnight, and her time ran out. She looked at the washroom door and thought about telling Remi she had to go, until the clock chimed again. Everything she wore would vanish, and she did not wish for Remi to see her in her pathetic, ripped gown.

Panic flowed in as she remembered her promise to the faery godmother, to leave before the final strike of the clock. She collected herself, slipping back into her underwear, then walked to the window. Though she was loath to do so, she knew she would be able to climb down. With the glass shoes clutched against her chest, she began to make her way.

Once on the ground, she realized she had dropped one of the slippers before she left. She figured it didn't matter since they would vanish or change back when the magic ran out.

The clock chimed again, and she rushed to the carriage. Thankfully, it was still parked in front of the entrance to the palace. She hopped in and cried for the driver to go.

Time was against them as they flew through the gates and onto the worn path that led to the woods. Luella looked back, grateful no one pursued them. She had no idea how she would explain this to Remi, as her thoughts were interrupted when the carriage began to shrink around her.

She managed to jump out right before it popped back into a pumpkin. The mice and lizards ran to her. She scooped them up into her remaining slipper and carried them.

The colony wasn't much farther. The guards were out, and though everyone returned late because of the ball, she knew she would be hassled for breaking curfew.

She placed the critters carefully into her pocket, climbed a tree near the wall, and scrambled across a branch. From there, she made her way down the wall and into the colony, before heading home as quickly as she could.

Thankful no one else returned yet from the ball, she warily made her way upstairs to her room. Her eyelids drooped as she dragged her feet. Exhaustion washed over her, and as soon as she made it inside, she collapsed in a heap onto the floor.

Luella finished her breakfast, washed dishes, then headed for the back door when the bell for the drawing room rang. She straightened her apron before going inside.

Sitting together on the sofa, the governor and Clara appeared quite cozy. The sight nearly sent Luella fleeing from the room.

"Governor, welcome. Would you like a cup of tea?" Her throat tightened, but she forced herself to speak.

"Oh, I'm afraid this isn't a social call." He turned to the countess.

Clara smirked, clutching something in her arms. "It's true, isn't it? You attended the ball last night?"

Unsure if Madison ratted her out, Luella couldn't risk being caught in a lie. "And if I did?"

Clara held up the remaining glass slipper. Luella had hidden it in the box under the floorboard, sure no one would find it. "Well?"

"Yes, I did attend. After all, it was requested by the king for all eligible women to go."

"Whether you attended or not isn't the issue," Langdon said as he stood. "But the slipper is proof you were there. Several women here commented on it. Now, the issue lies in the curfew. And the fact that you broke it."

Luella let out a nervous laugh. "Surely, you jest? Everyone returned after midnight."

"Can you name one person you saw breaking curfew as well?"

"No, but—"

"That's what I thought." He nodded, and Luella cried out when the guard grabbed her arms. Her body went rigid, and her muscles tensed as he bound her wrists. "Take her to the town hall and place her in holding."

"Yes, Governor," the guard replied as he pulled her toward the door.

Clara met Langdon's gaze. "You will not kill her, right? I need her for Henri, if I am to marry off Madison to him."

"She will be punished, but not killed." He smiled at Luella. "You will be punished for breaking the law, unless you wish to work with me."

"What are you talking about?" Luella asked, trying to appear calm despite her wide eyes.

"Tell everyone it was Remi who hurt you, not my sons. Let me punish him, in your place."

Clara studied them both as she attempted to piece everything together. She remained silent and listened intently.

Luella scoffed. "For starters, I will never lie about what happened to me. Secondly, nothing you say or do will ever make me turn against the one I love most."

Clara gasped. "You are with the herald?" she asked as she jumped to her feet. "You did lie, to me!"

"That was different," Luella cried out. "I did so to protect him, from the two of you. You threatened him, and I would do whatever necessary, including risking my own life and happiness."

"And you would do that now?" Langdon asked. "Here is the deal. Give me Remi, and you will go, with my promise to never come after you again. If you don't, you will be taken to the town hall, where only pain and torture await you. The decision is yours."

"Take my life, my heart, my soul. You will never take my love."

He looked at the guard. "Escort her to the town hall and lock her up, now!"

"No, please!" Luella begged as she struggled to break free. Aubrey and Madison ran in to see what the fuss was about.

Aubrey turned to her mother. "What is going on?" she asked in shock, staring at Luella. "Where is she going?"

"Nothing that concerns you. Go back to your practice."

"Yes, Mother," Madison said, gripping Aubrey's arm and pulling her away.

The guard placed a gag in Luella's mouth. He dragged her through the streets. She was grateful it was so early in the morning, so there were only a few colonists about to see her predicament.

Remi, please. I need your help.

Dread washed over her, chilling her to the bone, as she could not imagine what Langdon had in store for her. The guard escorted her into the town hall and took her to a panel on the floor, offset from the governor's chair.

Her chains were attached and her ankles shackled, forcing her to a kneeling position. A blindfold came next, and she trembled in fear.

Remi. Remi, please. I'm so sorry I left last night, but if you can hear me, I need your help. Now more than ever.

The silence penetrated the air. Her head hung, and she had nearly lost hope when his voice rang in her mind, as clear as though he were right beside her.

Luella, why did you leave me?

The palpable anger stung her.

Please—

Last night was one of the most important nights of my life, and you abandoned me! I walked out, excited about the next step of our journey, only to discover you left me. Why? I demand an answer.

There's no time for one. I'm so scared. I don't know what he's going to do to me. You have to help me!

Wait, what? What's going on?

His voice shifted from anger to concern.

The governor had me arrested this morning. He's going to punish me for breaking the law.

Are you in a dungeon?

No, I'm chained up in the town hall. A door behind her opened, and the hinges creaking echoed throughout the room, sending a shiver down her spine. *Someone is here. Please, come quickly!*

Luella, I have to shut this off so I can gather help. Do not despair. I promise, I am coming for you. I will be there.

Then silence. She swallowed hard and kept her head bowed. Her legs began to ache from the pose she was forced to be in. The air resonated with tension and the smell of fear.

"Soon, I will have my revenge for what you did to my sons. And the entire colony will be here to witness it firsthand."

Luella choked back her sobs, praying Remi would arrive in time to stop whatever Langdon had planned. The thought played through her mind, over and over. It was the only way to placate her fear. Lost in her head, she didn't even realize the room had filled with people.

"Citizens, thank you for coming. It was brought to my attention Luella broke one of our most sacred laws, returning to the colony after curfew." Murmurs spread out among the crowd. "You must be thinking, she wasn't the only one. This is true. However, since I am a kind, merciful governor, I decided to make an example of her. She is the only one to be punished."

"This is wrong," Tiernan said as he stepped forward. "This is not punishment. If it were, everyone who broke the law would be chained up beside her!"

"Silence," Langdon commanded. "Now, Luella, for your crime, I sentence you to eighteen lashings." He held up a short, black whip. "I will use my dressage whip, as this is fitting for you." He laughed at his own poor joke while ripping away the back of her gown.

"Please, will you show her some compassion?"

To say Luella was surprised by such a request from Clara would be an understatement. Her confusion was swiftly answered.

"Of course, dear Countess. For your plea, I shall lessen the number. The curfew is midnight, so I will punish her with twelve instead."

"How magnanimous. Thank you."

They performed their respective roles. She was the caring and concerned stepmother, while he played the governor who could be reasoned with. Luella hung her head lower.

"I shall count each one. Anyone faint of heart or with small children should leave or turn away." He raised the short whip, and with a flick of his wrist, he brought down the first strike. "One."

Through the blinding pain, Luella hardly heard him. Her back burned with fire while her cries were muffled through the gag. She waited for the next hit, only to realize he was drawing it out, to add to her suffering.

"Two!" he called out as he made contact.

Her mind spun, and though she knew he wouldn't be able to hear her, she cried out for Remi. She screamed through her mind, begging and pleading for his help with each strike. Hot tears rolled down her cheeks and soaked the blindfold. Her breathing came in rasps as the pain flashed like lightning with each hit. Luella's mind filled with a whirlwind of fear and desperation.

With every lash, her heart shattered into a thousand pieces, the weight of her suffering becoming unbearable. The crack of the whip reverberated through the room. Luella gritted her teeth, refusing to let the pain break her spirit.

"Eight," Langdon cried out, no longer attempting to hide his joy in watching her suffer.

"I demand you stop this at once!"

Remi's voice calmed her heart, even as her back throbbed with blood trickling down. His jaw clenched and his eyes went black at the sight of Luella. The anger burned within him. His wolf clawed to be unleashed to free his mate, but he had to remain calm for Luella's sake.

"You have no authority here," Langdon said with a scoff.

Remi let out an empty laugh, and the cold expression masked the anguish burning in his eyes. His calmness belied the storm of emotions swirling within him. "That is where you are wrong." The crowd gasped. Luella tried desperately to see what caused their reaction. "Now, step away from my wife, or I will kill you where you stand."

"Wife?" Langdon asked, his brow wrinkled. "She is not your wife!"

Remi walked up behind Luella and gently pulled down her sleeve, revealing the mark he left on her shoulder. "I have claimed her, and we spoke our vows. She is my wife. Now release her this instant!"

"She still needs to be punished," Langdon said as he clutched the whip tightly in his hands.

"For what crime?"

"She broke curfew last night."

"As I'm sure everyone here did. So, who is next after her?" Remi glanced around the room. "Surely, she is not the only one to be punished?"

Langdon shook his head. "Well, I mean, she…"

"Ah, I see. Petty revenge for your sons. This does not bode well for you. Not at all."

"I would never," Langdon replied with clear indignation at the suggestion.

"Then why is my wife the only one being punished?"

"Because she is a lowly servant girl I could use to make an example of."

Remi sighed. "That is not a valid reason." He turned to the crowd. Clara caught his eye. He thought for a moment before proceeding. "Countess, please step forward."

Clara warily approached him and bowed. "Yes, mi'lord?"

"What is your name? Your full name, that is."

"I am Countess Clara Alexander."

"Really? Because I believe you are Lady Claire Malvado." More gasps and murmurs erupted from the audience.

"I am unfamiliar with that name," she said, keeping her chin held high.

"So you've never heard of Princess Aribella Capulet?"

"Everyone has heard of her. What is any of this to do with me?"

Luella whimpered in pain. Remi knelt beside her. "Release her at once!" A guard ran to him and removed her chains, gag, and blindfold before retreating. "Luella, I am sorry."

"For what?" she murmured, barely conscious. Her eyelids fluttered as the pain began to ease, if only slightly.

"This." He gripped her arm, and she transformed into her wolf. The audience let out a collective gasp, with one woman screaming at the sight. "She is the daughter of Prince Caspian Capulet, who was married to Lady Claire. After she had him killed, she escaped their kingdom with the princess."

"How do you know I… She had him killed?" Clara demanded. "What proof do you have?"

"Why else would you flee?" Luella whimpered again, and Remi leaned down by her ear. "I'm sorry, mon trésor. Just another minute, I promise." He stood and faced the countess. "Who were you working with?" He noted her gaze drifting to Langdon. "Really, the governor himself?"

"What? No. I had nothing to do with it!" His eyes went wide, then he turned to look at the large black wolfskin hanging on the wall. He bent over, and for a moment, Remi thought he was going to vomit. "You lied to me!" he screamed at Clara.

"Shut up. There is no proof—"

"She told me a feral wolf attacked her and her daughters. She then told me where to find him. I swear on every deity we have, I did not know he was the prince!"

"You fool," Clara cried out. "Do you realize what you've done?"

"How did you not put two and two together?" Remi asked. "Surely, you heard of the death of the prince, of his wife and daughters who went missing?"

Langdon shook his head. "Yes, but my father must've figured out what happened. He hid the four of them away for nearly a year. By the time they arrived here and purchased the manor, nearly all talk of the prince and his family were no longer mentioned. Instead, talk swirled around whatever the latest scandal was at court or with the king himself."

"How did no one recognize her with her hair?"

Clara laughed. "Because his father helped spread the rumor that her hair was blonde, not white, so as to help hide her. Langdon is correct. His father helped me. He did it to protect his own son, not because he cared for us. I kept the message Langdon sent me and blackmailed his father to protect us."

Remi approached Clara and snatched the expensive silk shawl from her. "Guards, take them both away. Now!" He went to Luella, placed his hand on Luella's scruff, and she returned to her human form. With utmost care, he covered her bare back with the wrap. "Where are her stepsisters?" Aubrey and Madison stepped forward, keeping their head down. "Take her home. You are to clean her up and return her here in the finest gown you own."

"Yes, mi'lord," Aubrey said, approaching Luella and helping her to her feet.

She swayed for a moment, and Aubrey wrapped her arm around her waist. They followed Madison from the room.

"Guard, with utmost respect and care, bring that," Remi pointed to the wolfskin, "down."

"At once."

Remi gave his attention back to the crowd. "I should condemn you all for what you did to Luella."

"We didn't know," a voice said from the back.

"It doesn't matter. Princess or servant, she is still a person. You fed into Clara's lies, and you mistreated someone who was only ever kind to you. Every one of you who did so should be ashamed of yourselves!"

"You had our governor arrested. What will happen now?" asked a woman in the front row.

"We will choose a new leader for you. Everything will be all right, I assure you."

The guard removed the skin, rolled it up, and carried it from the hall. Remi paced while waiting for Luella to return.

Chapter 19

Home

uella clung to Aubrey as they entered the town hall. When her gaze met Remi's, her eyes were drawn to the small golden crown resting upon his head. Her eyes went wide as her breath sucked in, the disbelief written across her expression.

"Who are you?" Luella asked as she stepped up beside him.

"I am Prince Sebastian Remington Montague, youngest son of King Mikael."

"I don't understand."

"We will talk when it's just the two of us. Come, your home awaits you."

"My home?"

"Yes. You are my wife, and we will live together in the palace," he said, offering a warm smile as he extended his arm towards her.

"Your wife?"

"Yes. Those were marriage vows we said at the pond."

"They were vows, I know. It was just the two of us, so they're not legally binding, right?"

"Yes, they were. For us wolves, we only need to say we are mated, we are married, and it is so."

"I didn't know."

"Would you not have said them if you did?"

The crowd stared at them, and she couldn't take it much longer. She knew there wasn't another choice. The colonists would never allow a shifter to live among them.

"I believe so." Reluctantly, she took his hand and followed him to the carriage.

Resting on the plush seat, she shrank away from him, curling up as if to protect herself. Her heart ached, and when he reached for her, she recoiled further.

"Luella, what's wrong?"

She looked out the window and nearly fell onto his lap when the carriage lurched forward with a sudden jolt. She pulled back and kept herself in the corner.

"How could you do that to me?" she asked, her voice small and not much above a whisper.

"Do what? Save you?"

"I... Of course I don't mean that. Thank you for saving me from him. No. I'm referring to the fact you outed me to the entire colony. I trusted you, only for you to do that to me. Now, it will never be my home again."

"It wouldn't be anyway."

She sighed. "You can't be sure."

"But I am. Because as princess, you belong at the palace."

"Princess," she said under her breath. "I'm a lost princess and a shifter? This is so much to take in all at once."

"I know it's overwhelming. For now, let's focus on one thing at a time. As far as being a shifter—"

"A shifter you outed to the colony," she reminded him as she wiped her unshed tears.

"You asked why I did it? What did your stepsisters say when they cleaned you up?"

"That has absolutely nothing to do with what we are discussing!"

"Answer the question," he said in a steady, firm tone.

"Aubrey wiped away the blood and gasped. She said my wounds had already healed. Why is that?"

"Because I made you shift. We have a natural, accelerated healing. Mine works all the time, whether I am in this form or my wolf. Since your wolf was denied for so long, you had to be in that form for it to work. I was helping you."

"Why were you so sure it would work?"

"I didn't, but I had to take the chance."

She studied the crown. "And that?"

"What about it?"

"Why the lies? Why tell everyone you were a simple herald?"

"It was my father's idea. When one of the princes would visit a colony, everyone put their best foot forward. Even a surprise visit. He thought since I rarely left at an early age and most colonists didn't know me, I agreed to act as a spy for him. I could be his eyes and ears in the colonies, to see what the people really thought of him."

"Why not tell me, at least?"

"Because you were so forthcoming yourself?"

Her shoulders sagged. "Fair enough, I guess. Why didn't you tell me last night you were the prince we were celebrating?"

"I planned to. After we danced for the evening, I was going to tell you in private. Then we would make the announcement together. Instead, you became ill, needing to shift and going into heat. I didn't get the chance. Now, it's your turn."

"What do you mean?"

"Why did you leave me?" It took every ounce of his control to not sound angry, as he didn't want to risk scaring her away once more.

She swallowed hard at the hitch in his voice. "I didn't want to. You have to believe that. I mended my mother's gown to wear to the ball, but my stepsisters destroyed it in a fit of jealous rage." She looked down. "I'm not sure how much of this you will believe."

"Try me."

Luella's pulse pounded as she prepared herself. She told him everything, starting with running out to the courtyard, the faery godmother, and her magic.

"The spell broke at midnight. I promised her I would leave before then. Time got away from me, and when the clock chimed, I panicked. After all, she said there would be dire consequences if I didn't leave in time. I swear, I never meant to hurt you."

"That is either the most elaborate lie I've ever heard, or it is absolutely the truth." He thought about her story, and while he did, Luella could scarcely breathe. "I believe you. Still, why not tell me last night?"

"I was embarrassed," she admitted as her face went flush.

"Why?"

"Because I was unable to afford a fancy dress like theirs. I had to mend an old gown. Then for them to tear it apart the way they did…" Her voice trailed off, filled with a mix of sadness and frustration. She swallowed back her tears. "I don't have much that belonged to her, and I was so excited to wear it for you."

"You still can. We'll retrieve it from the manor, then you can do with it whatever you want." He noticed her smile, though she continued to keep her gaze lowered. "Luella, please look at me." When she did, he leaned in and kissed her softly.

"It still doesn't seem real."

"Everything you have suffered through… none of that matters now. Instead, you will be the one who is waited upon. Everything you have ever wanted or needed will be yours. Say the word, and I will give you anything in the world."

"All I've ever wanted was to be loved. Clara never rocked me to sleep, read to me, hugged me. For as long as I can remember, my sole purpose was to cater to her and my stepsisters. To see to their every need."

"That is my purpose now, to see to yours." He kissed her again, and she writhed under him.

"Hmm," she moaned softly. She froze. "Oh, no."

"What's wrong?" he asked, looking her over.

She bit her lower lip. "I think I'm still in heat."

"Let me help."

"I can't explain. Don't ask how I know, but I need more than your mouth or hands. I need all of you."

"You are my wife, and as I said, I will give you whatever you need."

"I'm grateful, but I don't want our first time together to be tarnished by this!"

"Luella, I have wanted to bury myself inside you for so long. You have no idea how much the thought itself makes me ache. I mean it. Tell me what you want, and I will do it."

She climbed onto his lap, straddling him as she whimpered. "I want this pain to go away."

"Then I will see that it does."

He sat her beside him, stood, and unfastened his pants. Her eyes trailed over him, full of hunger, as he lowered them to the floor. He sat on the seat and pulled her across his lap. His hand teased between her legs, eliciting a whimper that grew into a moan.

His fingers trailed inside the slender fabric separating them, then pumped in and out. The sensation made her writhe, her hips rising and falling with the movement. Before she became unraveled, he removed his fingers and sucked them dry. He ripped her underwear away, then seated her right above him.

"When you are ready, mon trésor."

She slowly lowered down, taking him all in. Pain flashed for an instant before switching to pleasure. He grabbed her hips and lifted her, moving with the motion of the carriage.

"Oh," she moaned, and he nipped playfully at her neck as he picked up speed. "Gods, yes!"

The world breezed by, unseen as she focused on being with him, being in this moment, giving him everything she could. He pounded into her, fisting her hair and roaring with his own release. When he filled her, she cried out again, then lay her head against his chest. Her vision blurred as stars erupted before her. She breathed heavily while he stroked her hair.

"Better?"

"Yes," she replied as she started to pull away.

"Wait," he said, holding her firmly on his lap.

"What is that?"

"I'm sorry. I didn't think this would happen so soon."

"What is it?" she demanded.

"We are… knotted together."

"Are you serious?" she yelled. "I thought that only happened during breeding?"

"I mean, isn't that what we just did? And how do you know about that?"

"Clara did have a decent library. I studied shifters, trying to prepare myself if I ever did have to face off against one." She sighed. "How long will this last?"

"Thirty minutes."

"Please tell me you are joking?"

"I am. It will go away soon."

He shifted his hips, causing her to moan as she ground her thighs over him. She kissed him softly, parting his lips. The way he filled her, stretched her, sculpted her to him, made her go into heat once more. Desire burned through her until she could no longer resist, giving in and giving him everything he demanded in return.

She bared her teeth, and on instinct, she bit his shoulder. He cried out in a mix of pain and pleasure. When she lapped at the blood, his wound healed on its own. She kissed him, and he sensed her fear.

"What's wrong?"

"I didn't mean to… I never want to hurt you," she said as a single tear rolled down her cheek.

Using the pad of his thumb, he swiftly brushed it away. "That was amazing," he said as she sat beside him. "And I'm grateful you claimed me. I've been waiting for you to do it, ever since we learned what you truly are."

"Will it be like that every time?"

He lifted his pants and dressed. "Possibly, and there may be more biting too," he added with a chuckle. He glanced out the window. "Oh, we are almost to the gate. Are you excited for your new home?"

"I am, but I have so many questions. What will my life be like? What are my duties? What if I don't like it here?"

"Luella, it's going to be all right. We will go to our room for privacy, and I will answer all of your questions."

"I'm so nervous," she exclaimed.

"Take a deep breath. Follow my lead, and you will be fine."

The carriage came to a stop, and the door opened. Remi helped Luella out, then up the steps of the palace. His hand gripped hers tightly, reassuring her as they went inside.

Luella kept her head low and avoided the people who stared at her as they walked past. The palace was lit up with the afternoon sun streaming in through the numerous windows. Banners of different packs hung along the walls, and people dressed from rags to fine silks also walked along the corridor.

Remi took her into the same room as the night before. Her heart raced as the walls closed in around her. She rasped in a breath as her body went clammy.

"What's wrong?"

"I need air."

"Come." He took her to the window and opened it. "It's a lot to take in. Wait here for a moment." He smiled at her. "No climbing out this time?"

She returned his smile, attempting to keep her composure. "I promise."

"I'll be right back." He kissed the top of her head before going into the washroom.

"Is this real?" Luella murmured softly. Her life would never be the same, and she didn't know if she was ready for everything ahead of her.

A knock at the door pulled her from her thoughts of the future. She opened it and stepped back. The king himself stood before her, dressed in fine silk with a massive, jeweled crown on his head.

"Your Majesty," Luella said with a bow.

"Who the hell are you?" he asked with a scowl. "Why are you in my son's room?"

"My apologies. I am his—"

He leaned down and sniffed her. "Remington brought home an omega? Where on earth did he find a stray like you?"

"Mi'lord, I—"

"Guard!" he called out. "Take her and have her examined with the other omegas. Then I will be down shortly to see to her myself."

Before Luella had a chance to protest, she was bound and gagged. Her spine stiffened as the cold metal wrapped around her wrists. Remi stepped out of the washroom and ran to them.

"Leave her alone! What is going on?" he demanded.

"Son, you know the rules about omegas in your private chambers."

"But she isn't any—"

"Oh, right. She isn't *just* any omega. She's 'special.' I assure you, she is like every other female. Only good for one thing." The king winked and laughed.

"Father, this isn't right. You must let her go."

"Silence, boy. Remember your place." He stepped up to Luella, gripped her chin, and examined her. "You will make a fine addition. I cannot wait to claim you for myself."

Luella looked at Remi with hope in her eyes, as she waited for him to secure her freedom. Her heart sank when his head went down, and he remained silent.

Her shouts were muffled through the gag. The king laughed and lowered it from her mouth. "What did you say?"

"I reject you, Remi! I reject you as my mate, reject our bond!"

The king's eyes went wide for a moment before he returned the gag. He turned to Remi. "What nonsense have you fed the poor girl? There hasn't been a mating bond amongst our kind in nearly a millennia." Remi didn't say a word. The king nodded to the guard. "Take her away."

"Remi, please," Luella begged once more, though her words were garbled. His eyes met hers, and he could see her pain and heartbreak.

Luella, you have to trust me.

Why aren't you fighting for me?

I'll explain later, I swear.

I don't believe you!

With a firm grip on her arm, the guard led Luella down two flights of stairs.

Chapter 20

Alpha to the Rescue

hey arrived at the dungeon. Luella could scarcely breathe, between the thick fabric stuffed in her mouth and the foul stench surrounding her. The guard snatched her gag away as he forced her to walk forward.

"What are we doing here?" she demanded.

"This is where all omegas are processed before they are sorted." He shoved her into a cell and removed the irons from her wrists. "The doctor will examine you to see if you are fertile. If you aren't, you will belong to the king, along with the other omegas."

The guard locked the door, then turned and walked away. Luella gripped the bars, desperation sinking in. She would not do whatever the king wanted, even if it meant attempting to escape. Regardless of the consequences, she would defy him to the very end.

A familiar laugh caught her attention. "Well, well. What's wrong? Did you and the prince have a lover's quarrel?"

Luella faced Clara. "No. The king has made a mistake. I won't be here long, you'll see." She prayed that was the truth.

"Right."

She decided she would take advantage of her current situation, to at least try and get answers out of her stepmother. "Why did you lie to me all of these years? Why did you never tell me I'm a shifter?"

"For starters, I didn't know for sure if you would be one or not. But I couldn't take the chance. Because if even one person in the colony found out, they would kick us out." She gestured around her cell. "Or worse. I had to protect both of our secrets."

"You killed my father!" Luella screamed. "You deserve to be in here."

"You don't know the first thing about him."

"Yes, I do, from reading my mother's journal. He was kind, and gentle, and loving. Because of you, I never got to meet him. How could you do that?"

"I didn't have a choice. Your mother died in childbirth, and he wanted a mother for you. I only married him because I became widowed. I did not have money and was about to be homeless with two young children. Becoming his wife guaranteed us a life of luxury. After we were married, he told me he wanted me to have a child with him. It was bad enough, having you around. I drew the line at giving birth to a... shifter."

"What do you have against shifters?"

Clara only smirked. "I have my reasons. As I said, I didn't have much choice when it came to marrying him. I was willing to do whatever was necessary for my daughters."

"Why didn't you tell him no?"

"I did, but his mind was made up. To make things worse, he decided we were going to move to a small, country chateau. He would take me away from the comforts of the palace. I would not live such a life. So I set everything up, then we fled."

"How is that any different than our life at the colony?"

Clara sighed. "I thought I had grabbed more valuables than I did. I intended to sell them at various colonies, to afford us a better life." Her jaw clenched. "Either I packed the wrong thing or dropped them in our travels. I did have enough to afford our house and to live off the first few years. Then we had to fire the staff, the gardener, the chef, the maid… You were probably too young to remember."

"It's a little hazy."

"I tended to the garden as best I could, until you were old enough to take over. Then you became all of those things, and more, for me and my daughters."

"I don't understand. At the town hall, Remi said my name is Aribella? In my mother's journal, she called me Luella."

Clara scoffed. "Luella was a nickname for you, it means warrior, and your father picked it out."

"Really?"

"Yes. Your father doted on you. He loved me and my girls, but you were his everything. I had to wear his dead wife's clothes while he had the most beautiful little gowns made up for you. Everything was for you and about you!"

"Wait, if my father was a shifter…" Luella closed her eyes as the memory played before her. "It wasn't a dangerous black wolf that attacked us but a memory of my father playing with me, wasn't it? You turned a joyful memory against me, to feed into your lies. My father loved me, and I was happy to play with him in his wolf form."

"That is true. You did have a hazy memory of a wolf, so I used that to my advantage."

"Why were you unable to love me?" Luella asked softly. "You are capable of it. I would watch you play with Madison and braid Aubrey's hair while she read to you. Why not me?"

"How could anyone love a mutt?"

Luella's breath sucked in. "Do I have any family at all?"

"You have a distant cousin at the colony. Fiona, I believe, is her name. I was unaware at that time, or I wouldn't have moved there. Thankfully, she never figured out who we were."

"Fiona, the baker's wife?"

"Yes."

"Do I even want to know what else you have kept from me?"

Before Clara could answer, the king and two of his guards entered. "Unlock her door," he commanded, pointing to Luella's cell. "The doctor is busy with a woman giving birth, and I am not a patient man. I am ready to claim you."

"I've already been claimed. You will not touch me!" Luella screeched.

He only laughed as the guard opened the door and proceeded to drag her out. She kicked and swung but to no avail. Fear rampaged through her, and her instincts took over, forcing her to shift. She wrapped her jaw around the guard's throat and thrashed. Blood sprayed everywhere when she ripped it out, and he made a gargling noise as his body hit the floor.

The second guard rushed to her, but she grabbed his leg in her large teeth and shook him like a rag doll. He started to shift, but she pawed at his chest, clawing him right in his heart.

Luella turned to see the king shift into the largest wolf she had ever seen. His coat was a solid black, with a glossy sheen, and he lunged at her. She managed to duck in time, as he snapped his massive teeth inches from her face.

The king sprung backwards, gathering his speed before attacking again. He anticipated her movement, and they collided together. Luella released a roar of pain as stars circled her vision. She regained her composure, then watched as he lunged for her once more.

She clawed for his eyes, but he lowered his head and backed away. As she figured, he used the momentum to pounce at her. She slid under him, intending to gut him. Instead, she used the opportunity to give him the same treatment as the first guard. His blood sprayed over her, coating her fur and matting it down with the coppery, sticky liquid.

The king shifted into his human form before landing with a thud on the floor. Clara shrieked at the sight.

"You stupid girl! What have you done?"

Luella couldn't respond, nor was she able to shift back to human. She huddled in the corner, shivering as the reality of her actions sank in. The king was dead because of her. Surely she would be executed for her crime. What would Remi say when he learned she killed his father? She dry heaved for a moment before everything went black.

Chapter 21

The Ceremony

emi ran in. His eyes widened as his mouth hung open. The coppery scent accosted his senses before he saw it. He followed the blood trail to see Luella curled up and covered in the crimson liquid. The sight made him freeze for a moment before his instincts kicked in.

"Luella!" He rushed to her side, sliding to his knees beside her as he checked for a pulse.

His own deafened him, making it impossible for him to find hers. The thought she could be gone sent a shudder through him. Determined to find out one way or the other, he tried once more, nearly falling backward when her eyes fluttered open. She let out a quiet whimper.

"Are you hurt?"

No. I'm so sorry. I didn't mean to kill him! It was like the wolf was in control, not me. I had to defend myself. He was… He wanted to…

"Shh, it's all right now. Can you shift back?"

No.

He gently gripped her scruff and helped her. She clung to him as tears streamed down her face.

"I'm s… so sorry!" she blubbered.

A clatter caught their attention, and two guards ran in. They examined the bodies before slowly approaching Remi.

"The king is dead," said one guard.

"Long live the king," said the other, as they bowed before him. He then walked to the body of the king, removed his crown, and presented it to Remi. "Your Majesty."

"Thank you," Remi said as he took it and placed it upon his own head. "As king, my first order is for all of this to be cleaned up. Second, all omegas are to be freed." He pointed at Clara. "And as for her—"

"I don't suppose you will show me mercy?" Clara asked.

"The only mercy I grant you, is that it will be quick. She is to be executed tomorrow at dawn," he instructed the guard nearest her.

"Yes, mi'lord. We shall see to everything."

Remi led Luella from the room. She trembled in shock, and her words would not come out. People quickly stepped aside and stared as they walked past.

Though it was a short walk, the hallway seemed to stretch on as Luella kept reliving what had just occurred. Remi noted she continued to tremble, but said nothing. Once in their room, he took her to the shower to clean her up.

"Luella, are you all right?" Remi asked, noticing the glazed look of her eyes, as if she were in a trance. "Can you hear me?"

"Why am I not being executed as well?" she asked softly while refusing to meet his gaze. "After all, I killed the king. I killed your father!" Tears sprung from her eyes and flowed down her face.

"That is one of the things we were going to discuss before everything happened." He reached up and gently wiped them away. "As I told you before, the sons of the king are expected to kill him, once he is old and weak. He wasn't quite there yet, but you did what I was supposed to do."

"I don't understand. What sort of kingdom is this?"

"One that will be filled with peace and prosperity, as long as we are on the throne. The old ways will die, and with you as my queen, all will be as it should be."

"But I rejected you," she reminded him as her head hung in shame.

"Did I accept it?"

"Well, no."

"Then it doesn't count. I have to ask, why did you reject me?"

"Your father threatened to hurt me, and you stood there! He told you to be silent, and you refused to help me."

"He didn't tell me, Luella. He ordered me."

"I don't understand. What's the difference?"

"The king is the ultimate alpha, and he can control all other wolves. I had no choice but to obey."

"I don't believe you."

"All right, I'll prove it to you." He stepped closer to her. "Luella, drop to one knee."

"No."

His face lit up in surprise. "Oh, by the gods. You're an alpha, too? That's impossible!"

"What do you mean?"

"Males can be an alpha, beta, or omega. Females are typically omegas. As king, I can control all ranks, even alphas. With exception, if the queen is an alpha, as well. Or so the legends said. There hasn't been a female alpha in nearly a thousand years."

"Is that why we have a mate bond, because we are both alphas?"

"It's one possibility, but I'm not sure. Whether you are a human or a shifter, alpha or omega, I love you just the same. I truly hope you believe that."

"I don't know what I believe anymore."

"Luella, you are my queen. We will do many wonderful things for this kingdom. Remember how you spoke of the people suffering in the colonies? We will start there."

"Really?"

"Yes."

"What happens now?"

"I will have food brought in, and we will rest in here for a few days. Then we'll have a proper coronation. After, we can travel to the colonies so you may see them, and we can begin to improve things there."

"That sounds wonderful!"

He helped her dry off and changed into a fresh gown.

"Where did this come from?"

"I had some brought in before coming to get you, not knowing if you would have time to bring anything with you."

"It's lovely. Thank you." She examined the pale pink gown in the mirror before she approached him. "Regardless of tradition, I am sorry for your loss."

"My loss?"

"Your father."

"Thank you. Being the youngest son, we weren't very close. I probably shouldn't admit this, but if he had denied me permission to marry you, I already had plans in place to kill him myself."

"Really?"

"You are mine, now and forever. Nothing will ever keep me from you again. Together we will run this kingdom, but I will do whatever is necessary. To keep you with me, to keep you safe, to keep you until I no longer have breath in my lungs."

"I love you, Remi. I love you so much, and I have a long way to go, a lot to learn, but I am excited to be on this journey with you."

She kissed him, her hands tangling in his hair as she pressed against him. He led her to the bed, then she sat before he joined her. Slowly, he lifted the hem of her gown and gripped her inner thigh.

"Tell me you want this."

"Yes. My blood is on fire for you. I yearn for your touch, for every piece of you. Please."

"Gods, every time you beg, I feel as though I will burst!"

She smiled as she bit her lower lip. "Please, Remi. Please give me what I want."

He nearly ripped his shirt off as he hastily undressed. She stood long enough to pull the skirt of her dress up to her waist, before he lowered her to the bed and claimed her.

His tongue teased along her clavicle as he pumped in and out. She writhed and moaned, riding the waves of pleasure with each movement of his hips.

She nipped his neck as he finished inside her, her own body trembling as the sensations overwhelmed every nerve. His name came out as a scream from her lips as he licked her throat.

"Gods, how am I so blessed to have you as my mate?" Luella asked.

He kissed her hand before wrapping his arm around her and holding her close while they each calmed their racing hearts. "Because we were destined to be."

Luella jolted awake, looking around, and remembering she was safe now, living in the palace with her husband, who snored softly beside her.

She slipped from the bed and went to the window, her arms wrapped around her waist as she looked out at the starry night.

"Are you all right?"

"I'm fine," she said softly, keeping her eyes forward.

"Bad dreams?" He gently gripped her wrist. "Your heart is racing, Luella."

"Yes. I still feel guilty for what happened in the dungeon. I killed people, and I can't…" Her voice trailed off as her breath hitched, and she pushed down the sob threatening to escape.

"You did what was necessary to protect yourself. You are so brave and powerful, and it only shows me that the goddess was right to make you my queen."

"But the dungeon—"

"Was violent and bloody, but if it helps bring about a new era, one with peace and equality, is that not worth it?"

"I murdered your father."

"No, you defended yourself. Luella, I promise you here and now, I am not upset with you about what happened. He tried to take what was mine, and had I been there, I would've killed him myself. I swear it." He kissed her forehead. "Please, come back to bed. You will be in heat for a few more days, and you need your rest. Let me take care of you, in every way I possibly can."

"Could we… Never mind."

"Luella?"

"We already said our vows by the pond, but could we have an official ceremony?"

"We can. That is part of the mating process, to have our vows in private, then to officially celebrate."

"I need something else."

"What?"

"Closure."

Remi tilted his head but said nothing as she went to the closet. They dressed and walked down to the dungeon. Langdon sat in his cell while Clara paced in hers. They both turned to watch Luella.

She went to Langdon first, speaking softly so Remi nor Clara could hear her.

"For what you did to me, you will die. However, for what you did to my father, you will suffer first. I will see to it you are drawn and quartered."

Langdon jumped to his feet and gripped the bars. "You can't do that!" He looked to Remi, his eyes wide with fear. "Please, grant me mercy."

Remi scoffed. "The same mercy you showed Luella? I do not know what she said to you, but I will assure you here and now. I support whatever she decides."

Luella smiled at Remi, mouthing her thanks before turning her attention back to Langdon. "So it will be. After tomorrow, you will be nothing to me but a bitter memory."

She walked to Clara's cell, who approached the bars. "What of me?" she asked, keeping her chin high.

"What my husband has commanded. At first light, you will be beheaded. When I leave you tonight and return to my room, I will never think of you again. I am where I am meant to be, where I am accepted, happy, and loved. Everything you've ever denied me."

"You don't deserve it," Clara hissed. "You are nothing but a scruffy, filthy wolf, just like your father!"

Remi stepped up beside Luella, taking her hand firmly into his own. "Don't you dare speak to my wife that way. I can change your sentence. All she needs to do, is ask."

Luella shook her head. "No, her life will end first thing. That is good enough for me." She kissed him softly, lingering for a moment to ensure Clara saw how much they loved each other. "Goodbye, Clara."

Remi led her up the stairs and back to her room. He let Luella shower alone, saying she needed the time to herself. Then she joined him in bed, snuggling in tightly with him. He loosened the blanket and wrapped it around her.

"You can have every blanket in the kingdom, if you need it to build your nest. Never again will you be denied your heart's desire."

"Right now, that is you," Luella said softly as she climbed on top of him.

Her kiss turned from gentle to passionate. He grabbed her hips and began to pull her forward, making her straddle him as the passion grew between them.

"Whatever my wife wants."

Luella smiled at Aubrey as she helped her into the shimmering blue gown. "Thank you for coming today." Aubrey kept her head down. "Is something the matter?" Luella asked.

"I don't suppose…" She trailed off while wringing her hands.

"Aubrey, please ask whatever it is you want."

"Well, since my mother died, and Madison took off, I can't continue the upkeep of the manor. I had to sell it, and given the history of its previous occupants, I didn't get much for it." She swallowed hard. "I need a job and a place to live."

"Aubrey—"

"I'm not looking for a handout. I messed things up at the manor, but I've been reading and studying these past two weeks, knowing I was coming here."

"What exactly are you asking?"

"Could I be your handmaid, in exchange for room and board? Simon and I are courting, and it would be beneficial for me in so many ways. However, after all that has happened, if you never wish to see me again, I will understand."

She gasped when Luella gripped her hand and pulled her into a hug. "You are always welcome here. If that is what you want, we will make is so."

"Really?"

"Really."

"Thank you, Your Majesty."

"Aubrey, that is fine when we are out of quarters, but in here, please, call me Luella."

"Thank you."

She finished helping Luella get ready and escorted her to the chapel. They stopped at the doors leading in. Luella faced Aubrey.

"Despite everything that happened, thank you for being here today."

"Thank you for accepting my apology and inviting me. I wouldn't miss this for the world."

"Wait!"

Luella saw Madison approaching, dressed in a lovely pink gown with her hair in an updo. She approached Luella, curtsied, and smiled at her.

"What are you doing here?" Aubrey asked. "Where have you been?"

"I had to do a lot of thinking, after everything that happened. Between losing Mother, our home…" She turned away. "Henri broke off our engagement once he found out my… sister was a shifter. I needed time to come to terms with everything." She looked at Luella. "But I'm here to tell you, I am truly sorry for the things I did. I am sure you will never forgive me, but I had to see you and tell you, just the same."

"How did you get past the guards?" Aubrey asked.

"I didn't know if it would work, but I told them I was invited. I told them I was you, Luella's stepsister. Your name was on the list, so they let me in."

"You're right, that I may never be able to forgive you," Luella said. "After the way you've treated me my entire life. Aubrey wasn't much better, but at least she showed me moments of kindness, especially in more recent times. You have been nothing but as cruel as your own mother."

"I know." Madison's breath hitched. "And for that, I am truly sorry. I wish to walk you down the aisle with Aubrey, if you will have me." She handed Luella her mother's journal. "Either way, here is an offering of peace. I found this after you left."

Luella clutched it tightly, scarcely believing what she saw. "Thank you, Madison. I can't tell you what this means to me." She handed it to Aubrey.

"I will take good care of it, then you will get it back after the ceremony. I promise."

Luella nodded before returning her attention to Madison. "Very well. You may walk with us. Once at the altar, you and Aubrey are to stand off to the side."

"Yes, mi'lady."

The doors opened, and Luella smiled as she walked inside. The chapel had four columns of pews branching out. She walked up the middle aisle, keeping her eyes forward as she did. Remi waited for her at the altar, dressed in dark slacks and jacket, with a pale blue cravat matching her gown.

She ignored the audience as she made her way to him, smiling when he extended his hand for her to take. His eyes went wide at the sight of Aubrey and Madison.

I'll explain later.

I am most curious to hear.

She laughed softly, then watched as they lowered her train and stepped aside. Remi squeezed her hand as they turned to the minister.

"Dearly beloved…"

They said their vows, had their kiss, then Remi lifted a small platinum and diamond crown.

"Today, I have the honor of officially declaring my wife, Luella, as queen of the Loup Kingdom." He looked at Luella, love and pride reflecting in his eyes.

Madison lunged at her, pulling her backwards, with a dagger aimed at her throat. "Nobody move!"

"What are you doing?" Aubrey cried out.

"I am taking my revenge. Because of Luella, we lost our mother, our home, my betrothed, and everything I have ever known!"

"What do you want?" Remi demanded, raising his hand and gesturing for the royal guards to stay back.

"Give me the crown."

Luella scoffed. "That's all it would be, a crown. It would not make you queen!"

Madison dug the blade in hard enough to cause a trickle of blood to flow down Luella's neck. "I don't care!"

A flash of white light erupted through the hall. The crowd directed their attention towards the source.

"Faery godmother!" Luella cried out.

Alyssa approached, and with a flick of her wand, the dagger transformed into a blue rose. Madison dropped it and stepped back.

"I apologize, Your Majesty, for my tardiness," Alyssa said with a bow. She looked at Madison. "And you? Who do you think you are, to attack your queen in such a way?"

"I—"

"Silence! I know exactly who you are. Now, kneel before your queen, beg for her mercy, and if she gives it, I will leave you in peace."

"She is a dirty shifter and conniving b—"

Alyssa flicked her wand, and Madison's mouth snapped shut. "Very well. If this is the path you choose, so be it. To your sister, Aubrey, who has shown pure openness and kindness, who has begged your sister's forgiveness, and received it, I offer my blessing."

"Thank you," Aubrey said with a half-bow.

"As far as Madison is concerned, she has made her decision. You say you hate Luella because she is a shifter? Would you hate yourself if you were no longer human?" Unable to speak, Madison's eyes grew wide as she vigorously shook her head, pleading silently.

"What are you going to do?" Luella whispered.

Alyssa aimed her wand at Madison, speaking softly, as a grey light shimmered around her. Aubrey watched in terror as her sister grew to over eight feet tall, her skin turning to grey stone, her teeth elongated and sharpened, as her fingernails stretched into claws.

"A gargoyle?" Aubrey murmured in shock.

"She will be a permanent protector of this palace. I will place her at the gate, where she will sit, poised and ready to defend the monarchs and their family throughout the centuries."

Once the enchantment completed, Madison's form solidified into stone. Aubrey wiped her tears away. "Must you be so cruel?"

"Multiple opportunities for redemption were offered, and she refused every single one. She did this to herself. But I am not without mercy. If a time comes when she no longer has a heart full of envy, greed, and hatred, she will become human again. That is up to her."

"I don't understand," Luella said as she stepped forward. "She is a statue now."

"But she is aware. She can see and hear everything going on. So she knows, all she needs to do to break herself free of this, is to let everything go that she is holding onto. Again, the decision is up to her." Alyssa flicked her wrist, and Madison disappeared.

"Where did she go?" Aubrey yelled as she reached for the place her sister once stood.

"Where she should be, outside the gate, keeping watch."

Luella pulled Aubrey to her. "Everything will be okay," she assured her. "We will help her find her way."

"Why would you do that?"

"To help you."

Aubrey nodded, then stepped back. Luella smiled at Alyssa, who gave another bow. "I must go now. We are having our own celebration. A beautiful princess has been born in the Earth Court, and I am going to bestow my blessing upon her, as per our tradition."

"Thank you for everything," Luella said, watching as Alyssa disappeared into thin air.

Remi cleared his throat. "Let us continue. I will crown my wife, and we will celebrate with a feast!" Cheers erupted through the audience. He raised the crown and held it over her head. "Luella, I declare you are now officially, Queen of the Loup Kingdom."

He lowered it onto her, then kissed her brow softly. As they turned to face the audience, Aubrey couldn't help herself.

"I present your King and Queen, husband and wife, rulers of your beloved kingdom."

Everyone stood and bowed as they made their way down the aisle. Luella couldn't hide her surprise when they returned to their chambers.

"The reception—"

"Yes. While everyone is making their way there and the final touches put on, we will stay in here." He leaned forward and kissed her cut, watching as it healed. "I see your healing is finally working how it should."

"I guess that's a good thing."

"It is. Now, I'm sure you must have a million thoughts racing through your mind, after all of that."

Luella smiled at him. "No, I only have one."

"What can I do for you, my love, my wife, my queen?"

She bit her lower lip as she led him towards the bed. Her heart thudded as she sank onto the soft mattress. He climbed up with her, lifting her gown, and trailing his fingers over her smooth skin.

"We have enough time."

She giggled and buried her face in her hands. "Gods, you make me feel like it's my first time every time. As if I've never known your touch, and it makes me long for you so when we are apart."

"This you will remember," he said as his hands explored higher. "Seeing you in this dress, it took all of my self-restraint to not claim you in the chapel." His fingers hooked in the lace and pulled down her underwear. Her fine hair glistened, and he licked his lips. "You look so ravenous, I want to devour you until my name is all you can scream."

She gasped when he lifted her legs and buried his face between her thighs. His tongue ravaged her as his fingers teased. Every time she thought she would erupt, his movements would slow. She groaned softly in frustration.

"Please, Remi," she begged, her hips shaking as she felt herself again coming close. "I can't take much more."

Without a word, he buried his tongue inside, probing and pushing, until she trembled in response. Her body shook the bed, and she screamed his name as she gripped his head in both hands. She fell back onto the mattress, her body still shivering in waves of euphoria, while panting for air.

He leaned up and kissed her, making sure she tasted herself as his hand cupped her chest and teased softly. Her back arched in response.

"Hmm, ready again so soon?"

"I want you on me, burying yourself inside me, joining our bodies in bliss."

"Then you shall have that." He slid off the bed, undressed, then joined her. He lifted her legs as he slowly slid himself inside, smiling as she took him inch by inch, her breath catching with each thrust.

"Yes!" she cried out. "Oh, gods, yes. Remi, please!" She moaned again as she dug her nails down his back. "I'm so close."

"Come for me, wife. Show me exactly how much you are enjoying this." He filled her, and as he did, her own body unraveled.

They lay together as their hearts resumed their normal beats. She snuggled in closer, breathing him in.

"My whole life, I've waited to be loved. Waited to be held, comforted, blessed the way my parents were. Thank you."

"Luella, I am the one who is blessed. You never have to thank me for that."

Remi's arm tightened around Luella's waist as they danced their first dance. She clung to him while the rest of the world melted away.

After the song ended, they sat to eat and watched other couples continue as the music played. She smiled at Aubrey and Simon.

"Do you think they will get married one day?" she asked.

"He told me he is ready, but she is still a little nervous, with him being a shifter. So they are taking it slow for now."

"I'll talk to her and try to help any way I can. I think they are great together."

"Yeah, about them…"

Luella told Remi about the letter Aubrey sent. "She seems sincere about wanting to be here, to be with us, Simon, and to be a part of my life. Time will tell."

"Alyssa seemed convinced of her sincerity." He took a sip of wine. "Tomorrow, we will leave early. Are you ready to travel to the colonies, to see where we can give aid and help improve their quality of life?"

"I am."

"Me, too."

Epilogue:
(Ten years later)

uella watched as Remi played with their son, Prince Caspian, who was named after her father. They ran through the field. Caspian, though small for his age at five years old, gave his father a good chase. Luella jumped to her feet, gripping the tiny bundle in her arms, as she watched Caspian complete his first shift.

A small wolf puppy, white with dark brown patches, ran to her. Remi chased after him, shifting as well, and playing with his son.

Luella smiled at the baby girl in her arms. "What about you, Aribella? Will you be a shifter like your big brother?"

Remi and Caspian shifted together. They approached Luella. Caspian looked at his younger sister before he took off running again. Luella's smile grew when Remi kissed her before giving chase after him.

Simon and Aubrey joined them, and she sat beside Luella, cradling her swollen belly.

"Still nervous?" Luella asked.

"It is my first."

Luella chuckled. "You'll be fine. And Simon?"

"Oh, I had to move heaven and earth to get him to let me come out here. He isn't just protective, he is overprotective to a fault!" Aubrey said with a laugh.

"Can you blame him?"

"No, I can't."

"Have you decided on names?"

"We're still working on that. No rush, since I'm not due for a few more months." Aubrey glanced towards the gate.

"What's wrong?"

"I thought Madison would've freed herself by now. It makes me feel guilty."

"Why?"

"Because, with this baby coming, I won't be able to visit her every day like I was. At least, not for a few weeks after giving birth."

"Then I will come out here," Luella assured her.

"Really?"

"I promise."

"I just realized, I never told you about Henri."

"What about him?"

"When Simon took me back to the colony, to finish up a few things with the sale of the manor, we heard from one of the barristers. Apparently, Henri was found in the woods with his throat ripped out."

Luella watched Remi and Caspian play. "I told Remi everything. I didn't think he would… Did he?"

"Knowing how repulsive Henri was, I don't blame Remi if he did. After all, he will do whatever he must to protect his mate. He has made that abundantly clear."

"Let's focus on happy times ahead, shall we?" Luella asked.

She observed as the two families played and laughed together. Remi was right, they would bring the people together in ways she hadn't imagined.

The king and queen had worked hard their first year, creating new laws, reducing taxes on the colonies, and earning the trust of their people.

Luella was amazed by the fact that she went from serving the greediest individuals to serving her people. People who loved, admired, and respected her and her husband. To Luella, she didn't see how life could get any more perfect.

Acknowledgements

To Kevin, my love and my biggest supporter
To my sister Lisa, for always being in my corner
To my editor, Stephanie. I couldn't have done this without you!
To my beta readers, Jess, Stephanie, Bonita, Ronda, Brittany, & Sam
To Samazon, for being the inspiration behind Alyssa
To my ARC readers, thank you
To my readers, who continue to support me
To Gran, who instilled in me a love of reading and fairytales

And thank you, God, for my love of writing and fantasy

I wish to thank the different authors who inspired my Cinderella retelling, from Charles Perrault to the Brother's Grimm, and the various movie adaptations as well.

And William Shakespeare, who penned Romeo & Juliet.

In Memoriam:

To Kimmy (ChubbyRomanceReader)

You will be missed!

About the Author

A.R. Kaufer lives in Indiana with her husband and furbabies. When she's not playing video games or watching movies, she is reading or writing. She can be found on Twitter, Instagram, TikTok, and Pinterest, and she is happy to hear from her readers.

Author Photo By:
Kevin Kaufer